27 04 83		
18 10 83		
23 10 83		
05 08 83		
08 03 80		

The
Bengali Inheritance

The
Bengali Inheritance

by

OWEN SELA

HODDER AND STOUGHTON
LONDON SYDNEY AUCKLAND TORONTO

for
Ann

K. SELA
100017897

Characters in this book are depicted as holding appointments in the Royal Hong Kong Police Force. These characters are wholly imaginary and do not represent past, present or future incumbents of these posts. The air crash in which Subhas Chandra Bose was killed and the students' rally in Hong Kong in 1973 are both historical facts. The interpretation of these events is, however, entirely fictional, as is the depiction of the use, discovery and location of the Bose treasure.

I

As HE WAS to report it afterwards in Cantonese, Police Constable Wong Kui was proceeding eastwards along Yee Wo Road in the direction of Jardine's Bazaar when he saw the taxi. It was 5.58 a.m. and PC Wong Kui had been on duty nearly eight hours. He had intended to walk as far as the Roxy Cinema and make his way back to Wan Chai police station along Gloucester Road, past the huddle of junks in the typhoon shelter, and the broad expanse of the harbour that separated Hong Kong Island from Kowloon and the Chinese mainland.

At that time of the morning the harbour was always peaceful, a cool, fresh breeze blowing off the flat sea, the ships riding high above their moorings, bereft of life, baring the red under-bellies of their water lines. It was the time of the day PC Wong Kui liked best, the time of calm and quiet hope, with light creeping softly along shuttered streets, the tall green Daimaru department store building, lined with gold.

PC Wong Kui walked on, watching the slow transformation of shadow into object. It had been a night without incident, and he had passed this way four times before. The last time, the taxi had not been there. Orange light danced along the tram lines to meet him as he stepped into the middle of Yee Wo Road and strode purposefully towards the offending vehicle.

The taxi was parked at an angle in the middle of the road, its bonnet and flopped over front wheels lying firmly across the tram lines. As he advanced, Wong Kui felt the early morning sense of elation evaporate. Of all the stupid, selfish, inconsiderate things he had seen in his short career as a policeman, this was the worst. In a few moments the trams would begin clanking their way up from Shau Keiwan and any fool knew that trams couldn't swerve round parked taxis.

He eased the baton at his waist and flipped the notebook out of his top pocket. Obstruction, waiting in a restricted street, and if the bloody thing had broken down, failing to maintain a public vehicle in a roadworthy condition. His mind raced through the list of offences — there was no end to the charges he would bring. He made a note of the taxi's licence number, noted that it was a Mercedes and that it was red. The light on its roof was out and it had a scrape along its offside wing, filled with grey primer. The taxi appeared to be empty.

PC Wong Kui was right up against the taxi when he saw the man asleep in the rear seat. Drunk no doubt, or insensible with opium. The gods alone knew how far the man had driven in that condition and he had obviously left the car where it had stopped. If PC Wong Kui had his way the man would never drive so much as a bicycle again. It was only good fortune that had saved him from killing somebody.

Killing somebody! Righteous indignation blazed through Wong Kui as he wrenched open the rear door of the taxi. The obscenity clawed in his throat and stuck. For a moment Wong Kui stared wide eyed in disbelief. Then whirling away from the open door he bent over and was sick.

*   *   *

It was 6.06 a.m. when the Emergency Unit whose job it was to deal with 999 calls heard a frail sounding police constable murmur that he had discovered a body in the

8

back of a taxi parked in the middle of Yee Wo Road, pointing eastwards.

The message was relayed to a blue Ford Zephyr cruiser which at the time was drifting slowly past the head office of the Hong Kong and Shanghai Bank in Central. Before the patrolling Ford Zephyr had screeched into third gear, the Emergency Unit was talking to the Duty Officer at Wan Chai police station. By the time the Zephyr had skidded to a halt in Yee Wo Road, its blue light revolving, its siren dying, the Duty Officer at Wan Chai police station was talking to Senior Inspector Richard Chan. The time was 6.13.

*   *   *

Senior Chief Inspector Richard Chan hunched forward as he drove, gripping the wheel too tightly with chubby, scarred hands, concentrating into wakefulness. The car was a new Ford Cortina, bought three weeks ago with a long-term, low-interest loan from the Special Police Fund, painted a bright yellow, Chan's auspicious colour. His lack of driving skill and experience made every iota of good luck necessary.

Chan was a solidly built man, just turned thirty-eight, with heavy shoulders and thick forearms protruding from the wide sleeves of his safari jacket, like the piston rods of a steam engine. He was five foot nine, chunkily compact, his body covered with a resilient mattress of hard fat, the body of a wrestler who now confined himself to infrequent exhibition matches. A fleshy neck was rammed firmly between the heavy shoulders, surmounted by a tough looking, square head, covered with springy black bristle, looking as if it could be used as a battering ram, and a face that looked as if it once had.

The nose was squashed flat and the smooth swollen olive skin around the eyebrows was shirred with tiny brown scars. It was a pugnacious, well worn face saved only from the gormlessness of the ex-pugilist, by the alertness in the

9

button bright eyes, the firmness of the jaw line and the indentations of humour in the soft flesh beside the mouth.

A determined man, Senior Inspector Richard Chan, you could tell it from the aggressive tilt of his head and the calculated manner of his driving. There was a kindliness about the mouth and the lived in face looked alert despite the scars, as if it had never been hit hard enough to jar the brain.

Chan kept his window down as he drove, smelling the vinegary odour of early morning Hong Kong streets, the squashed fruit tang from rubbish piled high outside restaurants. He drove over crushed leaves and the debris between tarpaulined market stalls. While still some distance away he saw the revolving blue light of the patrol car, surrounded by a knot of people. He accelerated along Yee Wo Road, honked his way through the crowd and stopped parallel to the taxi. Chan looked at his watch. It was 6.42.

He switched off the engine and studied the scene. A red Mercedes taxi was slewed across the tram lines in the centre of the road, as if it had lost its transmission halfway through a U turn. Two uniformed policemen stood on the near side of the car staring ferociously at the crowd. The offside rear door was open and beside it were an Inspector and two constables. They saluted as Chan walked towards them and Chan hastily altered the rubbing of his sleep roughened eyes into an acknowledgment.

"Bad business, sir," the Inspector said. "Shooting. He's in the back of the car."

Chan recognised the Inspector from last year's police dance. He was based at Arsenal Street and had been in cruisers two years. The Duty Officer at Wan Chai would have summoned an ambulance, doctor, fingerprint men and a photographer. Until they arrived there was nothing for Chan to do, except look.

Look! His stomach fluttered uneasily at the thought. 6.45 in the morning was far too early to examine the consequences of violent death. Chan looked about him and scratched the stubble at the top of his head, putting off the moment when he would have to examine the body.

"You'd better get this crowd further back," he said to the Inspector. "Bring your car alongside."

While the Inspector was doing that, Chan still hesitating turned to the constables. He recognised Wong Kui, one of the lads from his station, still pale from the shock of his discovery. No point in keeping the lad hanging around. Chan asked him to get back to the station and make his report. Then straightening his shoulders, Chan walked up to the taxi and avoiding the pool of vomit, looked inside.

A man lay half on, half off the blood-stained brown leather seat of the car. His legs were bent into a sitting position, the feet tilted in the well between the seats, so that only the sides of each foot touched the floor. The body was lying on its right, balanced along the front of the seat, the left arm trailing behind the buttocks, the right dangling to the car floor. The palms were open and the body was fully clothed in a pale blue cotton suit.

The man was slimly built, couldn't have been much more than ten stone seven, an Indian, aged about forty, good brown skin and a purple swelling on the right side of his face. His dark eyes were still open, staring at the brown leather of the seats.

The Indian had been shot in the back of the head about an inch and a half above the neck. The bullet had smashed through the base of the skull leaving a blackened hole ringed with dried blood and sticky, charred curly hair. The top of the man's collar was soaked with blood from the entrance wound and there were large splotches of blood on the back of his blue cotton jacket and along the car seat. *Ei ya!* It was a messy business. Gruesome crater of an exit wound too, as if the bullet had mushroomed out of the top of the skull spattering slivers of bone, silvery grey brain matter, blood and yellow fat everywhere.

Chan walked across to the police car. He needed UB men and movable barriers to keep the crowd back, a Detective

11

Sergeant and some Detective Constables. He made his request to Wan Chai police station over the radio telephone, also gave them the taxi's registration number, wanted the taxi driver found and held. At that moment the first tram of the day, tall and green, advertising Marlboro cigarettes across the full width of its top deck, clanked its way up to the police car. Chan sighed and made more requests into the radio telephone. A tow truck and a warning to the Traffic Department. They were stuck across the tram lines and there was going to be chaos in Hong Kong that morning.

Chan got out of the police car and walked back to the taxi feeling the eyes of the crowd on the top deck of the tram boring into his back. He took out his notebook and entered the time of his arrival, the taxi's registration, peered into the front of the car. No blood there, so the man must have been killed or transported in the back. Empty ashtray in front, taxi meter in the off position. Chan made a note of the figures on the meter and on the car's instruments. He took a little walk round the taxi, no skid marks, no dripping of oil, feeling as if he were some kind of public performer, noting the scrape on the offside wing, the position of the body, the precise location of the car. More trams had come up now, and people were crowding round. Chan felt hemmed in by their hot breath, the unyielding pressure of their bodies. He bent down and taking a piece of chalk drew the outline of the wheels on the road.

A few minutes later the police van arrived, bringing the constables and the Detective Sergeant, escorted by a grey Fiat 850 carrying the fingerprint men. Chan had the policemen set up mobile barriers around the scene and dispatched the Detective Constables into the crowd and the buildings in the immediate vicinity, looking for witnesses.

The photographer arrived in a travel-weary MG Midget, a slim Cantonese wearing an open faded denim jacket and high heeled cowboy boots. His neck was festooned with a Rollei, two 35 mm Nikons and a Polaroid.

"I'll need a hundred head and shoulders," Chan said. "Clear ones, so that even his fifth cousin will recognise him."

"Okay, okay," the photographer said. His eyes were still caked with sleep and there was a faint shadow of beard on his chin. "Let me have a look first, will you."

"Go ahead," Chan said. "But don't take all day looking. I want those pictures fast."

The photographer moved over to the taxi with a shrug of wiry, blue denimed shoulders.

Chan walked back to his car and climbed into the rear seat. Seven o'clock in the morning was a hell of a time to find the body of a murdered Indian. What the hell did he think he was doing getting himself shot in the back of a taxi in Yee Wo Road? Chan didn't know any Indians. There were only about five thousand of them in Hong Kong, a peaceful, earnest race, sharing the Chinese passion for hard work and making money.

He looked out and conscripted a member of the public to take his place in the rear of the car. Chan occupied the other seats in turn and finally decided that the man had been shot by someone sitting in the rear passenger seat. He sat in the rear passenger seat, brooding till one of the fingerprint men leaned in and said, "All clear, sir." Straightening his safari jacket Chan walked back to the taxi.

The medical examiner had turned the body on to its back, and it lay staring at the plastic shielded interior light. The glass in the rear door of the car was undamaged. Chan squatted down and looked up at the roof lining. There was a small tear about a third of the way between the light and the door. Chan stood up and looked at the metal skin of the roof. That was unmarked.

A Morris van flashing a yellow revolving light nosed its way through the barriers and pulled up beside the taxi. Chan turned and watched impassively as an impressively moustached European climbed out, clad in the khaki uniform of Hong Kong Tramways.

"What the hell's going on," the Tramways official demanded. "We've got trams stretching back all the way to Shau Keiwan."

A self-important, harassed man, Chan thought, whose carefully organised time table had been shattered. "Someone got shot," Chan said. "Want to have a look?"

The Tramways official hesitated.

"It's all right," Chan said. "Everybody else has."

The man approached the taxi gingerly, peered inside and turned hurriedly away. "It's awful," he said. "Bloody awful."

"That's what the police are there for," Chan said, "to clean up other people's messes." He looked at the man, pale now behind the florid moustache. "We'll be as quick as we can, meanwhile you'd better stop any more trams getting out."

"I'll do what I can," the official said.

There was no help for it, Chan thought, an Indian had been shot in the middle of Yee Wo Road and half the population of Hong Kong was going to be late for work that morning. He went back to the taxi and slid sideways into the front seat. The dead man stared up at the roof, slack jawed, the swelling on his face turned darker. His tie had now been loosened and the middle buttons of his shirt were open. Chan looked at the man's left hand now lying across his belly. There was a thick weal around the wrist and the nail of his index finger had been discoloured, leaving a dark blue ridge in the centre of the nail. Chan picked up the hand, cold and clammy, looked underneath the nail. A sliver of bamboo jutted out like a pinhead.

He let the hand drop and bent over the seat, looking at the right hand which still trailed to the floor. A quick wave of revulsion washed over him. The end of the man's fingers were a bloody pulp. There were no finger nails.

Chan waited for the wave of nausea to subside, glad that he had been called out so early and not had time to eat or drink. The man had been tortured. Why? By whom? He stared into the dead face as if looking for an answer. It was a thin face, sharp nosed, a full mouth, the eyes already going pale and fishlike. Dead men's faces usually kept their secrets, the act of dying seeming to drain the features of all character and the shape of a living past. A figure crowded through the window beside him.

It was the fingerprint man holding out a large envelope with the deceased's possessions. Chan opened it, extracted a blood-stained handkerchief, a crushed packet of Benson & Hedges cigarettes, a Ronson Varaflame lighter, a leather wallet. Inside the wallet were two ten dollar notes, a bill from an hotel in Taipei, an air ticket Tokyo-Taipei-Hong Kong. In a transparent plastic folder in the centre of the wallet were a Diners Club card and an out of date press card. Both were made out in the name of the *Asian Clarion* magazine and the user was one Debnath Raghavan.

At least he knew the dead man's name. Chan turned to face the Inspector, who asked, "Okay to move now?"

Chan nodded. He put Raghavan's possessions back into the envelope, picked up the taxi's log book and climbed out of the car. He stood and watched while the ambulance men took the body out, fitted it into a plastic bag, rolled it on to a stretcher and carried it through the crowd into the ambulance.

The tow truck backed up. The men locked the steering and lifted up the front end of the taxi. After the car had been moved, Chan had the photographer take pictures of where it had stood.

Minutes later, the crowd was thinning. The patrol car pulled away, followed by the fingerprint men's Fiat and the photographer's MG. The Detective Sergeant came up to Chan. "Found one witness, sir."

Chan said, "Bring him back to the station."

The trams clanked slowly forward. Chan climbed into his Cortina and reversed carefully away from the tram lines. The time was 7.55. Chan's day was just beginning.

2

CHAN DROVE BACK to the police station, thinking hard. Around him, Wan Chai woke lazily. It woke late, it woke slowly. The streets were still quiet and here and there men quietly removed the boarded shutters from the fronts of shops. People walked slowly along the pavements, under the huge Chinese signs, silent now, ash coloured, looking like dead men's eyes. Only the tea rooms were doing serious business. Far ahead of him a line of schoolgirls in white uniforms crossed the road.

Chan parked in Jaffe Road, behind the police station, hoping that the traffic police would recognise the new car as his. He entered the rear of the building and walked quickly through the lobby with its atmosphere of chipped paint and peeling 'Wanted' posters, passed the crush of uniformed men and civilians crowding before the lift and ran up the bare cement stairs to his office on the first floor.

Chan's office was immediately opposite the lift, and over the months he had grown used to the slam of its doors and the constant tread of feet. There was little privacy in a police station. It was almost as if the authorities wished to avoid scandal by compelling policemen to live their lives in the open.

It had taken Chan a long while to appreciate the luxury of his own room. His boyhood had been spent in crowded

.. ..

apartments and even more crowded classrooms, his adolescence in crowded streets, the dormitories of the police training school and open squad rooms. He had developed a habit of withdrawing into himself whenever necessary, but these withdrawals were not as complete or as comfortable as being able to shut one's own door. Over the months Chan had grown to like his grey hardwood door with its wooden slot and dusty card with *Senior Inspector R. Chan, OIC/CID* written upon it in laborious italics.

The office behind the door was small, nearly filled by the four-drawered wooden desk and Chan's straight-backed armchair. Opposite the desk were two straight-backed chairs without arms and beside them to the right, an open five-drawered filing cabinet in battered grey metal. Between the filing cabinet and the door was a small table on which rested a disused telephone and a portable typewriter. A chart above the table showed crimes in his area, comparing numbers of cases reported with those prosecuted. Lines of different colours distinguished between crimes against lawful authority, crimes against public morality, crimes against the person, narcotics offences and crimes against property. The same careful hand that had written the notice on Chan's door had marked the detection rate, 76. 5 per cent in 1971, 59.3 per cent in 1972; the consequence of more crime and fewer policemen to deal with it.

Chan sat down behind the desk, moved aside the battered plastic trays and drew the previous night's Incident Report towards him. It had been a quiet night, one knifing, one jewel robbery. Chan read the investigating officer's report.

The jewel robbery had occurred in Lockhart Road. It should have taken place in a television script. Thieves complete with guns and stocking masks, a stolen getaway car screeching from the kerb, a broken down lorry parked at the intersection between Lockhart Road and Percival Street, a second getaway car available safely beyond the

17

obstruction. It was the third such robbery in as many weeks.

Kids, thought Chan, ruthless kids, spawned in refugee camps, brought up in squalor, with too much time and too little education, the deprived no-hopers in a land of apparent plenty. All right, the softies would blame society for it. But stealing was stealing and it was not a policeman's job to understand why. There were enough sociologists to do that. A policeman's job was to see that people didn't steal, or carry guns.

Sergeant Yim had taken charge of the enquiry. A good man, experienced, he had found the getaway car abandoned, wiped clear of fingerprints. More television training, but then you couldn't ban television simply because a few people were unduly affected by it.

"Morning chief, you were late! What did you do? Come by tram?"

Chan looked up into Sergeant Lau's smiling face. Chan and Lau were friends, they had been through training school together and over the last four years, worked together at Castle Peak and at Kowloon City police stations.

"Where the hell were you?" Chan asked. "A man was found murdered in Yee Wo Road."

"And you'll find the killer and make superintendent."

Superintendent was the rank that went with the job. Chan's predecessor, Davidson, had been a superintendent even though he'd had two years less service. Chan studied Lau's face. There was no malice on it. "I'll make superintendent a lot quicker than you'll make inspector."

Lau laughed. "Me chief! I'm going to stay a sergeant all my life."

Fool you, Chan thought, with four children to bring up on a sergeant's pay. But Lau was like that, one of those people who would rather resign than be kicked upstairs to shuffle sheaves of administrative memorandums.

Chan said, "I've got something for you."

Lau came in, allowing Chan to relish the full splendour of his batik patterned shirt, moving lightly on the balls of his feet, legs splayed apart, thick muscular arms standing out from his sides as if he was about to grab somebody. Lau was a judo third dan and still gave classes twice a week at a boys' institute on Kowloon side. His happy, open countenance gave the lie to the impression that CID men were born with poker faces.

"A nice bit of poncing," Lau said. "That's what I feel like."

Chan said, "Get on to ballistics and tell them the bullet is in the roof lining of the taxi."

"What taxi?"

"The murder taxi, idiot."

"Oh you mean the red Mercedes in the Arsenal Street Garage?"

"You know someone else who was shot today?"

Lau looked blank. "Was there?"

"I know someone who will be. I want you to take as many men as you can spare, borrow as many buttons as you can, get over to Yee Wo Road and go and find me a gun."

"A gun!"

"You heard me. A gun."

"But chief that is *foki* work."

Chan glared directly at Lau. "So?"

Lau shrugged. "What kind of gun you looking for, chief?"

"A pistol or a revolver."

"Any special make or calibre?"

Chan shook his head. "I don't know yet, but I want you crawling through every *nullah* in the area, till you find it."

Lau groaned, held up two fingers in the gesture that Winston Churchill made famous, and went.

* * *

Chan picked up the phone and made four rapid calls. The first was to the Identification Bureau to whom he gave a brief description of the late Mr. Raghavan, the next to the General Investigation Office to whom he repeated the information and requested a hotel check. He booked a call to the *Asian Clarion* in Manila for ten o'clock and then called the officer controlling traffic through the tunnel which ran underneath the harbour between Hong Kong Island and Kowloon. No, the officer said, it had been a quiet night. Definitely no incidents. Speeding! Of course there was speeding. Everybody drove too quickly through the tunnel and one day there was going to be gigantic smash and three hundred and twenty million dollars worth of tunnel would sink into the harbour. All the officer prayed for was that he wouldn't be on duty when it happened.

The Detective Sergeant who had attended the scene of the murder came in. "I've got the witness downstairs, sir, in the detention room."

"I'll talk to him here," Chan said. "Bring him up, and then you'd better get over to the mortuary. They'll be starting the PM soon."

The witness was a frail, elderly Chinese with a wispy, Ho Chi Minh beard and surprisingly bushy eyebrows. He wore a tattered black *samfoo* and beneath its tattered pyjama-like exterior, his body looked as brittle as a bird's. He was frightened and kept darting anxious glances around the room. When Chan asked him to sit he perched nervously on the edge of a chair.

Chan reached for a statement pad, then pulled out a packet of cigarettes from his drawer and offered them. The Chinese took one, lit it and drew hard. He looked suspiciously at the brown mottled pattern on the outside of the cigarette and cupped it in his hand before placing his hand between his knees. His name was Leung Chan-Fai and he wasn't sure of his age. If the Inspector insisted, well he would say, eighty-six. Chan wrote down sixty-eight which was what the man looked like.

Chan asked the man to think carefully and tell him what he had seen that morning.

He screwed his face up and thought, looked suspiciously at the stale cigarette in his hand, then looked back at Chan and said, "A car. Two cars." He flicked ash from the cigarette into his palm. "There was a sharp noise and I woke up. There were two cars in the street. Some men got into one and they drove away."

"What direction did they drive?"

"Away." The man gestured, spilling ash over his legs.

"Where were you at the time?"

"Inside the doorway of the grocery store. That is where I sleep."

Chan asked him the name of the grocery store.

"Yuan Wo is my grand nephew. He lets me sleep in the doorway of the shop at night."

And saves hiring a watcher, Chan thought, that's what family togetherness was all about. "What direction did the car go? Did it come towards you?"

"No, away."

"Towards the cinema?"

"Yes."

Chan wrote that the car had travelled eastwards. "What kind of car was it?"

The man shrugged. "I don't know. A car."

"What was its number?"

The man shook his head.

"How big was it?"

"It was a car."

"How many men were there?"

"Four."

"How do you know?"

"I can count. One, two, three, four." The man held up a gnarled hand with large grimy fingernails.

"Did four men go from one car to the other?"

"No, three." The man held his hand up again.

"And with the driver, that made four."

"That was what I thought," the man said.

"What did you do then?" Chan asked. "After the car had gone."

"I lay back on my bed and went to sleep."

"Did you not see the taxi parked in the middle of the road?"

"Yes."

"Did you not think it would hold up the trams? Did you not think to call the police?"

The man stared wide eyed at the edge of Chan's desk. Slowly he shook his head. "I am an old man. I need to sleep."

"But you could have called the police."

"No," the man said. "I would have had to wake up my nephew."

"Why?"

The man hesitated. "I do not know how to telephone."

Chan sat back in his chair and tapped his pencil against the desk. "What happened next?"

"The police car came, whee, whee, and I woke up again." He smiled at Chan and repeated "Whee, whee."

Chan finished writing out the man's statement and offered it to him. "Is this what you said?"

"I can't read," the man said.

Chan got up and went to the door. He gave the statement to a constable and asked him to take the witness downstairs and have him put his thumb print on it. Then he thanked the man and went upstairs to the canteen on the third floor. His throat was parched and he was dying for a cup of tea. The time was nine-fifteen.

3

WHEN CHAN RETURNED to his office, Inspector Pete Winston was there, chair tilted back, feet braced against the side of Chan's desk, scattering cigarette ash on the floor and reading Chan's copy of the Incident Report. He raised a lanky hand in greeting as Chan entered. "Hi there, Charlie, hear you've got a murder case."

Chan waited for the crack about promotion and when it didn't come, snapped, "Cut out the Charlie bit. I've told you before."

Winston was Chan's second in command, a tall, gangling Englishman of twenty-eight, with shoulder-length hair and a handsome, arrogant face. He'd spent two years in the Leicestershire Constabulary and six months more than that in the Royal Hong Kong Police Force. Already he had reached a position it had taken Chan ten years to achieve.

Calling Chan Charlie was Winston's idea of a joke. Charlie Chan the famous Chinese detective, you know, ha, ha, quoting Confucius, sipping green tea and being inscrutably Oriental and all that. Ha! Ha! Chan, sensitive about his name, didn't find it at all funny.

His milk name had been Chan Yan-Wo, and at school he had changed it to Richard. It had been the first step in accepting Western ways and he felt the sense of betrayal still. In any case, Chan only joked with friends. He disliked Pete Winston intensely.

Winston was one of those jumped up ex-pats infinitely superior and irremediably ignorant. A few years ago Winston had been plodding the beat in some little-known English village and now that he had come to Hong Kong and become an inspector, felt that he had a God given right to rule the Chinese. The insult, *kwei lo*, crossed Chan's mind. Foreign devil. That's exactly what Pete Winston was.

Winston owed his present position to uncovering a spy ring amongst the hordes of Russian marine supervisors at Whampoa Docks. It had been a sensational case and now when Russian ships were refitted, the number of supervisors was limited to those strictly essential for the job. Winston made no secret of the fact that he should have been given his own command, and that if he had a number one spot at Wan Chai something constructive could be done about a detection rate of only 59.3 per cent.

Chan walked to his desk, snatching the Incident Report from Winston's fingers as he sat down. "There's something I want you to do," he said.

Winston's head lolled back with studied indifference. He looked at Chan from under half closed lids. "Shoot."

Chan told him about the discovery of Raghavan's body in the taxi. "I want you to find me the driver."

Languorously Winston looked at his watch, a solid Omega chronograph. "I'd like to chief, but I can't. Got a meeting with the AC in an hour about the rally a fortnight on Sunday." He straightened up in the chair.

Sucking up to the Assistant Commissioner accounted for the smart blue gaberdine suit and the freshly washed and combed shoulder-length hair.

"Actually, I dropped in to check if you were coming."

"I haven't the time to be concerned with student politics," Chan said. He made a wringing hand gesture that Charlie Chan might have appreciated. "My humble apologies to the AC. I've got a murder case to deal with."

"Sure," Winston said, standing. "Sure, I understand,"

implying the Assistant Commissioner might not. "Don't worry, I'll look after it. Don't you worry about a thing."

And somehow, Chan felt irritably, he had allowed his deputy to excuse him.

* * *

Chan was just completing his preliminary notes on the Raghavan case when the phone rang. It was Manila, a friendly voice saying, "*Asian Clarion*".

"I want to speak to the Personnel Officer," Chan said. "This is Inspector Chan, Hong Kong CID."

"I'm sorry, sir, we have no Personnel Officer. Could you please tell me what you are calling about?"

"It's about someone who works for you. A Mr. D. Raghavan. R for Roger, A for apple, G for German, H for Harry, A for apple, V for — "

"Mr. Raghavan doesn't work here any more, sir."

"I'd still like to to talk to someone about him."

"One moment please."

The moment extended into minutes. Then a male voice said, "Editorial".

Chan said, "This is Inspector Chan, Hong Kong CID. We are making an enquiry about a Mr. Raghavan."

"Go ahead," the voice said.

"I am speaking to . . ." Chan allowed himself to lapse into silence.

"Kenneth Wong, Deputy Editor. What's the trouble with old Raghi?"

A pompous voice, rich and fruity, accented at some English university, the voice of a wearer of poplin shirts with a gold Parker in the top pocket. Half Chinese perhaps, Chan thought, with thick-lensed horn-rimmed glasses, a man with a home whose furniture had been selected from *Good Housekeeping* and an elegant Chinese wife who could make bright dinner party conversation, with all the *amahs* she needed and who always looked elegant. Kenneth Wong, Deputy Editor, undoubtedly drank cocktails in the evening and wore a cravat when he went to the polo club.

"Old Raghi's dead," Chan said.

Chan waited while Wong went through the familiar exclamations of shock and surprise. "What do you mean dead?" As if there was any doubt about that. "How did it happen?"

"He was shot in the back of a taxi. He had an *Asian Clarion* press card in his pocket."

"He shouldn't have," Kenneth Wong said. "He left us nearly a year ago."

"Do you know where he went?"

"No," Kenneth Wong said. "He left Manila, you see. It was all quite sudden. He turned up one morning, handed in his resignation and left. He didn't really tell anyone about his new job. Unusual, because he was a gregarious type of chap. Always chattering, you know."

"Did he have any close friends?"

Chan heard the rasp of a match, a long inhalation. State Express 555 he guessed, in the flat tin, so convenient a shape for one's pockets. Kenneth Wong, Deputy Editor, would hold his cigarette near the end in long, tapering fingers stained with the pale black of rubbed off newsprint.

"Come to think of it, Raghi was strange about that. I mean, he knew everybody and liked everybody but he never had any special friends."

"Was he married?"

"No. I mean not that anyone knew of. There was a rumour that he had a family in Calcutta, but over here, we don't really pry into one another's personal life."

Prissy old fart, Chan thought, and said soothingly, "I understand".

"So far as I know, Raghi lived alone in Manila. Mind you he was always chatting up girls. In fact one or two of our own dear ladies took it rather seriously and complained."

"And?"

"What? Oh, I see what you're getting at. And nothing.

Raghi was told to keep his thoughts to himself and that was that. No jealous husbands or boyfriends."

"What about enemies?" Chan asked.

"With Raghi! Oh no. Impossible! If you knew him, you'd know what I mean."

Chan reflected that that was a pleasure that would now be forever denied him. He thanked Mr. Wong and put the phone down.

He could hear Winston pacing around the office next door. Chan looked at his watch. If he didn't hurry, Chan thought gleefully, Winston would be late for his meeting with the Assistant Commissioner, blue gaberdine suit and all.

Then Chan realised that he too might be late. He got up and went over to the squad room. It was a long room with ten empty desks and Reserve seated by the table at the end of the room where the phones were. Chan picked up the duty book from the table by the door and wrote that he was going to Victoria Public Mortuary. Then he went down the stairs into the bright sunshine and the steamy smell of Jaffe Road. As he walked to his car he rubbed his chin and thanked God he was Chinese and didn't have to shave every day.

4

PETE WINSTON PACING about his office heard Chan go out and wondered what he could tell the Assistant Commissioner about the phone call that had come seventy-two hours ago.

Seventy-two hours. Three whole days. It felt longer than that. Winston remembered that the air conditioning in his office had broken down that day and he had been feeling more than usually sticky with humidity.

"Ah Mr. Winson," the familiar voice had said. "I am in Macau. I have to see you quickly."

"Where in Macau?"

"The Bella Vista. You will lunch with me, yes?"

"I am not sure — it's such short notice. I have — "

"Is important for us to meet one o'clock." The receiver clicked sharply against Winston's ear, leaving him with the steady burr of a dialling tone, the echo of a sibilant voice whirling through his auditory memory. The Bella Vista at one o'clock. At the time he had thought it was a sodding nuisance.

Two and a half hours later, having shouted hurried instructions to Sergeant Lau and scribbled a hasty note in the duty book that he was checking out a lead on some stolen silver, he was in Macau. Immigration took him another hour and it had been a quarter to one before he was hurrying under the Northern Airways sign and speeding along broad shady streets to the pension-like hotel with its Moorish tiles and Scarlett O'Hara atmosphere.

Hiroshi Watanabe was seated amongst lush greenery on the shaded verandah, staring at the harbour, infuriatingly certain of Winston's arrival. On the chair beside him were an Asahi Pentax and a lens case, the appurtenances of a tourist or business man with a few hours to kill.

"You will have beer?"

"Let's eat," Winston said. The fast ride across the open sea had made him hungry. Besides he did have to trace that lost silver. He picked up a menu and looked at it.

Watanabe had not changed much in the two years since he had last seen him. He was still slim, still slope shouldered and scrawny necked, the black eyes behind the half rimmed glasses still immobile. Watanabe was wearing a pale brown tropical suit, a spotless white shirt and knitted green tie. His face was long, with a forehead that receded in multifold ridges of skin to a semi-circle of thin black hair. His eyebrows were thick slashes above the half frame horn rims and he wore a moustache, a straight pepper and salt affair above a narrow mouth that was full lipped and cruel. No, Watanabe had not changed much, but then if you are over seventy, you change slowly.

Winston beckoned a waiter over and ordered from the set menu.

Watanabe stared at him quietly. "You find any more Russian spies?"

Winston forced a grin. "No. You know of any more?"

Watanabe inclined forward, smiling and nodding gently. "We will see." He picked up his beer and sipped it. "We will see."

Winston felt uncomfortable. He had a sense of favours owed to a man he did not know well. He had first met Hiroshi Watanabe four years ago when he had been working with the SAS in Vientiane. Watanabe had been doing some mysterious administrative job for Air USA. Myles Brinkley, Deputy Head of USAID, had introduced them.

At the time Winston's contract had been near expiry. Renewal would have meant staying on in the war zone or a posting to Northern Ireland, which was a kind of insanity he could do without, especially if he were not to have the benefits of PX's and US Army rates of pay. He had consulted Brinkley on the problem and was wondering what it would be like working in England, without the comforting feel of the service around him or the exotic backdrop of South-East Asia.

Watanabe had bought whisky and listened politely. He had given Winston the name of two Japanese friends in London and some six months after Winston had left the SAS, he had been invited to cocktails at the Japanese Embassy. Nothing had happened for nearly a year after that, except one more invitation, but by then Winston had spent most of his savings and sick of pen pushing to nowheresville, had applied to join the Royal Hong Kong Police Force.

He had been in Hong Kong six months, when Watanabe contacted him. That summons had been less imperious. Like today, they had met in Macau. On that occasion Watanabe had told him about a Korean insurgence group operating on the island. There had been arrests and Winston had taken the first step on the ladder of rapid promotion.

Watanabe asked, "You have risen high, yes?"

Winston shrugged, his mouth full, eating rapidly without taste. "Can't grumble."

"You will go higher," Watanabe said. He ate slowly, cutting his meat into small pieces. "I do not work for the Americans now," stacking meat on to his fork. "Now I stay in Tokyo. It is time I watched my grandchildren grow." He smiled and nodded and slipped the fork into his mouth. "You are married, yes?"

Winston coloured at the implication of lack of virility. "No," he said. When you can buy milk, who wants to buy a cow, but he did not tell Watanabe that. "Not yet," he compromised.

"You will have many sons," Watanabe prophesied. Then without any sign of change added, "I have a house in Tokyo. With a garden. It is good for a man to dig earth at the end of his days."

"Is it a big house?"

"Enough. It helps me lay my spirit to rest." Then with another of those rapid changes of subject he added, "I want to come to Hong Kong."

Winston spread his arms in a gesture of welcome. "Be my guest."

Watanabe finished eating tidily, pushed his plate away and sat back in his chair. "You do not know, do you," he said, shaking his head. "You cannot know. You were too young to remember what that war was like."

"No," Winston acknowledged.

"All my life I have been in wars," Watanabe said, sadly. "In 1936 the Chinese, 1941 the British, 1963 Vietnam. Three wars." He held up the fingers of his right hand like an accusation. "In all of them I fought for what I believed. For the Emperor," he bowed low over his plate, "for Japan, for freedom. I think I fought with nobility, like a samurai."

Winston pushed away his plate and lit a cigarette. "It was a long time ago," he said. "Even the Yanks are getting out of Vietnam."

"All people are not as young as you," Watanabe replied. "There are many persons who remember. It is a question of attitude to war. With us Japanese it is total. In 1941 it was not a game. We were fighting for survival. You understand, we *believed* in the South-East Asia Co-prosperity Sphere. That belief, that totality made us offend others' code of behaviour."

"It was still a long time ago."

"I am still a wanted war criminal," Watanabe said.

"A lot of water —, look, it's all forgotten. We aren't interested in the Second World War any more."

"But they're still trying Germans."

"Not in Hong Kong."

"I want to be sure," Watanabe said. "I want assurances. There are things I have to do." He paused, the immobile black eyes looking past Winston, staring unseeingly at the harbour. "Christmas day 1941 I was in Hong Kong. My brother died in the New Territories, also other friends, comrades. Their bodies must be taken back to Japan before I, who was their commander, can find peace. That is the code of the samurai.

The waiter cleared away the dishes and brought coffee.

Abruptly Watanabe asked, "What is the strongest country in the world?"

"Militarily you mean? America of course."

"Why America?"

"They have the money, the manpower, the technology."

"Missiles," Watanabe said. "Do you know of the latest Chinese tests at Lop Wor?"

Winston shook his head.

"Up to five megatons. I have the details." This with quiet pride.

Winston went very still, smoke curling out of his mouth as he exhaled softly.

Watanabe nodded. "You think they are not a threat, that they have no aeroplanes to carry their bombs?"

Winston rapidly summarised his knowledge of the Chinese Air Force. Copies of Russian Mig-21's and medium range twin jet bombers. Not really sufficient for an airborne nuclear attack. "They haven't got the air power," he said firmly.

"They don't need air power," Watanabe said. "These tests were war heads for ICBM's, range six thousand miles, only forty per cent penetration needed to kill eleven million Americans. There are twenty-five launch sites."

"You should be talking to the CIA."

Watanabe smiled. "The CIA do not own Hong Kong. This is what I give the British, for my freedom and one hundred thousand American dollars."

Winston whistled softly. "That's a hell of a lot of bread."

32

"There's more. Hard facts. Details of the solid propellant power plant, details of MRBM launch sites, plans and personnel in the U-235 plant in Lankow." Watanabe leant forward, warming to his task. "Details of the Russian T-62 tank, a new electronic missile guidance system. I give you all. Is cheap."

Winston said, "I haven't got the authority to deal with this. I'll have to talk to people higher up."

Watanabe leaned back, satisfied. "I know," he said. "You will do that?"

"Sure," Winston replied, "sure."

Watanabe leant forward again. "And for you I have special present. Free. You have problems with students, yes?"

"We sure do, the bolshy bastards."

"Then be warned. Ogishima of the Red Army group was in Hong Kong only last week. He met with your student leaders. And there is a shipment of arms coming, arms stolen from US dumps, FN automatic rifles, ammunition, flechettes, plastic, number 8 detonators."

"Jesus Christ!"

"I am sorry I cannot tell you more. That is all I know." Watanabe stood up. "I will see you in Macau at seven o'clock tonight, at the Hotel Lisboa."

"Jesus Christ!" Winston exclaimed again.

*   *   *

Ex-DC Alec Thompson puffed steadily at his Dunhill, as Pete Winston told him exactly what he had learned in Macau. Alec Thompson was the Far East section head of DI6. He had been in Intelligence for ten years, and before that spent seventeen years in the Hong Kong Police Force, soon after three years in the war in Burma. He knew the value of careful listening, and the expression on his ruddy-cheeked face was one of interested unhurriedness; the air of a man who was not going to interrupt, and didn't.

Thompson was a robust framed fifty-four, a man who

33

with his outdoor complexion and semi-circle of silver hair looked more like a retired naval commander than the policeman he had been. His deep set blue eyes were firmly locked on to Pete Winston.

Winston couldn't stop shivering as he spoke. He had hurried straight from the Macau hydrofoil to Thompson's office above a bank in Central, no great distance, but it was a Turkish bath of a day and even sitting in the taxi had made the sweat pour off in streams. Now Winston hoped his shirt would dry out before the air conditioning gave him pneumonia and tried to keep his story as short and as interesting as possible.

Behind Thompson's kindly, almost school-masterish facade lay a shrewd and analytical awareness of matters criminal. Thompson had been the youngest District Commissioner in the Hong Kong Police and he suffered fools less than gladly. Winston could feel Thompson's interest growing as he spoke, the puffs of smoke from the Dunhill growing slower and more rhythmic, a kind of warmth seeping out of the piercing blue eyes. Winston felt bold enough to ask to be placed in charge of the arms operation.

Thompson took the pipe out of his mouth and looked steadily at the mound of smoky ash in its bowl. Big, strong fingers. Big, roughened bowl. "I agree with you," Thompson said when he had finished contemplating the pipe. "It's fair that you handle it. You've done well for us before and after all, it is your contact. But Special Branch won't like it."

Thompson's jacket lay rumpled over a chair, his unfashionable tie was yanked down the front of his shirt, and his open cuffs trailed links over the crowded desk. Thompson was not a man who liked rules or precedent for their own sake.

"I'm not sure, sir, that Watanabe would like the Special Branch."

"I've thought of that. But you will need some assistance from SB — the files at least."

"I was thinking of co-operation, sir, not exclusion."

"Very well. I'll speak to SB about it. I'm sure it will be all right." He paused to smile briefly at Winston. "It isn't as if you are totally inexperienced in this kind of work."

Winston smiled back, thinking warmly of Whampoa.

"Now tell me, what do you think of all this?" The pipe scattered ash over the papers on the desk, as if they were Watanabe's story.

"I believe the man."

"He's a crafty swine," Thompson said. "Trustworthy as a bankrupt's cheque. He was a war criminal all right. Here, Guadalcanal, Batavia, Malaya. And we want him badly. Wanted him." Thompson shrugged. "Don't suppose we could try him now, though. New generation and all that. Young people have no memory of that war, and the Japanese are now our best trading partners."

The old man was uncommonly loquacious, Winston thought, perhaps it was Watanabe and the war triggering off youthful memories. He wondered whether one day he too would be looking back on his service career as the high point of his life.

"You know, I nearly had Watanabe once. It was just after the war. He was hiding out in Shatin Temple. But he got away. Someone tipped him off before we got there. I believe he went over to the Americans. Isn't that where you met him?"

Winston nodded.

"Look after him, he's been good to you."

"He can come to Hong Kong, then. And the money?"

"Hong Kong's all right. Do you know why he came to us?"

Winston shook his head. "Only what he said. Money and freedom."

"And all that bullshit about burying his comrades. It's not right, Peter. He could have done the same deal with the Americans and got more money out of it. Oh yes, they could have leant on us to let him into Hong Kong."

"His information in the past has always been accurate."

35

Thompson was having ignition trouble with his pipe. It was making sucking noises and he put it down on the desk.

"In this game Peter, one doesn't trust anybody. People are basically selfish, out to satisfy their own needs even when they appear to be fulfilling yours. Remember that."

"You think Watanabe is working as a double?"

"With Watanabe quadruple is more likely, but there you are. You've got to work with what you've got. It's a right old rag bag. Russian tanks, Chinese missiles, Japanese arms smugglers. Somebody's been dredging a barrel for this stuff. A big deep barrel mind you, but still dredging."

Winston looked at his watch. If he was to get back to Macau by seven he would have to leave soon. "What shall I tell him?"

"Oh, invite him to Hong Kong by all means. But we're not going to part with a hundred thousand dollars till we're damn sure we've got what we want. He'll have to give us samples and they will have to be checked out by London. Tell him that will take at least two weeks. Meanwhile he can be our guest."

*　　　*　　　*

The next day, despite some indignation from DI6, Watanabe had moved into a suite at the Peninsula Hotel, and Special Branch had agreed, albeit reluctantly, to the exercise in co-operation. Now all Pete Winston had to do was obtain the Assistant Commissioner's approval to his part in the operation without, at the same time telling him too much, or letting him know of his connections with DI6. There was nothing like inter-departmental rivalry to screw things up and as Winston paced about his office in Wan Chai Police Station, he hit upon an idea. Actually idea was too good a word for it. It was simply a matter of technique.

5

IN THE MORTUARY they were still dissecting Raghavan's cadaver; a group of white clad figures bending earnestly over a high table, glimpses of peeled back flesh and shiny talons of bone. Beside the body, its organs were set out on grey zinc, little bloody parcels like a butcher's shop, only not so well displayed. Deep brown of liver, pale yellows, a mound of intestines brilliantly coloured blue and bright purple, flashes of red; the interior of the body was a kaleidoscope, Chan thought, leaning against the cream wall, trying not to breathe too deeply.

Death was always ugly, always messy, liquefying tissues and gas distention, the skin coming away from the bone in damp patches. There was nothing dignified nor spiritually uplifting about the brutal act of dying. God in his wisdom could surely have chosen a less revolting method of bringing man closer to him, Chan thought, feeling a sharp twinge of guilt at questioning familiar dogma.

Chan was a Roman Catholic. His parents, believing in the fundamental and equal good of all religions, had accepted without qualm his compulsory conversion to an alien faith. It was a small price to pay for the advantages of an education. They had reckoned however without Father Loyola or Chan's own need for a systematic belief. It was the sheer logicality of the faith that had first attracted Chan, the application of reason to known fundamentals,

37

like an approach to a murder enquiry. He had grown to appreciate the sense of unerring rightness, the belief in rules and order and ritual, in defined purposes, the sense of belonging to an esoteric community. It was much like being a policeman, in fact, only better.

Mackenzie, the Senior Pathologist, saw Chan and moved away from the group around the body, hands covered by stained rubber gloves held away from him as he walked, clutching a blood-stained scalpel. He brought with him a stronger odour of death. Chan knew that already the smell would have seeped into his clothing, blended with his skin, his eyes, and his hair, that the odour of open cess pits and rotting fruit would hover insidiously about him for days.

"I suppose ye'll be wantin' to know what time he died."

Chan eased away from the wall. He couldn't see much of Mackenzie's face above the mask. A pair of bright grey eyes, sandy brows, freckles that mottled his forehead and the bridge of his nose. A tall man with a slight stoop as if he was forever entering low doorways.

The time of death was relevant, not crucial. Chan waited for Mackenzie to tell him.

"You found him at what time — six in the morning?"

Chan nodded.

"I'd say he died about then, give or take an hour. He's been as pliable as a wee bairn all morning. Look, he's only just beginning to stiffen."

Chan glanced towards the table. His sergeant was standing a discreet distance away. Chan glimpsed the sheen of skull threaded between streaks of blood and cobweb like hair. "How did he die?"

"The bullet killed him, man. Not that he wouldna' died anyway."

"How do you mean?"

"We're all going to die, man."

Chan winced at the pathologist's hoary joke, winced at letting himself get caught for the umpteenth time.

38

"But this one would have died quicker than most. He were a hard drinking laddie. Liver corroded like the bottom of an old barge."

"Was he drunk when he was shot?"

"I cannot say if he were drunk or no, but he'd been drinking all right. At least a half bottle of guid scotch, I'd say. Shagged himself dry as well."

"How do you know that?" Chan asked quickly, anxious for data that would show how Raghavan spent his last hours, hoping to find some trace of a jealous husband or boyfriend.

"Simple, laddie. Collapsed scrotum, stained underpants and pubic hair that weren't his."

"What about the torture?"

"Bad," Mackenzie said. The grey eyes were grave. "Splinters under the fingernails, two ribs kicked in, cigarette burns all over the body, like a Jap POW. But it weren't the torture that killed him. It was the bullet."

At six o'clock in the morning, in the middle of Yee Wo Road. Still no clue as to who or why. All Chan knew was when and how, but he'd known that all morning. He left the mortuary and went back to the station, clutching the idea of Raghavan's sexual proclivities like the end of a thread in a maze.

*   *   *

Chan returned to the station to find Sergeant Lau confronting a slightly built, pale blond man, pink from the sun, wearing a lightweight suit, horn rimmed spectacles and an expression of total bewilderment.

"You are Inspector Chan," Lau was saying.

"No, no, I am not. I want to *see* Inspector Chan."

"You are Inspector Chan and you would like to see Inspector Chan. There are two of you, yes?"

"I am *not* Inspector Chan. My name's Snaith," the man said. "I want to see Inspector Chan."

"If your name is Snaith why are you pretending to be Inspector Chan?"

"I'm not pretending to be anybody. I only said — "

"But you look like Inspector Chan."

"Do I?"

"You aren't wearing a disguise are you?"

"No," Snaith said. "All I want to — "

It was an old CID game, whose purpose was nearly as obscure as its origin. Chan stepped between the men and said, "I am Chan."

Snaith looked even more bewildered. Then as if doubting the sound of his own voice he said, "I am Snaith from Ballistics," and waited for something disastrous to happen.

Chan took Snaith into his office and offered him a seat.

"The bullet was in the roof lining of the taxi," Snaith said.

"I'm glad you found it."

Snaith took out an envelope and emptied the lead bullet into his palm. "Ever seen one of these?"

"Oh, yes. I've seen bullets before."

"This is the first time I've seen one of these," Snaith said.

"Hell, I thought you were an expert."

Snaith said, "It's an 8 mm. A very unusual calibre."

"Ah," Chan said. "I see."

"First time I've seen one of these," Snaith repeated.

"Are we to look for a very unusual gun, then?" Chan asked.

Snaith pursed his lips and wrinkled his brow, considering his next statement carefully. "It may not be that unusual," he said at last. "Not in Hong Kong, anyway. The only 8 mm weapon I know of, is the Nambu. It looks something like a Luger, though the locking system is pure Mauser."

"What kind of gun is it?" Chan asked tersely.

"It's a pistol. It was the standard Japanese sidearm during the war." Snaith shrugged. "I suppose there would

40

be quite a few Nambus knocking around Hong Kong."

A few Raghavans too, Chan thought, saying, "I suppose so." As soon as Snaith left, Chan leant through the doorway and shouted to Sergeant Lau in the Squad Room, asking him if he'd found the fucking gun yet.

*   *   *

Lau came into Chan's office clutching three large envelopes. "From the photographer," he said. Chan slit one of the envelopes, took out a photograph and looked at Raghavan, blank eyed and secretive in death, the bruise on his face heightened by the graininess of the print. "So you didn't find the gun," Chan said.

Lau shook his head violently. "Sorry, chief. We looked everywhere."

"If you did, you would have found it. In case you find you've been sitting on it, it's a Nambu."

"What the hell's that?"

"A Japanese gun, stupid. Looks like a Luger. Hell, I don't know why I put up with you."

Lau smiled. "Because you like my shirts."

"Oh God," Chan said and masked his eyes as if avoiding a direct light. Suddenly he became serious again. Mackenzie had said that Raghavan had been tortured like a Japanese prisoner of war. Altogether there was too much Japanese involvement in this case. Raghavan had come to Hong Kong from Tokyo, he had been killed by a Japanese gun, he had been tortured like a Japanese POW. Abruptly Chan stood up.

"Where are you going, chief?"

"Central. City Library. Our body once worked for the *Asian Clarion*. I'm going to look at a few back numbers."

*   *   *

The girl in the City Hall Library said they didn't usually keep three years back numbers of any magazine, even the *Asian Clarion*. She said she would have to obtain them.

"How long will that take?" striving to keep the impatience and disappointment out of his voice.

"Not long, twenty minutes, half hour."

Chan decided to wait, staring around him at the serious-faced students, at the notice boards filled with announcements of exhibitions and the dust jackets of books. The girl didn't take half an hour. She was back in fifteen minutes, leaning over him to place the volumes of bound magazines on the table, hitching the mauve mini skirt further up her slim thighs. Chan felt a flash of friendly desire, resisted it and an urge to touch, began to read.

Kenneth Wong, Deputy Editor and wearer of poplin shirts and cravats, had told him that Raghavan had left nine months previously. The most recent piece by Raghavan was seven months old, but then it might well have been written before he left. It was an article about corruption in Manila, interviews with government officials, businessmen and gangsters. Rather close to home that, Chan thought. Motive for a killing, but surely not in Hong Kong. Chan remembered the little publicised family in Calcutta and wondered if Raghavan had ever had a home. Wondering still he turned over the pages. No, Raghavan hadn't done an article on corruption in Hong Kong. Nothing as easy as that. Nothing unusual either. Raghavan's subject matter and style fitted easily into the magazine. An interview with a Filipino pop star, an article explaining why the Chinese would never be a nuclear power (inability to produce U-235 required for triggering off a hydrogen bomb), an interview with a painter on Asian life styles, an account of American foreign policy towards Taiwan. A mixture of news, views and all the background you need for gracious living as the editorial banner proclaimed.

A few months before he left the *Clarion*, Raghavan had done some pieces on Japan. Excited, Chan took out his notebook. Articles on wife-beating, Sumo wrestlers, Kabuki, the Japanese obsession with gross national product, a stage by stage description of the manufacture of a Toyota. Harmless,

42

innocuous, just the kind of stuff that made the *Asian Clarion* a status symbol for every trendy Asian executive.

There were five thousand words on secret right wing movements inside Japan. 'Once again the Japanese are digging Emperor worship,' Raghavan had written in the hip journalese the *Asian Clarion* favoured. 'A powerful caucus of former Imperial Army Officers and dedicated young men, disillusioned by Japanese dollar worship, self immolating neutrality, and the ever swifter erosion of tradition.'

Raghavan had described the method of one of these movements — the *Ao Arashi* — the Blue Storm — blue being the symbolic Japanese colour of purity. Training in judo and aikido, the use of weapons, riot control and demonstrations. There was a photograph of a group of young militants demonstrating outside the Emperor's palace, wearing white headbands emblazoned with the bloody red circle of the rising sun. These people stood for a return to the old ways, the creation of a powerful army, the rebuilding of national pride. They were opposed to Communism, foreign manners, trade unions and the industrial exploitation of their country. The leader of the *Ao Arashi* was one Hiroshi Watanabe.

Raghavan had not been able to interview Watanabe. Nevertheless the facts he presented were chilling. Born in 1907, Watanabe had graduated from the Tokyo Military Academy with honours and remained there as a Morals Instructor. He had participated in the China campaign where he acquired a reputation as a burner of brothels and the officer whose army massacred the civilians at Shansi.

Chan remembered his parents' tales of hordes of refugees pouring in from the north, their tales of atrocity and the word that had been on everyone's lips. Nanking. Nanking, the city that had been allowed to burn for twelve days, while Japanese soldiers murdered thousands, raped and pillaged. With the imperfect memory of childhood he remembered huddling on the deck, his father's arms around

43

him as they crossed to Hong Kong, still fleeing the Japanese. Anger grew inside Chan and he had to tell himself that this was an old war. This was no way to solve a murder. He read on.

In 1940, the year of Chan's crossing, Watanabe had become Deputy Head of the 82nd Bureau. Together with Colonel Yoshihada and Colonel Yamashita he had formed the plan that saw most of Asia succumb to the Japanese invasion. What else Watanabe had done during the war, Raghavan had not known. In 1952, Watanabe had apparently reappeared in Japan, become a member of the Diet, and then a journalist. Raghavan implied strongly that Watanabe's fear of Communism had temporarily overcome his xenophobia, and that he had joined the CIA.

Chan looked up subsequent issues. There had been no apologies, no withdrawals, no libel suits. He went back again to the pre-Japanese period. Visits to Singapore, an article on the effect of long hair on drug users (most users and pushers in Singapore now wore their hair short), the debt of Mandarin hit songs to rock and roll, an interview with a Chinese singer, cock fighting in Bangkok, tin mining in Malaya, all innocuous. Chan wondered whether if Raghavan had not been killed with a Japanese gun, the piece on the right wing movement would not have appeared just as innocuous, and leaving the magazines on the table, smiled at the librarian and went out.

6

OUTSIDE REFULGENT TRAFFIC crawled, tall buildings stood slabsided under turgid grey cloud, the air was as clammy as a steam bath. Chan strode across the road into Statue Square, filling up now with lunchtime strollers, slim-hipped secretaries and shirt-sleeved clerks, young, smart, neat as new pins. Chan hurried along, going nowhere, his hands thrust deep into his pockets, heavy brows knitted together, face screwed up pugnaciously, thinking.

No libel writs, no apologies, no corrections. Was that because the Japanese knew the answer lay in a gun? But then why waste six months before killing the man? If Raghavan had known too much he would have had ample opportunity to pass the information on. In any case why kill him in Hong Kong when killing him in Tokyo would have been easier? Raghavan had been in Tokyo recently. Why? And why had he come to Hong Kong? Escape? But then why the detour to Taiwan? A man on the run doesn't stop off sight-seeing. And where was Raghavan's passport anyway? At his hotel? With the killers?

Chan saw the bean-pole figure towering above the swirling Chinese clerks and secretaries, peering into the plate-glass window of a camera store, his khaki uniform sagging about his spare frame like old clothes on a scarecrow. Chan stood on tiptoe and whispered, "The students have blown up Wan Chai Police Station."

45

Superintendent Brian Hanson's deep socketed blue eyes raked over Chan's reflection amongst the cameras in the window. He turned, smiling. Chan settling down on his heels reflected how deceptive Hanson's build really was. Close to, Chan was uncomfortably aware of the breadth of bony shoulders, of wiry arms and a hard muscled body.

"Hello Richard," Hanson said. He flapped an arm towards the window. "What do you think of the new Takumar wide angle?"

Chan looked. "Good," he said. Because of the police custom that required a uniformed man to be in charge of a station, Hanson was nominally Chan's immediate superior. But Hanson was experienced enough to know that Chan's work and his were dissimilar. He rarely interfered with Chan and never pulled rank.

"Bloody expensive!" Hanson said.

"Put up the take from the mini buses," Chan suggested. They turned away from the window and walked along the pavement.

"That isn't funny, Richard. Not with the anti-corruption boys hanging round like leeches."

"In one year's time we will have anti-anti-corruption boys hanging around the anti-corruption boys like leeches," Chan said.

"God, you make it sound so depressing."

"Depressing Brian? This is the romantic Far East. *Tam woo* is a way of life. It is an old Chinese custom. Nothing for nothing. Even if you don't take, you have to give."

"What are you saying? That we should all be corrupt? All take bribes?"

"We all do," Chan said. "We're all on retainers." The retainer was the monthly share out, the market price for overlooking petty crimes. Everyone, but everyone was involved in it.

"How's your stomach?" Hanson asked. "Fancy *dim sum*?"

Chan remembered with a sense of shock that all he'd had

that morning was a cup of tea, well over three hours ago. "Let's have steak," he suggested. "Now."

*   *   *

They ate in a steak bar off Des Voeux Road, all red shaded electric candles and dark wood the colour of sherry casks, the kind of place that would be described as intimate at dinner time, but just now, crowded and noisy, full of bustling waiters and fledgling taipans from Jardines.

Chan ordered a medium rare fillet for Hanson, tartar for himself, San Miguel and lemonade.

"How the devil can you mix lemonade and beer?" Hanson demanded, venting his irritability at Chan's digs about bribery. Bribery was a very dirty word in Hong Kong just at the moment, especially amongst policemen. A few months previously Chief Superintendent Godber, formerly second in command of Kowloon Police District had left hurriedly for the United Kingdom, leaving behind him an unanswered query from the anti-corruption squad as to how he had amassed a small fortune in the last five years. Godber's departure had been embarrassing to the police in more ways than one. It was rumoured that lots of little pigeons were coming home to roost and everyone was walking around trying to look as pious as the Pope and making no comment about Godber. Except of course, the students.

Chan said reasonably, "Lemonade and beer is sweet. Beer is bitter." He liked Brian Hanson. No fancy graces about him, no feeling that he had come to rule. A good honest experienced cop doing his job as best as he knew how.

"But you never take sugar with your tea," Hanson said. "Or milk."

"I'm different," Chan said. "I'm just an ignorant Chinese prick."

Hanson smiled, a big, frank smile, full lips parting under the pencil-line moustache. The glow from the lamp gave his face a ruddy colour, taking away its customary yellow

47

pallor. Hanson was the sickest looking fit man Chan knew. He always got A at his medical just as he always looked as if he was recuperating from a serious illness.

"You weren't at the meeting with the AC," Hanson said.

"I should leave a murder enquiry to talk to the AC about students?"

"Wish I had a murder enquiry," Hanson grumbled. "Those damn students are nothing but trouble."

Chan grinned. Those damn students were organising a rally, calling for Godber's return, using the fact of his continued sanctuary in Great Britain to highlight the exploitation of Hong Kong by the British. The rally was a source of grave distress to the administration, the ex-pats and most of all to the police. It kept Godber's name before the public eye, despite the fact that the hastily erected hand drawn posters were just as hastily torn down. Perhaps something would come of it to end the system that allowed corruption to flourish, but Chan thought not.

"How's your murder going?"

Chan sipped his drink. "Nowhere and fast."

Chan thought about Godber. Everyone was talking about a hell of a lot of money. And the reports had said not by luck or inheritance. Not by writing out parking tickets either.

Chan remembered the first time he had been offered a retainer, $150 in an envelope from a civilian clerk. He didn't have to do anything, just spend it. A friendly gesture from a well wisher. At the time Chan had been aware he was being tested. Someone wanted to know if he was one of the boys. He had left the envelope in his locker for three days while he reflected. Being a cop meant working within the system, and then, being a cop had meant more to Chan than anything else in the world. In the end he had kept the money. But despite his retainer, he had done his best to be careful. Careful never to need the money, never to take too much, careful only to overlook petty offences or those created by stupid, artificial laws. It was necessary

48

absolution for venial sin, Chan thought wickedly and asked, "How did the meeting go?"

Hanson frowned into his beer. "Bad. Good. Depends how you look at it. Your friend Winston was there. Apparently someone's shipping arms to the students."

"For the rally?" incredulously.

"So Winston said. Sounded pretty convincing too. The AC is behind him."

Chan felt his throat go dry and drank some more shandy. "I don't believe it," he said. "I don't see how anyone can believe it. All the students want is Godber back in Hong Kong and on trial."

"Don't they know Godber cannot be extradited from the UK?"

"No," Chan said. "That is something you and I know because we work with the law. For a simple Chinese it is difficult to understand." He stopped while the waiter brought their food, and began to eat, hungrily. "For nearly a hundred years you people have been telling us that your Queen is our Queen, you've been making us observe laws passed by a Parliament in London where we are not even represented, you've even tried to persuade us to think of UK as home and now you want us to believe that England is a separate country which does not recognise Hong Kong's anti-corruption laws, and therefore cannot extradite Godber!"

Hanson said, "It's tough. I see the problem. How do you feel about Godber?"

"I want to see Godber brought back and tried. It might make a few million people believe that the law is the same for everyone including Englishmen and policemen. It will also stop us looking such bloody fools."

"Fools is right. We look a right bunch of nanas."

Chan put down his cutlery and spread his hands out. "How the hell could they have let him get away, Brian. Tell me that. How *could* they?"

"A simple, administrative cock up," Hanson said

equably. "It is gratifying to know our superiors and betters are human too."

"They should have had him under twenty-four hour surveillance," Chan said. "And confiscated his passport."

Hanson laughed. "Godber was an instructor in surveillance techniques. He would have rumbled them as easy as pie. And then what? Cries of harassment and protests from every liberal in the Colony about personal liberties."

"Too bloody British," Chan said.

"I don't know, Richard. It isn't a bad system, inconvenient, as we both know and also allows us to be made monkeys of. But it's better than a lot of other things. Godber wasn't charged with anything. He was and still is innocent. I don't think our chaps have done a bad job anyway. I mean, they checked out something like four hundred and eighty-seven banks, they moved into HQ without Godber sussing anything, they put him on a stop list at Kai Tak, they got all the evidence they thought they needed, and — "

"And then someone forgot about asking him for his passport or that he had a Red Card allowing him to go anywhere in the airport."

"A simple cock up," Hanson said again. "It could happen to anyone."

"And now we've got armed students?"

"According to Pete Winston."

Chan looked out past the red-curtained window, at the traffic clotting the street outside.

"Winston was very persuasive," Hanson went on, "And I must say he handled the meeting superbly. References to the principle of confidentiality of sources, his eagerness to do his best, he had the AC eating out of his hand at the end. Winston's got carte blanche on this operation, as he will undoubtedly tell you."

Chan looked back at Hanson. "Winston's looking for promotion," he said dully. "That's all. Even if what he says is true, he's too inexperienced to be in charge of such an operation."

"Not my decision old chap. AC's already made up his mind." Hanson's tone was firm, non-committed.

"Winston's too unsure of himself," Chan said, "too absorbed in how things affect him. He's also too involved with security and revolution and things like that and can't and won't understand the people he is dealing with — the Chinese."

Hanson settled back in his chair and lit a cigarette. "There's something else I want to talk to you about," he said pointedly. "You've got approval for a rally at Victoria Park the same day as the students."

"Have I?"

"Yes. I got the papers this morning. I've vetoed it."

"That's all right," Chan said. "They can have their rally the following week." He finished eating and sighed deeply, replete.

Hanson's face behind the spiralling smoke of his cigarette was watchful. "Tell me Richard, how carefully did you check these people out?"

One of the less interesting jobs of the CID was checking the status of organisers of public meetings before the Urban Council gave their approval. Chan remembered the Indian gentleman who had called on him some months previously and who had introduced himself as Mr. Datt, Secretary and Treasurer of the Delhi Foundation. Datt had been a quiet, self-effacing, excrutiatingly polite man. Chan had only checked on him cursorily. He had offices on the seventh floor of a building in Lockhart Road, and the purposes of the Foundation were charitable and educational. Chan could not believe that anyone as meek and grateful as Datt had been could start any trouble.

"We checked them out briefly," Chan said.

"I thought so," Hanson replied. "Do you know why they are holding this meeting? It is to sanctify the memory of Subhas Chandra Bose. You know who Bose was, don't you?"

"No. Should I?"

"I suppose not. You are a little too young. He was a bloody traitor. If you doubt me, ask ex-DC Thompson."

Chan was already on his feet, spilling notes on the table. He'd had another idea. The Indians in Hong Kong were a small community, and like small groups of exiles everywhere, everyone knew everybody else. Perhaps, Chan thought, the self-effacing Mr. Datt could tell him something about the late, and presently unlamented Mr. Raghavan.

7

THE OFFICES OF the Delhi Foundation lay behind stencilled panes of frosted glass, situated half way down a dismal corridor, fuzzily blue with low key neon. Through the door, a secretary's cubicle, battered Underwood typewriter, shrouded Roneo duplicator, cluttered grey filing cabinet, boxes of stationery on the worn lino. Chan had not checked these offices himself. Sergeant Yim had done that, hadn't said anything about the smell though, or the secretary, middle-aged woman, fat, myopic, rummaging in her handbag before settling down for the afternoon. She looked too fresh to have worked all day. Part time probably.

There were no chairs for waiting visitors. Chan stood in the crowded office and looked at the calendar on the wall. Beautiful, oval-eyed, smiling sareed girl with skin like brown silk. The date for Sunday fortnight was ringed in red.

Datt appeared at the communicating door, over-effusive, insistent on shaking hands, murmuring, "How are you, please come in, how nice to see you, Inspector Chan." A small man, three inches shorter than Chan, with the build of a wiry spaniel. Spaniel eyes too, and brown skin roughened with acne scars, not at all like silk more like taffeta. He was in his late forties or early fifties, though the immature face made him look a good deal younger. Neatly dressed, blue lightweight suit and red tie, wearing a jacket in that heat, a man seeking reassurance in presentability.

His office was much less presentable, crowded with over-stuffed filing cabinets and papers strewn over a small wooden desk. The green leather of his chair was stained. There were two upright chairs for visitors, old and somewhat infirm. Above Datt's desk was a photograph of a moon faced bespectacled Indian, wearing a Nehru cap and an expression of carefully posed blankness. A dusty paper garland was draped across the picture. Obviously Subhas Chandra Bose himself, thought Chan, what a po-faced creature.

Chan sat down on one of the chairs and looked at the afternoon sun slashing through drawn venetian blinds. It had turned fine outside. Inside, the air was thick, smelling of seed oil and extinguished joss-sticks. Chan thought of bugs and moved his thin trousered thighs cautiously.

Datt was still murmuring, "Good afternoon, good afternoon, would you like a cup of tea."

Policemen always aroused such sub-conscious guilt. Chan belched softly. "I've just had lunch," he said, thinking that the tea cups might not be all that clean.

Datt smiled hesitantly, uncertain whether he had been rebuffed. The Foundation obviously operated on a shoestring, Chan thought. The walls needed painting, even though Yim had said the office had only been taken fifteen months ago. The rent was thirty thousand dollars a year. That was good money, even though it didn't show.

"I have bad news for you," Chan said.

"Ah-ha! Bad news, ah! What bad news?"

"Permission for your rally has been refused."

Datt blinked, hurt and incomprehension succeeding each other in the round black eyes. "But you said — " Timorous now, Datt was a man unused to fighting back.

"I know I did. But the students are using Victoria Park on Sunday week. They're trying to bring back Godber."

"Ah yes. Ah yes, I see. Bring back Godber. That would

54

be good, no . . ." His voice tailed off as if he had suddenly realised that Chan was a policeman, too. "Bad?" Datt was twisting his fingers together and cracked a knuckle. "But we can have our rally the following week, ah."

"You'll have to make another application," Chan said, cool now, bureaucratic. It wasn't professional to be involved with a witness, especially over rally permits.

"Another one!" Datt slapped his forehead with the palm of his hand and repeated, "Another one! Oh, disaster! Disaster! That will take months!"

Chan felt a stirring of sympathy. "Not months," he said. "A week or two. Can't you postpone your arrangements?"

"Postpone? No, no. Impossible. It is too late, too late." Datt looked devastated. "Our President is arriving from Kuala Lumpur," he explained. "He is arriving tomorrow. Mr. Suresh Banerjee, Chairman of the Alor Setor Group. He is the founder of our organisation. It is all his."

From the way Datt said it, Banerjee's name should have meant something. The Alor Setor Group, too. But Chan's mind was blank. That could wait, he decided, he could always check who they were, if it became necessary.

"Send him a cable and tell him to wait till next week."

"Impossible, impossible. He is coming anyway to Hong Kong." Datt cracked another knuckle, Banerjee was obviously very important to him, possibly overbearing too.

"Disaster, disaster," muttered Datt disconsolately.

Chan said, "I didn't come about the rally." He placed Raghavan's photograph on the desk. "Do you know this man?" He kept his voice flat, his expression set. A shock enquiry.

It worked. Datt's eyes stared, teeth tugged at his lower lip, knuckles cracked furiously and he wriggled in his chair as if he would like to twist away and run. Raghavan's photograph was proving to be a greater disaster than the postponement of the rally.

"He is dead."

Genuine shock or defence mechanism playing for time?

"You know him?" Chan had to handle this carefully. Too much firmness, too much aggression, and Datt could panic into incoherence.

Datt looked up from the photograph and closed his eyes as if trying to erase the image of Raghavan's bruised face. He nodded vehemently. "I know him. Not well. He was a journalist and he came once or twice to Hong Kong. Oh tragedy, tragedy. He is murdered, no? You are asking me to help you in the investigation of which you are in charge?"

Confused syntax. Poor, confused Mr. Datt. Chan lowered his voice, injecting gentleness and patience into its tone. "When did you last see him?"

"Over a year ago. Truly."

Unnecessary emphasis on veracity, Chan thought. "So he was a good friend of yours?"

"No, no. Not a good friend. Oh no, no. Simply an acquaintance."

"Did you know if he was married? Did he have a family?"

"No, no. I know nothing. I only met him once or twice."

"Has he ever visited your home?"

"Once. He came to my place for dinner."

"What did you talk about?"

"This and that. He did not stay long. He was not a vegetarian." The point obviously still rankled with Datt. "He was not even a good Hindu. He had thrown away his sacred thread and he told me he never did *puja*."

"He drank, too."

"Oh yes. Good drinker. One bottle of whisky was nothing to him."

A slight note of pride, there, strangely like a schoolboy boast. Unusual. Raghavan must have been more than a casual acquaintance for Datt to know his drinking habits.

"You don't drink?" Chan smiled now, teasing gently.

"No. It is forbidden. My religion — "

"When did you last see Raghavan?"

56

Datt frowned. Brows wrinkled in contemplation. His voice was low. "One year ago."

"That was the time he came to dinner?"

"Yes, yes. I think so."

"Aren't you sure?"

"Yes. I am sure."

Chan knew he damn well wasn't. "Do you know what he did after he left the *Asian Clarion*?"

Slow shake of head, but no show of surprise. Datt must have known that Raghavan had left the *Asian Clarion*, must have been in contact with Raghavan since he resigned. Raghavan had left the *Asian Clarion* nine months ago. Nine months was less than a year.

"You saw him last week?"

The shock effect didn't work. "No, no. Not last week."

"This week?"

"No, no. Last year."

"How did you first meet him?"

"I don't remember."

Another lie. Datt didn't look as if he had that many friends that he could forget his first meeting with a hard-drinking, meat-eating journalist.

"You must remember. Surely you remember how you met me?"

Datt nodded his head and smiled, as if to show that Chan was different. "A friend introduced him, with a letter. Mr. Chaterjee from Bangkok."

"What did the letter say?"

"That he was a journalist. That I should help him."

"Did you?"

"No. I only invited him to dinner, but that first time, he couldn't come."

"Do you remember why?"

"He was busy, he said."

"Was Raghavan a member of the Delhi Foundation?"

Hesitation, a prolonged pause for thought. "No. No. He

is not a member." But even the triple negative was less emphatic, a cause for concern.

Chan said softly, "This is a serious matter. A murder enquiry."

"I am helping. I am helping."

Chan decided to leave it at that. He was a great believer in the effect of time on an uneasy conscience, an old fashioned belief perhaps, but more effective than lie detectors, specially when someone was as frightened as Datt.

Chan stretched his legs in front of him and yawned. Rich smell of oil and joss-sticks. Sickening. Perhaps they opened the windows once a year to let the smell out.

"Who is Subhas Chandra Bose?" Chan asked looking up at the garlanded photograph, trying to assess the character behind the rigid face.

"A good man, a great man. He was our leader."

"A yogi?" No, that couldn't be right. Yogis wore loin cloths, and Bose looked too fat to be an ascetic.

"No. Our founder. He led us on the road to Delhi. Chalo Delhi! He made us free."

"Who," Chan asked, "and from what?" The air inside was getting too much for him. He should leave soon.

"He made us free, we Indians. We Bengalis. He brought us freedom from the British." Suddenly Datt shot out of his chair, rummaged in a filing cabinet and thrust a glossy pamphlet in Chan's hand. "Netaji's life story is there. Read it. You will like it."

Chan glanced cursorily at it as he stood up. 'Netaji — Saviour, Fighter, Martyr and Patriot'. About as interesting as the life of a saint, Chan thought stuffing it into his pocket. "What is the Delhi Foundation?" he asked.

"It is in memory of Subhas Chandra Bose." Datt looked up from under his eyelids, reverentially. "We spread his teaching to the Third World. And we do things in his memory."

"What things?"

"Scholarships. We help the poor."

"And the rally?"

"That is to focus attention on Bose's way. It was Mr. Banerjee's idea."

"Mr. Banerjee of the Alor Setor Group?"

"Yes, yes," Datt said, smiling, seemingly suddenly at peace.

*   *   *

The charge room was deliberately cheerless. Pale blue walls, stark upright chairs, a wooden desk devoid of everything but a lamp, a writing pad and a telephone, a waist high table by the door where, if necessary, a suspect could be made to empty his pockets. Lau was seated behind the desk, his face in shadow from the window behind him. The taxi driver was seated opposite.

Good, they were working fast. The pad in front of Lau was covered with ideograms. Chan went over, stood behind him and looked. The taxi driver's name was Lin Yu, aged twenty-four, married, two children, lived in Kennedy Town, the oldest part of the Colony and nothing whatsoever to do with the former American President. Lin Yu, if he was lucky, lived in a four-storey tenement with three hundred other people, or else squatted in a hut on the roof. He looked more like thirty than twenty-four, narrow, bony face, peaked forehead, close cropped hair and if the yellowish brown stains on his protruding teeth were anything to go by, smoked too much. He looked in need of a bath and a meal, his creased grey cotton shirt and slacks giving off a stale, unwashed smell. Understandably, he was nervous.

At two o'clock that morning Lin Yu had picked up three men near —

"What the hell is Narrow Way of the Biscuits?" Chan asked Lau.

Lau grinned. "Lane Crawfords, Lane — Way, Crawfords — "

Lane Crawfords was a big department store in Central. Chan read on. The men had been Chinese, not European.

59

The one who had spoken to Lin Yu had done so in fluent Cantonese. They had given him an address in Happy Valley, and he had taken them by the shortest route, along Queens Road East. There they had asked him to stop, put a gun to the back of his neck, and stuffed his face full of ether. When he woke up it was daylight and he was lying on a rubbish dump near Fanling, on the other side of the harbour.

A credible story, apprehensively told. Chan picked up the taxi driver's log book from the desk.

"What were you doing at Central at two o'clock in the morning? Nothing happens there, then."

The taxi driver's chair had been placed so that he couldn't touch the desk. He sat slouched forward, hands dangling between his thighs, uncomfortable. He kept his gaze at desk level. "I was — I had a fare to Morrison Street. I was on my way back."

Chan flicked open the log book. "No fares to Morrison Street," he said, simply. "What have you to say about that?"

The taxi driver had nothing to say.

Chan leafed through the book, took out his own notebook. "You're on the fiddle, my friend," he said. "You don't record all your hires and you tell the passengers your meter is broken."

Reluctantly, as if it weighed as much as a cannon ball, the man nodded.

"Your last hire was Kings Road to the Excelsior Hotel, right?"

The man nodded again.

"Go on friend, speak. That's what your tongue's for. Twelve forty-five? That was before you took the fare to Morrison Road?"

"Yes," the man said.

Chan tapped Lau's shoulder and eased into the chair. "You're lying," he said softly. "You've only got four miles on the clock since the Excelsior. You are a taxi driver. Tell me what is the distance from the Excelsior to Morrison Road?"

The man stared at Chan, face going white, as if he had been hit between the eyes.

"Tell me," Chan repeated softly.

"The speedometer cable must have broken."

"Didn't you know that? You drive without looking at your speedometer?"

"I don't know," the man said, "I don't remember. It was broken — perhaps."

Chan pushed Raghavan's photograph across the desk. "That man was killed in your taxi," he said. "We're talking about murder, my friend, and your speedometer cable was not broken. We checked."

"I know nothing," the man cried. "I don't remember."

Chan tapped the photograph. "Was he one of the men you picked up near Lane Crawfords?"

The taxi driver leaned forward and looked. "No," he said. "The men were Chinese."

"Why are you lying? You know it is dangerous to lie to the police."

"Not lying, not lying." Vehement shake of the head. "Speedo cable was broken."

Chan got up and walked round behind the man. "You can hang for this," he said. "You can be hung by the neck until you are dead." Chan stepped up to the taxi driver and grabbed him by the throat. The man gasped, started to tremble uncontrollably. Chan squeezed gently. "They put the noose round your neck like this," he said, "and stand you on a trap door. The door springs open and you drop. Most people shit in their pants then. Did you know that?" Viciously he jammed his hand against the man's windpipe. The man choked and tried to struggle. Chan held him easily, listening to the dry sobs of air, watching the face flush, the big vein in the forehead swell. When the man was on the verge of unconsciousness Chan released him, walked back to his own side of the desk. Chan felt unclean, the smell of stale perspiration and unwashed flesh clinging to his nostrils.

"It isn't worth it, is it?" Chan asked. "You dead, your wife becoming a whore, your children stealing food. Whom are you trying to protect?"

"No one," the man said. "Believe me, please, no one."

"Why did you lie?"

The man stayed silent, rubbing his throat.

"Your friends don't care," Chan said. "*They* are not going to hang."

Before the man could reply, the phone rang. Chan swore under his breath. The spell of the interrogation was broken. Lau picked up the phone, grumbled a few yesses, and said he'd be down there as soon as possible.

"Hotels have found where Raghavan was staying," Lau announced. "The Harbour."

Chan looked at his watch, "Better get down there," he said. "I'll join you as soon as I can."

But twenty minutes later, the taxi driver hadn't said anymore, adamant in his duplicity.

8

THE HARBOUR HOTEL was a few blocks from the police station, along Gloucester Road. Chan walked there, past provision stores and narrow motor repair shops, just wide and just long enough to take two cars front to back, past drowsy bars advertising '*Any kind of mixed drink four dollars. Welcome American servicemen*', past the grey and staid Luk Kwok Hotel, once the boisterous home of Suzie Wong.

Chan stopped at an open window to buy a blandly sweet cake wrapped in rice paper, giving the photographers and fingerprint men time to get over to the Harbour Hotel and out again. Wan Chai, in the thinly bright afternoon light looked industriously sober, the thrum of traffic along the Gloucester Road dual carriageway sounding quietly efficient and the sun dappled harbour busy with ferry boats, junks and darting *wallah-wallahs*.

There was bamboo scaffolding outside the hotel, fresh paint and a smell of turpentine, spread tarpaulins, a mixture of brightness and salt stained scruffiness. An eager, pill-boxed infant of a bell boy told him reception was on the right, the bar on the left by the dining-room. Senior Constable Ko stood in the spacious reception area on the right, incongruous in his khaki uniform, amongst the line-up of empty chairs and vulgar red carpeting. Ko broke off speaking to the moustached, blazer-clad Chinese reception clerk and walked over to Chan.

Thank heaven they were changing the police uniform, Chan thought. Even someone as perfectly proportioned as Ko, captain of the police gymnastics team, looked unfashionably graceless in those knee length khaki shorts, black puttees and wide sleeved khaki shirts. Chan remembered that there had never been enough pockets, and what pockets there were, never big enough to stuff all the things a constable needed.

Senior Constable Ko was a highly competent policeman. His verbal was concise, starkly factual. Raghavan had checked in the previous Thursday, at two-thirty in the afternoon. He'd made his reservation from the airport and requested the next to cheapest room at $70 a night. He had hired a typewriter through the hotel and eaten there on Thursday night, signing for the meal together with three bottles of San Miguel beer and one of Haig Dimple whisky. He had gone out on the Friday morning, returning after lunch, and according to the floor boy had been heard typing all afternoon. He had returned the typewriter at about seven that evening and gone out. He had not been back to the hotel since, and they were wondering what arrangements had been made about the settlement of his bill.

Ko showed Chan Raghavan's registration card. Neat, spidery writing, more than a hint of flamboyance. Raghavan had been born in Calcutta on September 27th, 1920, and travelled on a Malayan passport, issued three years previously. He'd had his passport with him when he had gone out of the hotel, on the previous night.

Chan took the brightly lit lift to the sixth floor. Raghavan had been over fifty. Funny that, his corpse had looked a good deal younger. Probably said a lot for the preservative properties of alcohol. What could he have been typing so industriously? And where the hell was his passport?

Raghavan had occupied room 612, down a short corridor to the left. The corridor was in darkness, and a gang of workmen had taken down the partition of another room, milling around the open space in a mass of wires and naked light bulbs, looking enquiringly at Chan as he passed.

Room 612 was full of bed. A green armchair and a strip of fitted wood serving as a dressing table flanked it, together with Raghavan's open suitcase on a small occasional table. Sergeant Lau stood in the bathroom opposite the entrance, surrounded by pink porcelain, and the fingerprint man was squatting on the floor saying, "A hell of a lot of prints including his, but no fucking use, I'm sure."

"Hello, chief," Lau said and the fingerprint man rose to his feet, sheepishly explaining that the room had been cleaned that morning and that in most cases like this, he'd found that the fingerprints belonged to hotel staff and to previous visitors.

Light poured in from two bare windows, flecked with paint, overlooking a construction site and a forest of television aerials, just about a $70 a night view. Inside, a fluorescent strip over the dresser, two beehive patterned shades on either side of the bed. Chan flicked a switch, sickly blue neon, switched off. *Playboy* on the bedside shelf, a lurid paperback, *Time, Newsweek, Asian Clarion*, a half empty bottle of Haig. The sound of hammering from the workmen down the corridor. Chan went and stood over Raghavan's suitcase.

It was a canvas lined affair, decorated with a vivid flower pattern. Half a dozen shirts, two still in the shiny packing of a Tokyo laundry, handkerchiefs and socks, underwear, in a cellophane bag a clutch of soiled smalls.

More hammering. They sounded as if they were tearing the hotel down. Raghavan must have been used to working surrounded by noise. Chan walked into the small corridor between the entrance and the bathroom. At the end was an open space, a head high wooden shelf and below it, a row of suits and empty hangers. Three suits, two bright chocolate brown, one a vivid electric blue. Shiny patches on the seats and elbows, missing button on one, frayed cuffs on

65

another. There were a pair of brown shoes on the shelf, worn heels, leather creased over the toe, scuffed, deformed by wear to the shape of the foot, certainly not expensive.

Lau came out of the bathroom. "Taxi driver tell you anything?"

"No."

"Let's go back and do some ball bashing."

"Not yet," Chan replied. "Give the man a night to think it over. He'll tell us more if he wants to talk."

The bathroom was a vivid pink, the colour of icing on cheap cakes. On a glass shelf over the wash basin was an electric shaver in a worn plastic case, a comb with fronds of greying, curly hair, a bottle of Brylcreem, a tin of Cuticura talcum powder — did Raghavan suffer from prickly heat — a neatly squeezed tube of Colgate toothpaste, a frayed toothbrush. Nothing unusual or lavish there.

Back in the bedroom, a goblet of water and glass on the dressing table, both covered with caps marked, 'Sterile'. Inside the drawers, hotel stationery and telephone directories. Indentations in the stationery? Raghavan's? He handed the pad to Lau. "Let's see what the lab boys make of that."

In a corner of the dressing table, tucked neatly against the wall in a thin black case, a Philips cassette recorder, dictaphone type, that operated off two rectangular spools. A grey fingerprint right in the middle of the roughened black chassis seemed to stare at Chan. Chan picked up the recorder. Battery operated model, old and much used, plenty of sideways play about the rewind tab. Chan opened the case and clicked the transparent plastic cassette shield. There was only one cassette, and that empty.

"Yes," Lau said. "No cassettes anywhere. I've looked."

"Fuck," Chan said. The cassettes were what it was all about. Raghavan was a blackmailer. He had come to Hong Kong to meet his victim, exchange cassettes and typescripts for money. But the victim had behaved in a most unvictimlike manner. He had grabbed Raghavan, tortured him and then murdered him. Who?

"Let's look again," Chan said. They searched meticulously for twenty minutes, moving the vast bed over, peering into the crack where the dresser joined the wall. It was an easy room to search. Not many places to hide anything, except in the low level flush, which Chan urinating frustratedly, opened. At the bottom of the tank a rectangle of plastic gleamed under seven inches of water.

*   *   *

The moustached clerk downstairs said yes, he had been on duty yesterday evening. He worked from — no, the occupant of room 612 had not come back to the hotel since he'd checked his key in at about seven, the previous night. The clerk would remember if he had. It was impossible that anyone else could have asked for and been given that room key. The clerk knew all their customers and he was a very experienced reception clerk. His blazer and his suavity showed that, Chan thought, looking at the former with barely concealed distaste.

Raghavan had not received any visitors during his short stay. His room service bills were those of a solitary man, coffee, beer, tea and sandwiches, all in singles. Phone calls? As the Inspector undoubtedly knew, local calls in Hong Kong were free. No separate record was kept of those, and there had been no long distance calls whatsoever. Now there was this matter of the bill.

"Shove it," Chan said unpleasantly, using a succinct Cantonese expletive to tell the clerk exactly where. "The bill is not our business. We're only concerned with who killed him."

*   *   *

Every uniformed constable going on beat duty was given a copy of Raghavan's photograph. A special squad of plain clothes men had been marshalled to visit Wan Chai's brothels, massage parlours, girlie bars and nightclubs, to find the woman with whom Raghavan had spent his last night on earth. It was a difficult task. There were about eight thousand prostitutes in Wan Chai, a similar number of bar girls, masseuses and hangers on. If his little squad worked twenty-four hours a day, every day, it would take them nearly six weeks to check out everyone and even then, they would miss out on the casuals.

Chan turned and slapped the taxi driver hard across the face. No time for psychological pressure now. Only bare physical coercion. The man's head whipped sideways, his cry broken by the speed and sting of the blow. Lau holding him, let him roll, then grabbed him and twisted him upright.

"Okay friend, ready to talk?"

The taxi driver moaned. Lau held him, arms trapped behind his back, bare chest facing Chan. Chan hit him three times quickly, short, vicious, boxer's jabs that slammed the air out of the man's body. Lau relaxed, allowing the man to fall on his face on the floor. They watched him lie there, sobbing.

"I heard something crack," Lau said. "I think you've broken one of his ribs, chief. Careful, when you hit him again. It might puncture a lung and choke the bastard to death." Lau stooped down and lifted the man up, holding him again in front of his body. Chan moved easily into the man's line of vision, left shoulder hunched up, dancing on the balls of his feet, fists churning before his body.

"Never mind the ribs," Chan said, shadow boxing. "We can always throw him in the harbour, afterwards." Almost casually he slammed the man in the stomach. Lau's grip didn't let him bend and the taxi driver brought his legs up in agony. Spittle frothed around his mouth, his body was glazed by clammy sweat and he gasped heavily, "Aaah — aaah — aaah." Then the taxi driver said, "It was the man."

Chan stepped up close, fists still clenched. He was sweating too. He yanked the taxi driver's head back, "Who?"

"One of the people who took my taxi to the Excelsior."

"Go on."

"They gave me *yut cheen*, one thousand dollar, to give them my taxi for three hours. I went to a mah jong parlour nearby."

Chan motioned to Lau to ease the taxi driver into a chair. "Who was the man?"

The taxi driver shook his head desperately. "I don't know . . . I don't know." There were tears in the corners of his eyes.

"You mean you give your taxi to anyone who offers you a thousand dollars?"

"What do I care? It was only for three hours." Free of immediate threat, his truculence was showing. "He gave me one thousand dollar." A shrug. "It wasn't my taxi."

A thousand dollars, one month's money, and no need to produce passport or driving licence like when you hired a self-drive car. The man's story was probably true.

"I didn't know this would happen," the taxi driver sobbed.

"Probably not," Chan said. Chan went out of the room and asked two constables to take the driver back to the cells.

That done, he came back into the charge room, still sweating and rubbing his knuckles. He sat down behind the desk and stuck his feet up on it. Hitting prisoners wasn't his way. It was crude, shameful, too much like bullying and he a trained fighter. But assault was an unpleasant fact of a policeman's life, necessary sometimes, like now, with the need to get information quickly and the taxi driver wanting to show others what pressure had been brought on him to make him talk.

They hadn't got much out of him, Chan thought, an unidentifiable man with a thousand dollars to spare to preserve his anonymity. Useful chain of evidence, if they ever found him. Hardly worth the beating, though it would have been much worse for the taxi driver if Chan had been one of those psychopaths who used electricity.

"Well, chief, what do we do now?"

Chan's eyes flicked away from his bruised knuckles. "Now?" He looked at his watch. He'd been on duty nearly fifteen hours. "Let's go home," Chan said. "It's nearly nine o'clock."

9

Nine o'clock. The city was a frozen explosion of light. Vivid patterns of Chinese characters smouldered unwinkingly as far as the eye could see, slashes of red and yellow and pale violet, streaks of green and black and ochre, that clawed up the sides of buildings and jostled untidily over the streets.

Chan drove slowly, concentrating on the traffic. The streets under the kaleidoscopic signs were filled with people. Slender-legged girls in mini skirts and cotton denims, sloe-eyed, elegant young men in shirts and dark slacks, families crowding around restaurant entrances, vendors huddled in doorways, children playing along the pavements, bare bodied porters moving huge loads in baskets balanced over their shoulders on shafts of bamboo.

Light and sound and people. Hong Kong. His city. Chan could sense the subterranean gaiety that filled the humid air, think that it seemed a lifetime ago that he too had been part of that Saturday night throng, moving through the congested streets with his friends, shadowing groups of chattering girls. They still moved around in packs, Chan thought, that at least had not changed. He smiled softly, a settled family man now, two children and on the verge of becoming a Superintendent. A lifetime ago. Even this morning seemed a lifetime ago.

He parked in front of the block of flats, switched off the

engine and the lights and sat in the half dark, squeezing his eyes. Another day. A man had been killed and he was slowly gathering the threads of the enquiry as to how and why, spinning a neat little web. Somewhere in the teeming streets below him, men were still working because a stranger had been killed. Men were sitting in bars sipping San Miguel and asking questions, showing photographs in horrid cubicles, staring challengingly at faces that did not or did not want to know. Hell, Chan grinned. He loved being a detective.

He locked the car carefully, went up two flights of bare cement stairs and rang the bell of the flat, already sweating again. The door swung open on its short length of chain, stuck and Li-li's alert, gamine face appeared in the crack, her shoulder length black hair shining in the light that fell behind her.

"Police," Chan said. "Open up."

The chain rattled. She let him in, standing to one side, smiling quietly, making no move to touch him. Li-li worried about his job and the gun he carried. For eight years she had greeted him exactly like this, standing to one side, smiling quietly, glad to have her man back, but not touching him till he put away his gun. Crazy, illogical, lovely woman, Chan thought happily, mother of his children and creator of his home. Did she really think that crime on the streets would disappear if only you treated villains kindly?

She preceded him into the living-room. Through sheer force of habit Chan checked the position of the furniture, the sofa and the three easy chairs that formed the suite, the record and cassette player which the children were not allowed to touch, the speakers at each end of the room, the chest of drawers topped with photographs of his parents, her's, the children, the formal depiction of their second wedding.

Li-li was much smaller than the rest of her family, all delicate bones, fragile wrists and ankles. Even the loosely worn spotted blouse could not hide her hand span of a waist and under the dark slacks, her legs were as slim as a boy's. Very Cantonese, Li-li, despite her northern parentage.

Chan strode past her into the bedroom, locked away the gun, dropped off his clothes and went into the shower. When he came out his body vibrant from the sting of the water, the flat smelt of food. He changed into fresh clothes, peered into the children's room, touched a kiss of air over Blossom's forehead and her teddy bear, stroked Tony's hair, went into the dining-room where Li-li had brought their dinner.

"They went to bed without any trouble?" nodding towards the children's bedroom.

Li-li smiled happily, serving out rice and pork and bean sprouts. "Blossom was fractious, over-excited at the thought of seeing her grandfather tomorrow."

Chan made a face and began to eat. He ate quickly, hungrily, spitting out rice stones and slivers of bone into the area around his bowl. "It was a murder case," he said somewhat self-importantly, referring to the telephone call that had woken them both at six o'clock that morning. "An Indian, shot in Yee Wo Road." Li-li's dark eyes widened in alarm and Chan added smiling, "It was before I got there."

"I heard about it on the radio," Li-li said, looking at his bowl to see if it needed replenishing. "Everyone was late for work."

Chan laughed and told her about the Tramways Inspector. "Very white faced he was, too."

"That was mean," Li-li said. "Everyone isn't like you, used to seeing dead people."

Chan grinned at her, went on eating. He said, "It is a very interesting case. The dead man was a journalist. I think he was blackmailing someone in Hong Kong. He had all this information on cassettes, and they tortured him and took it away from him. Except one cassette. We found that in the hotel." Chan frowned. The lab technician had said the tape would have to be removed from its cassette and air dried. It wouldn't be ready until some time on Monday afternoon. Chan thought the fellow really wanted his Sunday off. Nice to be a civilian, and work fixed hours.

Chan went on eating, told Li-li more about the case, as much to involve her in his work as to clarify his thoughts. Li-li's expression became glazed. "A very awkward thing," Chan said, "A stranger getting killed on your patch. With someone who lives in the area you've got whole areas of knowledge to work on, people who knew the man, who knew what he did, where he went and so on. But with a stranger, nothing."

He held out his bowl for more. Perhaps the tape would solve the mystery for him on Monday. Perhaps by Monday he would have a clearer idea of the kind of person Raghavan was.

Li-li smiled confidently. "You will solve it," she said. Chan was her man and she had total confidence in his ability as a detective, in his capacity for capturing wrongdoers. She smiled shyly. "Then you will get promoted," wanting it for his sake, not her's.

"I hope so," Chan said. "I think so." There had already been news about the murder on the radio. Tomorrow's papers would contain the official police version, and even in Press Office bureaucratese the story was dramatic enough to attract public attention. The officer who solved the murder would inevitably be in the public eye for some time. It would be difficult to say that such an officer did not merit the grade of superintendent, especially when all his predecessors had held that very rank.

Ever since he had been appointed in charge of Wan Chai CID Chan had tried to avoid thinking it was unfair. There must be something in his record, and he knew it wasn't blameless, to have prevented them from giving him what he reckoned to be his due. The police were never knowingly unfair to their own. They must have good reason. He was too impetuous perhaps. But they would soon have to give him the rank he thought he deserved. He was certain of

74

that and content to wait, though there would be advantages in being a superintendent right now.

From this term Tony and Blossom were attending school on different shifts. Li-li had to make four trips a day, accompanying them, instead of two. If he was a superintendent he would be entitled to an official car and a chauffeur and like most superintendents did, he could use the car for at least two trips, saving Li-li inconvenience.

"How's the arm?" Chan asked.

For the last three months Li-li had been complaining of stabbing pains in her right arm. The doctor suspected arthritis.

"I saw Doctor Ling today," Li-li said. "He gave me different tablets." Her tone was unbelieving.

"Try them and see."

"They won't do any good," Li-li said, convinced.

Chan laughed. "You still want to see this quack with the needles?"

"Don't make fun of him," Li-li said. "He has cured many people."

"Try the tablets," Chan said again. "If they don't work. we will think about the quack."

Li-li tossed her head at him, reached out and began to clear the dishes away. Chan stuck a tooth pick between his teeth and walked to the lounge, switched on the television and sat in front of it. Through the large windows of the lounge he could see the fairy lights that dotted the Peak. Here on the small hill, it was peaceful, quiet, so different from the hubub of Wan Chai, though hardly three miles away. They must have taken Raghavan somewhere in Wan Chai, Chan thought, if the taxi had only four miles on the clock. Where? Nearly impossible to check, nearly half a million people in a few square miles, crammed into tiny apartments. Surely someone would have heard Raghavan's screams.

Chan put the thought out of his mind and looked around him. He was not going to think about the case any more.

75

He did not have enough information and risked treading familiar ground too often, consequently missing out important details.

They were lucky to have the flat, lucky to live away from a police station. The flat was large, originally built for European PWD engineers, two bedrooms, two bathrooms, lounge, kitchen and a small terrace outside the dining-room where sometimes Li-li sewed and Chan read his newspapers. There was also a spare room and a separate lavatory for an *amah*. Li-li and Chan could not afford an *amah* more than two days a week. Still, they were lucky, living in such a comfortable place at only $300 a month.

The television began to boom. They were already five minutes into the big fight. Muhammad Ali was dancing about like a flyweight. What a boxer! Over two hundred pounds and he moved like a dragonfly. Great man too! It must have taken a lot of courage to have watched them take his title away, deprive him of his livelihood, to accept not doing what he had been born to do, because he believed deeply in something.

Li-li came in carrying a tray with an ornate teapot and two cups of green tea. Chan took a cup, still absorbed in television. Li-li sat by him, watching too.

In a break between rounds she said softly, "About your murder case? My father would like to see the children tomorrow."

Chan's attention was riveted. Sweaty faces being mopped, pencils being applied to the split brow of Ali's opponent, Ali unruffled as usual, baring his mouth for the gum shield. Chan thought, if he'd lived a thousand years he would never have been able to box like Ali, move like that, get out those long raking lefts. Li-li had said something about seeing her parents tomorrow.

"Lunch?" Chan asked.

"I'm afraid so."

Chan made a face, almost as pain-wracked as Ali's opponent.

"Father is old," Li-li said. "And I am his only daughter. He *does* like the children."

"But not their father," Chan said, without rancour. He reached out and took her hand in his big, scarred paw. "We'll go tomorrow," he said, "murder case or no." He allowed himself to be sucked once again into the battle being waged on the screen in front of him.

* * *

Shrilling phone, knifing through warm multilayers of sleep, jarring comfortably ensconced bodies apart. Chan reached out an arm, pulled the receiver to his face, eyes still fast shut. "Chan here," he said in a voice like gravel.

It was the Duty Officer at Wan Chai and it wasn't another murder. Chan opened his eyes at bright sunlight through thin curtains. He groped for his watch.

The Duty Officer was saying that Cameron Wah was at the police station. The Duty Officer sounded impressed. Cameron Wah was demanding the release of the taxi driver. Eight o'clock on a Sunday morning, Chan thought, bugger it.

Li-li had turned away from him, dark hair spread fan like over the pillow, hand in front of her face, breathing softly. In the next room he heard the voices of the children. Chan got out of bed and went across to them. Cameron bloody Wah could bloody wait.

He played with the children till the noise of their laughter woke Li-li. He drank his tea, took his time getting dressed, took his time getting to the station. The streets were magically still, shops boarded up, a few early risers arranging fruit in the market, lonely people scurrying singly along the pavements and under the arcades, the multi-coloured ideograms silent and still.

Cameron Wah was in the squad room talking to Sergeant Yim, dressed even at that unearthly hour as if he were appearing in court, black jacket, stiff collar, striped trousers, gleaming pointed shoes. Naturally, Wah was taller than average, mid-thirties, overweight, as smooth in manner as in dress, carefully manicured hands, graceful head thrown back, a mouth that curled down at the corners with disdain. The law suited Cameron Wah. Even at school, Chan remembered, he had been a pompous prick.

"Ah Richard, sorry to drag you out like this. It's a simple enough matter but the good sergeant here insisted I should talk to you."

Grumpily Chan led the way to his office. Wah's trouble was that he was Eurasian, Chinese father, Scots mother, educated partly in Hong Kong, partly in UK, a confusing situation for one of his limited mental resilience, a confusion resolved by Wah adopting the guise of a British gentleman while remaining unalterably Chinese.

Must be tough being a half-caste Chan thought, never to know who you are. Sudden horrifying thought. Wah was not the only half-caste. All of them, every Chinese he knew was half-caste too. Why else did Chan know more about Henry VIII than the Manchu Dynasty, more about rainfall in Birmingham than Kowloon. Chan was full-blooded Chinese, but his education had been British, his training had been British, he was working in a British way in a British police force and some of the time he even thought like a *kwei lo*.

Wah sat down opposite Chan, snapping his trouser creases straight between fingers and thumbs. "This taxi driver," Wah said, "Lin Yu. I have been instructed to get him out."

"Who by?"

"His family of course, old boy. Very worried they are too, I can tell you. He is the sole bread winner, you know, two sets of parents to support and all that. I must say you police chappies are pretty unfeeling about that kind of thing."

The sun was streaming into Chan's office, full and golden. It was going to be a gorgeous day. Everyone would be out in boats or on the beaches at Stanley and Shek-o, while he, Chan, would have to suffer lunch with Li-li's family.

"We have our job to do," Chan said, the age old excuse. He watched the sunlight gleam off Wah's gold cuff links. When had Cameron Wah acquired a social conscience? Hell, he should have been thinking of Wah's involvement instead of the beaches and the deprivation of his heritage.

"You've seen the man?" Chan said.

"Oh yes, oh yes. Rights of the citizen and all that. No complaints on that score."

Wah's father had himself been a successful lawyer, Chan recalled. Young Cameron had always been ushered to school in large limousines and they'd had a large house overlooking Repulse Bay. But all that was gone now. Cameron's father had gambled away two fortunes, and Cameron himself had been nowhere as good a lawyer as his father was.

"You've been a naughty boy, Richard, but we won't say anything about that. Lin Yu will make a statement about illegally hiring his taxi and you will let him go, right?"

"Naughty? You can't prove a damn thing," Chan said. "And I can hold this taxi driver of yours as long as I like. Material witness in a murder case and all that." Shit, he was beginning to talk like Wah.

"Really, dear boy, let's not be difficult. I don't have to explain the law to you. You can't hold him indefinitely against his will without charging him. And then you will have to request remand in custody and we will oppose it. We mustn't forget habeas corpus either, must we?" Cameron Wah wagged his finger archly in Chan's face.

Chan glared at him, poker faced. No taxi driver could afford the services of Cameron Wah, in a matter like this, and Chan was prepared to bet ten cents to a million dollars, that Wah wasn't representing him for nothing. "Habeas corpus?" Chan asked softly. "You'd apply for it?"

"Only if I have to, Richard. Only if I have to."

Wah was going the limit on this one. That at least was

obvious. The question was why. Wah's work was largely commercial, though lately he had been doing more and more criminal work and was supposed to be on a retainer to certain triads.

"How are his family finding the money to pay you?"

"Richard! Don't be impertinent. Let's say it's all taken care of. My liberal conscience if you like."

Liberal conscience! Cameron Wah wouldn't know what liberal conscience was, even if he found it clearly labelled in a box of cornflakes.

"You will undertake to produce him if I need him?"

"At any reasonable time, old boy. We always do our best to co-operate with the police. You know that."

"All right," Chan said. "He can make his statement and go."

Chan went into the squad room and spoke to Sergeant Yim. There was only one man free. How on earth was he expected to run a police force without enough men. Still, Chan had to take what was available. He asked the man to follow Wah and Lin Yu.

Chan became aware of Pete Winston in the squad room. Not the usual scruffy Winston in jeans and sandals masquerading as a tourist, but an elegantly suited, well-groomed figure, looking as if he were about to call on the Commissioner of Police himself.

"Ah, just the man I wanted to see." The self-satisfied drawl grated on Chan's nerves. Chan fixed him with a look full of Sunday morning biliousness.

"What do you want?" Chan asked.

"Firstly to tell you about yesterday's meeting with the AC."

"I already know," Chan said, thinking that Winston sounded like a head prefect announcing that the school had just won an away match.

"That's cool. Then you can let me have fifteen good men and true for a surveillance op."

"No," Chan said. "There's none to spare."

"But — " Winston said.

"No buts about it. Every man I have is working on a murder enquiry." Chan brushed past Winston's suddenly thin-lipped figure and went into his office where Cameron Wah was staring out of the window at the harbour and the taxi driver was already making his statement to a detective constable.

10

THERE WERE SEVENTEEN of them seated around the circular table staring at small dishes of segmented fruit, nuts, reddish brown sweet sour sauces, giblets, and shiny black thousand-year-old eggs looking as if they had been rolled in oil. Chan, seated between five-year-old Blossom and a visiting cousin from Singapore, wondered why even though he had been married to Li-li for eight years, and was the lawful and only begetter of two children by her, he was still treated as an outsider by Li-li's family.

The family were never rude to him, rarely impliedly offensive. Their rejection took the form of a scrupulous politeness, the kind that is reserved for dealing with total strangers.

Naturally Chan resented his non-acceptance. He had often sworn never to attend another claustrophobic family luncheon. However, six weeks after the swearing, the inevitable invitation would arrive. Li-li would plead, cajole, sulk, cry and Chan would finally relent. These were, after all, the only times when Li-li saw her family, as she would never visit them without Chan. It was her special way of insisting that her family accept her man, and her man, her family.

Over the years the meetings had become progressively easier, the feeling of exclusion less intense. Something akin to a family bond had been forged by the sheer strength of

Li-li's determination. Li-li was unusually strong willed for a Chinese girl and Chan reflected, he knew more than enough about that.

Li Tam, Li-li's eldest brother, seated across the table with his family, observed Chan being temporarily ignored in the merry round of family gossip. Now he leaned across and asked, "How do you like your new Ford?"

Li Tam had been to England and qualified as an accountant. He was a big, steady looking man, with a reputation for shrewdness in his business dealings. He now ran all the family businesses, in jewellery, ivory, and property, and was beginning to look more like his father every day, developing a pompous paternalism that would be fully fledged by the time he became head of the family.

Chan said, "The Ford runs very well. It's very comfortable," reflecting that Li Tam had arrived that afternoon in a new Mercedes.

Li Gng, the second brother said, "I had a Ford once, a big Capri. I grew to like it very much."

Li Gng had been born soon after the family had escaped from China and had been, according to his mother, a disturbed child. In adolescence this disturbance had reflected itself in a succession of misadventures with young women and in early manhood, a series of spectacularly unsuccessful ventures on the Stock Market. Now, at thirty-three, Li Gng was relegated to managing the ivory factory, and given an adequate, though not extravagant, allowance. He kept a mistress in a flat in Kowloon, a fact Chan had accidentally discovered during the course of a routine enquiry.

Li Gng had repaid Chan's silence with a cloying obsequiousness. Now he held up the remnants of a pre-lunch whisky and said, "To your good fortune." Chan smiled and busied himself with arranging Blossom on her chair.

Li-li's father suddenly said, "There have been a number of jewel robberies. Have your people found the criminals yet?"

"There has been only one," Chan said sharply, and immediately ignored Li-li's eyes.

"Two," Li Tam protested. "There was another one last night."

"Yes, it happened at about ten o'clock," Li Gng said.

Chan forced himself to control his irritation. The old man was not being critical of the police. He owned jewellery stores, his son-in-law was a policeman. A jewel robbery must have seemed to him to be the perfect conversation piece.

Chan remembered Sergeant Yim's report and said, "We think this will be a difficult case. The people are first-timers, without records."

"How do you make that out?" Li Gng asked.

Chan explained about the Method Index and how they used the style of a robbery to narrow the field of search to twenty or thirty suspects. Li Gng was suitably impressed.

A steaming bowl of sharkfin soup was placed in the centre of the table. Li Tam spoke to his father about politics and his wife shouted across the table to the cousin seated by Chan. Chan caught Li-li smiling at him and for a while there was the sound of slurping and smacking of lips. Chan told Blossom that if she had any more soup, she would not have room for the rest of the meal.

The meal proceeded majestically. Fried rice, a casserole of squab and mushrooms, sweet sour chicken livers, abalone in oyster sauce, Peking duck, tender and tangy, the flesh seeming to melt in the mouth.

Chan wiped Blossom's chin and rescued her chop-sticks from behind her ear. She would grow up to be like Li-li he thought, small and wilful. Li-li was so unlike the rest of her family. They were all big boned, flabby northerners. Li-li was so trim, she might have been a Cantonese. The only northern thing about her was her tenacity.

When they first met, Li-li had been seventeen and Chan, then fresh out of training school, had been directing traffic outside the convent. The exchange of smiles and heart warming eye contact turned to reality during the school sports meet, when Li-li running in a relay race had her foot spiked by her partner. Chan had administered first aid and

84

single handed carried her to the ambulance. A few days afterwards she had limped across the road to thank him, and after that they began to meet regularly. Li-li would leave school after the other girls, about the time Chan's spell of traffic duty was ending. They would go to a tea house, or walk along the streets, occasionally touching each other's hands, feeling inordinately conspicuous in their respective uniforms.

After Chan became a Detective Constable things became easier. He could wear civilian clothes and had greater freedom as to where he went and when. Inevitably there was talk, and inevitably Li-li's father found out. He wrote a letter of complaint to Chan's superiors and made sure that Chan was informed that Li-li was too young to think of men. Chan understood the implication. When Li-li did think of men, she should think of the son of a wealthy northern merchant.

Li-li left school and they continued to meet surreptitiously, until Chan was sent to England for a year's stay. They met for the last time in a coffee shop in Central. Li-li had cried, and they had promised to remain faithful to each other. Chan remembered that when he came back, he had not been able to reach her and that in the last three months of his stay in England, she had not written.

He did not see her for two months after his return. He had been promoted to Detective Sergeant and was sitting in the squad room, two mornings after Li-li's twenty-first birthday, when she came in. There, oblivious of the amused glances of his colleagues, she had insisted that he marry her that day.

Chan had taken her out of the station and for an hour they had driven round in the back of a taxi while Chan had attempted to persuade her that they should wait. Li-li had been adamant. Time would not solve anything. In five years he would still be a policeman and would not have accumulated a fortune. In five years he would still be unacceptable to her parents.

They were married that afternoon by Father Loyola who, with a totally uncharacteristic rebelliousness, used all his influence to persuade the Governor's Department to give them a special licence. They had signed the register in the sacristy behind the altar, celebrated the occasion in cupfuls of warm red wine, and then Li-li had gone home.

For three days Chan heard nothing from her. On the fourth, Li Tam came to see him. He first offered Chan money to go away. He had pointed out that he could never keep Li-li in the style to which she was accustomed and that it would be better for both of them. Later, he threatened Chan with a charge of abduction, with a complaint to his superiors, and with nullifying the marriage.

At that point Chan lost his temper. He rushed out of the station and rode up to the Li residence on his motor bike. There he forced his way into the house, past an hysterical Mrs. Li and broke down the door of the room in which Li-li was being held. There was more shouting, more hysteria as Chan asked her to leave with him. Despite her tearful protests, he was dragging her away with him, when Mr. Li returned, accompanied by a car-load of workers from his factory.

The scene was ugly. Chan in a blind rage had whipped out his police revolver and had lined the men beside their car. Li-li's father was preparing to hurl himself at the gun, and Chan had quite made up his mind to club the old man with its butt, when Li Tam arrived.

Li Tam had been calm and resourceful. He came between Chan and his father, wiser than both of them, saying, "What's done is done. We must make the best of it."

Two weeks later, Chan and Li-li were married again, with due ceremony. An offer was made to Chan to leave the police and join the family business. Chan refused. A month afterwards, when they had returned from a honeymoon in Manila paid for by Li-li's father, they began to live together in a squalid one-roomed flat behind the police station.

"The Japanese," Li Tam was saying, "are achieving with transistor radios and motor cars what they couldn't achieve with soldiers." He smiled across at Chan. "They're selling so much, they can even refuse us cameras."

It was an old gripe. Because of its free trade policy, cameras in Hong Kong were usually cheaper than in their country of origin. Many Hong Kong dealers had therefore gone into the mail order business, in direct competition with the manufacturers. The Japanese now only supplied cameras on a quota system, which compelled the dealers to obtain supplies from unofficial sources. These goods were identical to those available legally except that the guarantees that came with them were not international, and they had not been approved by the Japanese Camera Institute.

"Do the Japanese still make guns?" Chan asked.

Li Tam said, "Yes. People don't talk about it very much, but the Japanese do have a large arms industry. Mitsubishi for example, produce Sparrow missiles."

"For defence purposes only," Li-li's father said sarcastically.

Chan asked, "What about Nambu pistols? Do they still manufacture those?"

Li Tam looked blank.

His father asked, "Why do you want to know?"

"It has to do with a case I am investigating."

"It's an old gun. The Japanese used it in the war."

Chan asked, "What was it like during the war?"

The old man looked keenly at Chan. "We were always hungry," he said. "That's what the war was like." He launched into an explanation of how the Japanese had long lines of supply and how they had been a poor country and dependent upon the territories they conquered being self supporting. He spoke of atrocities, mainly against the English and Communist Chinese, of Japanese waywardness, and how he had escaped being executed through the carelessness of a shooting party who had allowed him to wander free in a forest.

As he spoke Chan remembered that the old man had come to Hong Kong with only his family and his skill at carving ivory. He had just got a business together in Hong Kong when the Japanese had come. After the war he had started again with nothing and expanded from an ivory factory into a jewellery store, into six jewellery stores that sold cameras and watches as well. As his business had grown, he had gone into property and two years ago had retired from the empire he had built. To do that sort of thing, Chan thought, called for guts and determination. The old man must have had plenty of that.

"How did the people live?" he asked.

The old man shrugged. "They lived as best they could. As a treat, we used to eat at the market stalls. You could get a big bowl of noodles for a dollar."

"What about night life?"

"There was that too. But only for the Japanese."

"And gangsters?"

"Oh yes, there was crime as usual. The Japanese executed a number of Cheu Chow who had escaped from Shanghai. But there were others who did business with them, even triads." He looked directly at Chan. "Why are you interested in all this?"

It was Chan's turn to shrug. "It's all part of a murder enquiry."

The old man smiled. "And I thought police work was all muscle."

Chan said, "And I thought all there was to making a fortune was greed."

Afterwards, the old man accompanied them to the car. After he had given the children their customary dollar each, and Li-li had got into the car, he turned to Chan, "I have a lot of time, now. If you want to talk more about the past, do come round."

"I will," Chan said. "Perhaps there are other things we can talk about too."

II

THEY SPENT THE rest of the afternoon by the pool at the
Hong Kong Football Club, the children splashing merrily
in the water, Chan spread out luxuriously on the roughened
tiles wearing only swimming trunks. Li-li stayed seated by
him, wearing a sleeveless mini dress and barefoot, her sole
concession to the foreign practice of sunbathing.

Afterwards they walked up the hill to the flat, ate lightly
and Chan helped Li-li put the children to bed. The warm
shadows of the day were quickly thickening into night.
Chan watched the emerald green of the Peak grow rapidly
dark, the pin points of light prickle out along it, one by one.
The roads of the Colony would be clogged with traffic, he
thought. It was not a good time to be a traffic cop, not on
a warm Sunday evening.

The phone rang. It wasn't especially good to be a detective on a Sunday, either. Sergeant Lau said they had found
the girl who had been with Raghavan the night he was
murdered. She worked as a hostess in a bar off the Jaffe
Road.

It wasn't much of a place, standing near the foot of the
Canal West flyover, a long queue of traffic grinding past its
shaded windows. Open-sided lorries that had brought produce to the markets crouched by the kerb between pick-up
trucks and off-duty taxis. An illuminated barber's pole in-
dicated a beauty parlour further down the street, the outline

of a small palm tree in white neon, a nightclub. The entrance to the bar was heavily curtained, dark, beyond it a stairway lit by garishly coloured bulbs, a sign on the landing in spidery red neon, FRISCO BAR.

Off the landing a wide room, a large bar counter and raucous music from a juke box. Raghavan's type of place, without doubt. It had the same atmosphere of shady flamboyance, dimly lit, smoky, formica topped tables in booths arranged around the walls. To the right in a more conventionally lit area, a huge refrigerator, two girls standing by a darkened window, talking.

Lau was straddling a high stool at the bar, sipping beer. Chan clambered up beside him, aware that the two of them, big, tough, slow eyed, couldn't be mistaken for anything but cops in plain clothes. Two youths in a booth eyed them cautiously. Further along the bar a pale-suited European drank steadily.

Chan ordered beer and lemonade. The barman frowning churlishly served him. Cops were no good for business, and there was precious little action as it was tonight.

Opposite the bar was a curtained off passageway. Now it opened, a glimpse of narrow corridor between a row of hardboard partitions. Three men came into the bar, Japanese, neatly dressed in identical blue suits, wearing tags on their lapels to assist identification, looking identically sheepish.

Lau nudged Chan as a girl followed them into the bar, still fastening her blouse. Quite a small girl; what on earth could she have done to make three Japanese look like that. She tottered across to the other side of the room on high wedge heels, a slight flounce to the brown maxi skirt, a satisfied smile on her face.

Chan beckoned the barman over and quickly closed the transaction. It was better to talk here than at the station. The girl would be more relaxed here, less worried about the money she would be losing while she was away from the bar.

The girl led Chan through the curtains, into the dim-lit corridor, into an even more dimly lit cubicle. A vinyl covered bunk, small table, chrome pegs let into the hardboard partitions for hanging one's clothes — the bare essentials of commercial sex, functional, cheap and not at all nice.

Music from the juke box filtered through the thick red lighting. Chan sat on the bunk, uncomfortable and marble smooth, hardly conducive to any kind of sex, feeling in the murkiness a sense of sweat and hurried lust, a sense of being vaguely unclean. So this was where Raghavan had come two nights ago, looking for a good time, poor, pathetic bastard.

The girl smiled at him, took off her blouse, draped it over one of the pegs. A scrawny figure, breasts like egg cups, arms only slightly fleshier than sticks, her fingernails bitten to the quick. The rough brown weal of an untidily stitched scar peeped above the waist of her maxi.

"My name is Heiki," she said. "What's yours?" She sat beside Chan, resting her hand gently between his thighs. Under all that make-up she looked no more than about twenty, a pleasant face, snub nosed, not hard or bitter yet. Chan eased her hand away and thrust his warrant card before her face. "Police," he said. The girl started, tried to get up, but he kept hold of her hand and pulled her back on to the couch.

She protested vibrantly, fear giving her voice a particularly mewing pitch. "Shut up," said Chan. "I am not interested in what you do with your body." Or your life either, he thought. I suppose at some point she chose to live this way. Presumably, even if you lived in a squatter's hut with ten other people, you had freedom of choice. He should ask Father Loyola about that.

He took out Raghavan's photograph and a fifty dollar bill. The girl's alarm evaporated. She had a nice smile, pert little dimpled chin, no business in a place like this, but then

Chan had no business, either, to want a different life for her. She lit a cigarette and inhaled deeply.

"You remember this man?"

"Oh yes. He come Friday night."

The fifty dollars had disappeared into the waist of the maxi.

"How do you remember it so well?"

"That it was Friday? That is two days ago, no. So I remember."

"And the man? Why do you remember him?"

"He was Indian. Two girls from the bar would not go with him."

"Why not?"

"He was drunk. They were feared he would hurt them." She gave Chan a mischievous smile. "Big size. Too big for Chinese girls."

"And you were not frightened?"

"Yong Po promised me fifty dollars extra to go with him, to give him good time. At first he no liked me. But afterwards, all okay."

Chan knew Yong Po. A pimp who worked the hotels in Causeway Bay. A long record as a juvenile delinquent, and two adult convictions for shop lifting and procuring. Not the sort of person you'd introduce your sister to, Yong Po, a nasty little Chinese with a gold tooth who wore loud sports jackets and two-tone shoes.

"Do you remember what time they came here?"

"Yes, about twelve thirty, one o'clock. I was tired that day and would have gone home, if not for Yong Po."

"The Indian stayed with you till when?"

"Till two o'clock. Till we closed."

"Afterwards, the Indian left alone?"

"No. Afterwards he stayed here, drinking with Yong Po. That lying cheating bastard, he only gave me forty dollars."

"The Indian must have talked to you. What did he say?"

Heiki frowned. So many men, so many stories, most of them false, as if she cared, anyway.

"Did he tell you about his job? That he worked for a magazine?"

"Yes, yes. He worked for a magazine and he was going round the world. He was going to visit England and France and America. He told me about his girlfriend also. She is from Taiwan. She was going with him, too."

Chan remembered that Raghavan had asked for the next to cheapest room at the Harbour, that his clothes were old, his shoes worn, that he had spent his last night on earth in a cheap brothel. His only extravagance seemed to have been whisky. So what was this about trips around the world? Pillow talk, or had he been certain that his fortunes were changing?

"How was he getting all this money?"

"From his work," the girl said. She lit another cigarette. "He had come from Japan and Taiwan and he had been very clever. He had found out what nobody else knew, and he was going to sell that information to many newspapers."

Chan frowned. Selling stories to newspapers was the obvious way for Raghavan to make money. But a fortune? And what was there to kill about that?

"Did he mention any names?" Chan asked. "Please, think hard."

The girl made a great show of thinking hard. "No," she said at last. "I don't remember. I don't think so."

Chan placed another fifty dollars on the table, watched it disappear into the folds of the maxi. "If you remember something, you will tell me. I am at Wan Chai police station, Inspector Chan."

"If I remember," the girl smiled. She stood up and drew her blouse over her scrawny body. Chan watched the scar wriggle across her smooth skin, fascinated.

"How did that happen?"

"An accident," the girl said.

"A knife?" Chan's voice hardened. "Yong Po?"

She shook her head. "No. Please, it doesn't matter."

She finished fastening her blouse and came and stood in front of him. "You like for me to wank you?"

There was a childlike kindness in her offer, a peculiar kind of honesty. "No," Chan said. "My wife would not like it."

Heiki smiled at him as if she understood.

*   *   *

Back at the station, Chan put out a general call for a pimp called Yong Po. Then he asked Lau to check whom the Frisco Bar paid protection to.

"Us," Lau said.

"Not us, you idiot. Who gets paid off on the other side?"

"You think — "

"Yong Po paid that girl to screw Raghavan, stayed drinking with him afterwards. That isn't how a pimp operates. The taxi driver gave his cab to an unknown man for a thousand dollars. That isn't how a taxi driver operates either."

"I'll check out the taxi company."

"Good idea."

"You think a big man is behind this?"

"We'll see."

"Where you off to, chief?"

"Family business," Chan said. "I'm going to see my father-in-law."

"I thought you didn't like him."

"I feel different now," Chan said and went downstairs to his car.

*   *   *

Li-li's father was surprised to see him coming alone. Surprised and then alarmed.

"There's no trouble," Chan said, reassuringly, "Li-li and the children are fine."

The old man frowned at him, puzzled. They sat together

94

on the verandah. A servant brought tea. Around them the city was bursting with light.

"I want to find out more about the time the Japanese were here, father," Chan said.

"More? What do you want to know more for? Is it about your case?"

Chan nodded. "It would help."

The old man sat back in his chair, sipped his tea. "It was different from now," he said softly. "Not so many people moving around, not so many lights."

"What did business people do? What did you do?"

"We kept on working. We paid more taxes, made less profit, importing and exporting was very difficult and for everything you had to ask favours from the Japanese."

"But crime went on?"

"Yes. Crime went on. Is that what you wanted to know?"

"More. Tell me about the protection rackets, if there were still organised gangs?"

"Yes. There was all that, too. I told you how some of the Cheu Chow were shot by the Japanese. Well, they were betrayed. The gangs were fighting about opium, about racketeering here in Hong Kong."

"What happened afterwards, when the war was over?"

The old man laughed. "The same thing, in reverse. If you live long enough, you know that nothing really changes."

"You mean the Japanese collaborators were betrayed to the British?"

"Some of them, yes. Others left."

"Is there no one here now who was big then?"

The old man thought carefully. "No, I do not think so. Unless of course you count Wan Liu. He wasn't as big then as he is now, but he collaborated with the Japanese, all right."

Chan felt a cold shiver run through him. Wan Liu, the III K Society. Raghavan's murder looked like being big trouble.

*   *   *

95

Lau had left a note for him at the station. The Frisco Bar and the taxi company were protected by the III K. Lau had written. "Take it easy, chief. This may be bigger than both of us."

Chan sat in his office a long while, thinking. How had Raghavan got himself involved with a Hong Kong triad? If Datt was to be believed, Raghavan hadn't been in Hong Kong for at least nine months, he'd been travelling in Japan and Taiwan. What had he found out in those places about the III K that made it necessary for them to torture and kill him?

The III K was no longer the anti-imperialist political organisation it had been in Manchu times. Nor was it a benevolent society, aiding Chinese exiled from their homelands, as some triads had later become. In present day Hong Kong the III K was purely and simply a criminal organisation, with heavy interests in gambling, vice and protection.

In present day Hong Kong, the III K did not officially exist. No triad did. They had been outlawed in 1955 and so did not exist. That too was pure and simple. Except they controlled gambling, vice and protection.

Criminal though they might be, they broke no laws unnecessarily. They did not indulge in violence just for kicks. Crime was a far more serious business than that. So if they had killed a stranger, he must have been a serious threat to them. Or done them dishonour. Had Raghavan insulted a chief's wife or daughter? But in that case honour would have been satisfied, bloodily and quickly. And the torture, if it had been thought necessary, done differently. Not Japanese style, not like a Japanese POW as MacKenzie had said. Besides, vengeance did not explain the loss of the cassettes, what Raghavan had been typing, or his hopes of a fortune. No, information had been taken from Raghavan and suppressed. Information, that was it. Has Raghavan found out about the III K collaboration with the Japanese or perhaps their involvement with the murder of the Cheu Chow? Possible. That would have made an interesting

96

newspaper story, but surely, not Raghavan's fortune.

Still puzzled, Chan turned over Lau's note in his hands. Bigger than both of us, he re-read. Dangerous too, he thought bitterly. Where a triad was concerned, you walked lightly, even if you were a Senior Chief Inspector in the Hong Kong Police.

12

FROM THE STREET you couldn't tell there was anything there, an ordinary office building decorated with small signs, one that glowed, Sun Sun Trade Association. The Sun Sun Trade Association was on the fourth floor, and as the lift slowed, Chan heard the stream of music, stepped out on to a landing that was the darkened foyer of a nightclub.

Chan stepped up to the ticket window, gave his name, tried to look lost and lonely as the ticket seller eyed him keenly, then took his money and gave him a fake membership card. Inside, at 11.45 on a Sunday night, it was all happening.

A couple cavorted on the low stage in front of the band-stand, surrounded by a semi-circle of intent Chinese. The man on the stage wore nothing except thigh length boots and a leather jock strap. The woman was completely naked.

As Chan followed the waiter to his table, the man lifted the woman on to the back of her shoulders and stepped be-tween her legs, pressing the shiny leather pouch against her in time to the throbbing music, while her suspended legs fluttered behind him and her sighs, magnified by a multi-directional mike floated susurratingly around the room.

It was sexy all right, outrageously so. The music reached a violent crescendo, stopped with a jarring clash of cymbals. A collective release of breath emanated from the men around the stage, a gushing cascade of lust washing round the room. Then the music started again, wailing, insinuating, controlling the writhing bodies. The girl went on her knees and placed her lips against the man's leather pouch.

The whole performance was illegal. Strippers were not allowed to move once they were naked, a typical British compromise. Not that many British people came to the Sun Sun. The Sun Sun was an essentially Chinese affair.

It was run by the III K Society, a meeting place for gangsters and occasionally cops. Chan had been there a few times before, but never to see someone as important as now. He ordered a coke and refused a hostess. The band and the couple reached another gasping climax. A titter ran round the room as the girl attempted to release the man's leather pouch. Chan backed against a wall and stared through the spaces between the crowding heads.

The girl had a perfect body, smooth as cream under the lights, full breasts and large nipples, like flowers. Her magnificent thighs were coiled round the tight haunches of the man, pulling him to her in time with a single exhilarating drum beat. Chan watched fascinated, a raw need for a woman clawing at his insides, a need for someone strange and brutally passionate, someone to be taken violently and anonymously and then abandoned. He grinned and thought that would be a mortal sin. Li-li would never forgive him, whatever the priest might do.

The act finished in a proliferation of drum beats and sustained trumpet notes. The men around the stage applauded wildly as the naked girl and her dark companion mounted the bandstand, acknowledging the cheers. A girl in evening dress came on singing a lilting Mandarin tune. The men went back to their tables. The lights dimmed. Couples moved on to the blue lit dance floor. On the further side of the room, Chan saw Pete Winston.

Winston was sitting opposite a pert young blonde, whose eyes were spread wide apart in her elfin face, whose mouth had the texture of an over-ripe peach. Too pretty to be true, Chan thought, too curious about what was going on around her to be a local. The neatness about her dress made him think of a nurse, or more probably, an air-hostess. She was smiling across the table at Winston, and from where he sat, Chan could see the glint of the revolver, protruding above Winston's waist band.

That gun worn so obviously told Chan a lot about Pete Winston. In a place like the Sun Sun Trade Association, guns were something you hid, unless you were licensed, or were a cop. In neither case did you expect to be given a bill at the end of the evening.

Nothing for nothing, Chan thought. That was the rule and Pete Winston had been long enough in Hong Kong to know it. Chan wondered what Winston would have to do to pay back his favours. As Chan watched, Winston leaned across and whispered to the girl. She nodded and took her handbag from the table. Winston picked up her scarf. They both stood up and walked towards the exit. Pete Winston shook hands with the guard by the door.

Wan Liu, the man Chan had come to see, arrived forty-five minutes later. He was a small, dapper Chinese in his late sixties, wearing a Piaget watch and a gold capped Parker in front of the silk handkerchief in the top pocket of his jacket. He was accompanied by two younger men, selected for their big and brutal physique rather than for their flat squashed faces and studious eyes. All three sat at a table near the bar, and while Wan Liu whipped through a wedge of invoices, the others gazed casually around the room and at the stage.

A rubicund woman with a plastic crown was allowing a statuesque young man in a bearskin to undress her. She protested horror and helplessness and writhed melo-dramatically in his grasp. This act was as ridiculous as the previous one had been erotic. Chan remembered that his bill was calculated by the number of floor shows he watched, and walked over to the table of the man he had come to see.

Wan Liu did not look up from his accounting as Chan

approached. One of the guards allowed his gaze to float casually over Chan. "What do you want?"

"A word," Chan replied. "A friendly word." He palmed his warrant card so that the bodyguard could see it.

The bodyguard spoke to Wan Liu who remained checking invoices for three whole minutes. Then still not looking up he said, "Sit".

Chan remained standing. "It would be easier alone."

For the first time Wan Liu looked at Chan. "I know you," he said slowly. "From Wan Chai Police Station, is it not?"

"Yes," Chan replied.

"What do you have to say?"

"Alone," Chan said, the word catching in his throat. "Please."

Wan Liu motioned to the guards to leave. They went out of earshot, their backs to the wall, looking at the couple on the dance floor. The woman had overcome her simulated horror and was now applying herself assiduously to the man. The music had become a rhythmic wailing. Feet and hands and bodies thumped on the stage. The woman screamed, a sound of mixed pleasure and anguish.

Chan said, "There are rumours about the III K."

"There's nothing new in that."

"Rumours that they were one with the Japanese during the war."

"Even if that were true, of what importance is it now?"

"A man was murdered two nights ago. You could say it was a ritual killing — Japanese style. He was set up for his murderers by a pimp called Yong Po, a prostitute at the Frisco Bar called Heiki and a taxi driver named Lin Yu."

"And what have they to do with the III K?"

"The man was taken somewhere in Wan Chai and tortured. For that his killers would have needed help. Afterwards, he was shot in a taxi in Yee Wo Road and his murderers drove away, free. That too would have needed help."

He had Wan Liu's full attention, now, the tiny black eyes fixed on his face like limpets. "And you want help from us in finding these assassins?" He hardly seemed to move his lips when he spoke.

Chan felt his body grow rigid with tension. Now, he thought, now. "Not help. Answers. The man was killed because he found out something that happened during the war. Something that had been done by the Japanese. We are looking for tape recordings that he had and which were taken by his killers."

"So?"

"So, there are people looking at who was friendly enough with the Japanese then, to commit murder for them, now."

"And what is any of this to do with me or the III K?"

Nothing, Chan thought, nothing except a series of casual connections. Nothing except that Wan Liu had allowed him to talk so far and made a discreet offer of help. "There was a man called Rodrigo in the war. He was a business man, living in Macau, and through his friendship with the Japanese Ambassador, he obtained contracts for the supply of rice. One day when he was attending a funeral, four men with sub machine guns killed him and his entire family. Do you remember that?"

"There was some talk of it, yes."

"There was also talk that it was a revenge killing. Triad revenge against the Japanese."

"So it might have been."

"If these investigations proceed, a lot of information will be made public about casual relationships with the Japanese. That might worry some people. Many members were executed by the Japanese. They left sons, brothers, families. Such talk might make people remember, especially if it looked as if old friendships were being revived."

Wan Liu fidgeted with the pencil torch on the table.

"There are people who have not forgotten," Chan went on.

"You are in charge of this enquiry?"

Chan nodded.

"And you want help?"

"Yes," Chan said.

Wan Liu smiled, revealing three gold teeth in his lower left gum. "You will take some drink?"

"No, thank you."

"Some girls maybe?"

"I am married," Chan said.

"And you are faithful to your wife?"

"I do not like girls who smile too easily," Chan said.

Wan Liu nodded, contemplatively. He pulled the wedge of invoices towards him and wrote a figure across the top. US $20,000. "I can give you help," Wan Liu said. "Any kind of help, but there are things I cannot talk about, you understand. There are things about which I might know, which I might have done, but about these things, my lips are sealed by an oath of silence."

$20,000, Chan thought. A lot of money. He had sometimes wondered if he would be strong enough, if the necessary absolution for venial sin had not been more corrupting than he knew. $20,000. He could take Li-li and the children to America with that, away from a country whose lease expired in twenty-five years. He was surprised when he heard his voice say, "It is too late for that. A man has been killed."

"Was this man so important?"

Chan thought of Raghavan thrusting his loneliness at Heiki, buying the companionship he needed. Old Raghi, Kenneth Wong had called him with the intimacy of casual acquaintance, old Raghi, a man unknown, unloved, with no one sure if he had a family in Calcutta, not even sure if they cared he was dead. What had made Raghavan important, was the manner of his dying. Murder was important. It was the ultimate crime, and there could be no compromise. Not at any rate for Chan.

"The man wasn't important," Chan said. "He was simply a man, no more, no less."

"So?"

"I want the killers," Chan said. "I want to know why."

Wan Liu said, "There are other things than solutions to problems."

"Not this time," Chan replied. "Not for murder."

*   *   *

That night, Chan checked that his Colt .38 Detective Special was loaded and placed it beside his bed. Li-li peering out at him sleepily came wide awake. "The children — " she started to say. "What's wrong?"

"Nothing." Chan sat down heavily on the edge of the bed and started to undress. "I might have to go out again in a hurry."

"In that much of a hurry?"

He half turned to look at her and said, "Yes."

After he had finished undressing, he turned off the light and lay beside her, staring into the darkness. Anything could happen, now. The III K could get him, or worse, get at his family. Chan felt sick with fear as he remembered Wan Liu ask if he was faithful to his wife. Alternatively, they could seek to influence someone in the police. Chan thought about that. The only way someone could yield to such influence and still protect himself, would be by removing Chan from the CID, possibly even from the police force. They would have to go pretty high for that, but it was not impossible. His life or his job, and Wan Liu had asked if Raghavan was important. Chan stared a long time into the darkness and wondered.

A long while later, he fell into a restless, worried sleep.

*   *   *

It was soon after two o'clock, when the girl came into Jaffe Road, thinking of the extra hundred dollars she had made. She teetered on high wedge heels, holding the brown maxi skirt away from the pavement, looking for a taxi to take her across the harbour, to Kowloon side. *Ei-Ya!* She was tired, and there were never any taxis about at two o'clock in the morning when the nightclubs closed.

She walked up the darkened street, neon signs dying all around her, past the black Toyota parked amongst the trucks at the kerb. A door opened. A man got out. She recognised the checked, seersucker jacket, the brown and white shoes. Yong Po.

"Heiki nay hoei beendo a?"

"Ook kkay." Where else would she go at two o'clock in the morning but home.

"Nay mo dik-see?"

Of course she hadn't a taxi. And she wasn't going with him either, not even to a party. She was tired. *Gwooi!* Then she saw the other men get out of the car and remembered.

Quickly she turned and started to walk away, the high heels a hindrance, now. A car crept down the street, its roof light glowing weakly. *"Wai! Dik-see!"* she screamed. Then Yong Po's hand clasped her elbow. She heard footsteps and stood still, feeling the sweat breaking out all over her body, her mouth going dry with fear. It was going to be like the last time, she thought, she should never have spoken to the policeman, remembering the gleaming pointed blade of the knife, knowing it was useless to resist.

*   *   *

Hours afterwards, Chan reached across the blackness for Li-li, finding security in the familiar warmth of her body, relief in the regular thrusting of his own.

Afterwards the thoughts returned. Incongruously he wondered about Li-li's arm and whether she had been to see the acupuncturist, just as so often he wondered, whether despite her professed Catholicism, she was taking the pill. He reached a hand out for the gun and was only half reassured by its lethal coldness. He remembered Wan Liu's gold teeth and his offer of help and fell asleep, dreaming of Raghavan's corpse erect in the arms of the girl in the Sun Sun Club, the stumps of his fingers trailing blood over her naked bottom, while his sightless eyes stared out of a head that bobbed and swayed and sometimes seemed to look at Chan and smile.

13

MONDAY MORNING, GREY mist twisting damp veils around the verdigris-hued Peak, shiny umbrellas bobbing between the full-bellied droop of drab tarpaulins, tyres splashing muddy water, the air steamy and close and stifling like the embrace of an ancient whore, the whole city drying out like a launderette. Not a day for working, a day for staying in bed and pondering the meanings of life and death, a day to drink Russian tea, a day that never should have begun.

Chan went heavily up the stairs to his office, glared testily at the correspondence on his desk. Paper, they would bury him with paper. Post mortem reports, ballistic reports, fingerprint reports, photographs, reports from every single policeman concerned with the Raghavan enquiry, a telex from Kuala Lumpur CID.

Kuala Lumpur CID did not know much about Raghavan. He had become a citizen in 1968, been granted a passport three years ago, worked for the *Straits Times*, and was still thought to be working for the *Asian Clarion*. No known next of kin, no knowledge of the family in India, no convictions and the address shown on his passport had been demolished two years ago. Chan snorted. Paper! A file as big as the Bible and still no closer to solving the mystery of Raghavan's death. Not much closer, anyway.

Let's see what depressing things had happened yesterday. Chan picked up the incident sheet, bland, black type face,

107

dirty grey paper. The jewellery robbery Li Gng had mentioned was there, together with fourteen assaults, four break-ins, one man practising dentistry without a licence, two requests for assistance in tracing missing persons, a raid on a grocery store selling spirituous tea labelled Courvoisier cognac. Crime, like sickness and death, had taken no heed of the sabbath. Never mind the sabbath, what had happened this morning?

At seven o'clock that morning, Pete Winston had raided the homes of two student leaders and arrested them. Seven o'clock in the morning; horrifying overtones of the secret police. That sumbitch Winston would go far in Russia. Had the students down in the charge room, without doubt, showing them he had ways of making them talk. Wonder how the parents had reacted to seven o'clock in the morning arrests. Parents had to have money these days to support student leaders at university. Poorer students were too concerned with studying to play politics. Soon the lawyers would start filing in. Winston would drop in the —

What on earth was he thinking about! There were two kids in the charge room having the life beaten out of them. Winston had broken a man's arm once, acting as a decoy in a drug raid. Superintendent Tang Lun had told Chan about that pointless exercise in violence. Resisting arrest, Winston had explained afterwards without remorse, pushers deserved worse than broken arms. Ignorant sumbitch! Didn't he know that Hong Kong had been founded so that the British could more easily push opium to the Chinese? The lawyers would be only the beginning of it.

Chan hurried down the narrow corridor, strong smell of Jeyes from the lavatories at the end, ignored the engaged sign and pushed open the door. Winston was under his command, whatever the AC said, the students were Chan's responsibility. They were stripped naked, cuffed tightly to upright chairs, faces swollen, bodies marked by black bruises. Young men, comfortable layers of puppy fat over the scarred ribs, used more to debate than to violence.

Vomit on the floor, a tooth glistening from a globule of blood and spittle.

"Morning," Winston said, leaning against the table. He looked pale and tense, sweating slightly, wearing his tourist gear, jeans, soiled bush shirt and sandals. There were two other men in the room with him, not from Wan Chai, obviously from Special Branch.

"Outside," Chan snapped. "I want a word with you."

For the smallest fraction of a second Winston hesitated. Then with a wave of his hand that was both a signal for an interval to the proceedings and a hippie sign of peace, he loped towards the door.

Chan led him away down the corridor towards the lavatories. "What the fuck do you think you're doing?" he demanded.

"Trying to make two crappy little arms smugglers talk."

"You have evidence?"

"They're high ups in the student movement," Winston replied. "They know how the arms are being brought in."

"And that is what you're charging them with? Arms smuggling?"

Winston leaned against the grey wall. A constable came in, saw them and went out again. "Don't be stupid," Winston said. "They're accessories to Saturday night's jewellery robbery. Of course they weren't anywhere near the store, but it'll do, for a holding charge."

"Get them out of here," Chan snapped. "Now."

"After they've talked."

"I gave you an order, Inspector Winston."

Winston drew himself away from the wall, a coiled, controlled movement. Snake like. "The Assistant Com —

"You have written authority from the AC to bash up suspects like bloody footballs?"

Winston threw his head back, looked down at Chan from under half-closed lids, lazily. He gave Chan a crooked grin. "You know the score as well as I do, chief." he said. "We've got to make them talk."

"Not this way," Chan snapped. "Not if they're innocent."

"Well, we don't know that yet, do we." He made to move round Chan. Chan blocked him with his shoulder.

"They're marked."

"They tried to resist arrest and they used foul language. They called me names, they even insulted the Queen."

Chan took a deep breath. It would be so easy, so refreshing, to hit Pete Winston. Resisting arrest, indeed. *Yut, yee sarm . . . bah gow sap*, no point in violence yet. "Their parents must have sent for lawyers," Chan said.

"So?"

"Don't you realise what's going to happen next?"

Winston's smile was patronising. "No, you tell me."

"They're going to hold their damn rally outside this police station. We're going to have to call the Riot Squad and we're going to look like the people who framed the student leaders because we were embarrassed about Godber."

Winston took it in, slowly. There was a brief flash of panic in his eyes, then he said, "Nonsense. They'll never do that. Even if they did, our chaps can soon disperse them."

"And the AC will send you a get-well card." Chan had the pleasure of seeing Winston flush.

Winston was still going to be stubborn, though.

"An uprising will endanger the whole colony," Winston said.

Big talk, small boy shouting to himself in a dark room. "The students aren't going to start an armed uprising."

"Oh! You're sure of that, are you?" Still defiant, but more careful, now.

"I am a Chinese," Chan said. "I *live* here." He had difficulty keeping his voice level, his face still felt flushed. "There isn't going to be an armed uprising. Forget that."

"They're bringing plastic and detonators — "

"It isn't for them. They don't want a revolution. We're all refugees. My family came over in 1940 and there are millions like us who have come here to live, to work, to find peace. We have struggled for what we have and the last thing any of us want is Chairman Mao taking over Hong Kong."

"This rally isn't about Chairman Mao," Winston said. "It's about kicking us out."

"As far as we Chinese are concerned, you are the lesser of two evils," Chan said. "We have been a long time together. There are things about you that we do not like, things that we will seek to change. But these changes will not be made by students at a rally to bring back Peter Godber."

Winston's eyes narrowed.

Heavens! The sumbitch was thinking that *he* was a revolutionary.

Winston said, "I have to find out."

"You'll have to do it some other way, Inspector Winston," Chan said. "Enough talk. Do they go or do I charge you with assault?"

Winston looked away from Chan, his face hard, angry. "Put like that, I have no choice."

"No," Chan said. "Go back to your office and stay there."

Afterwards Chan sent for Lau. Lau worked with young men at the boys' institute where he taught judo. He would be better able to deal with the students.

"Square them somehow," Chan said, "anyhow. But get them out of here and return them to their parents." He also told Lau to kick out the SB men on their sumbitching arses.

14

SURESH BANERJEE, CHAIRMAN of the Alor Setor group of
companies, President of the Delhi Foundation, came
through immigration with the harassed air of one whose
life was plagued by the incompetence of minions. A tall
man, handsome in an Aryan way, with a large hook nose,
a firm full mouth, vivid black eyes. His skin was deep brown
and glossy and he wore a pale cream mohair suit that hung
over his plump figure the way a good tailor intended it to.
He was a brisk walker and came quickly down the steps
into the reception area, eyes darting restlessly.

He recognised the young lout of a chauffeur still wearing
the same coxcomb hair style, still affecting tight striped
shirts with collars that were raised and pointed. Banerjee
went up to him and dropped his hide case and airline bag
at the man's feet. The chauffeur wheeled away a freshly lit
cigarette, picked up the bags and wordlessly led Banerjee
to the car park.

Little *goonda*, Banerjee thought eyeing the chauffeur's
insolent back. Deserves a bloody good kicking about. Then
he remembered that now he was more than a business man.
As a politician he should learn to love the masses, even
horrible little gangsters like Chiao Te's chauffeur.

Chiao Te was waiting in an olive green Audi, a busily
idling engine keeping the air conditioner streaming cool
air. The chauffeur dumped Banerjee's case in the boot

and allowed Banerjee to open the rear door by himself. Banerjee folded his palms in front of his chest and bowed to Chiao Te in an Indian style greeting.

Chiao Te's extended hand dropped, his ritual smile wavered. He asked, "Did you have a good flight?"

Banerjee settled himself and looked at Chiao Te with the air of a man who always had a good flight. "Yes," he said. "How is everything?" He wanted to get this business with Chiao Te over as soon as possible. There were very important things for him to do in Hong Kong, like reviewing the arrangements for the rally, and finding out what he could about poor Raghavan's death.

Banerjee was thrust back into the seat as the chauffeur accelerated sharply between rows of muddy cars. Now if the man had been driving Banerjee's own Benz, he would have sacked him on the spot.

Chiao Te however remained unperturbed. "I thought you might be hungry," he said. "There's a good restaurant in Kowloon. I have made reservations."

Banerjee studied Chiao Te's face with its lick of dark hair flicked well back from the forehead, the creases of fat in the cheeks that now looked like dimples, the expressionless eyes behind the rimless glasses. "Lunch," Banerjee said as if he'd never heard of the word. "All right."

He looked away at the ugly columns of apartments with their shabby pale green paint and thick layers of grime, long brown scars from broken water pipes. These omnipresent Hong Kong apartments reminded him of wartime newsreels, washing fluttering from the balconies like flags of defeat, an air of abandonment, as if the town had recently suffered a bombing raid.

There was only one reason for Chiao Te to invite him to lunch, Banerjee thought. He was unable to pay for what he had bought. His relationship with Chiao Te had always been formal, their business always straightforward. Their relationship did not call for a ritual sealing over food. All the way to the restaurant Banerjee worried about Chiao Te's inability to pay.

The restaurant was small, unpretentious, busy, calendars and scrolls on the walls, tables of plain wood covered with white cloth. The food would undoubtedly be good, Banerjee thought without relish. Chiao Te obviously liked eating well, and the meal would be unnecessarily long. Already Banerjee regretted accepting the invitation.

Then he had his second surprise of the day. Seated at their table was an attractive woman, well filled out, mid-thirtyish, dark hair pulled tightly back over her ears, her lipsticked mouth parted in a welcoming smile. Chiao Te introduced her as his wife.

Second wife, Banerjee thought, sitting down and ordering Coca-Cola. If it was unusual for Chiao Te to invite him to lunch, it was unique that he should bring his wife to it as well. Chinese wives did not participate in men's business. And it wasn't as if he and Chiao Te were friends. He'd only met the man twice previously, and that since Banerjee had gone into the business of arms smuggling.

Arms smuggling! It was Gopal who had shown him such things were possible. Gopal who had come back into his life in a creased white *dhoti*, bringing with him poignant memories of the INA, of a time when they had all been dedicated, involved, prepared to lay down their lives for a cause. Those had been great, wonderful days!

They were not over yet, Gopal had said. The enemy still thrived. He had come because the junta needed Banerjee. They needed Banerjee to lead them, and if he would only say yes, Gopal would pledge the entire movement to him.

Banerjee had been surprised, flattered and finally, taken aback. All his working life he had been a follower, usually in his father's footsteps. He had married a girl selected for him, he had dutifully bred two sons and a daughter, he had carried out his allotted tasks obediently, and even now, though he was Chairman of the group, he did very little leading. The companies were riddled with relatives, uncles, nephews, cousins, experts and accountants, who ensured that nothing could be done unless it was in a manner of which his late father would have approved.

Gopal had said, his people needed help. Pakistan, that perfidious state created by the perfidious British Raj, was splitting apart. Remember how Netaji had described it as the most monstrous act of treachery, how he had reviled those traitors, Mountbatten and Jinnah and Nehru and Gandhi, remember how he had foreseen that the partition of India would not last. The Bengalis of East Pakistan were in revolt and were being ruthlessly repressed by the West Pakistan Army. They needed money, they needed food, and most of all they needed arms.

Gopal had a friend named Andersson, a big blond Swede with piercing blue eyes, a vast fund of dirty stories and a very second hand Dakota. Andersson was flying meat into Vietnam. It was not too difficult, Andersson said, to fly arms out.

In the six months of the Bangladesh war they had moved four boat loads of arms through Thailand to certain islets at the mouth of the Ganges. It was novel, it was exciting, it gave Banerjee a heady sense of power. For the first time since his seventeenth birthday, he felt of use.

Then, India faced with a massive influx of refugees, with the prospect of a continuing guerrilla war on its borders resolved to settle once and for all the differences of its military commanders with the West Paks. The campaign lasted only a few days. The West Pakistan Army, beleagured, tactically inferior, and dependent upon supplies a continent away, surrendered. The new State of Bangladesh was declared and the patriot in Banerjee was fulfilled. But what to do next? He was President of his own, newly created Delhi Foundation, he had visited Dacca and ridden triumphantly through the streets in an open car, surrounded by a Mukti Fuj guard of honour, he had made wild, revolutionary speeches, crying we shall not rest until all Bengal is united, *Chalo* Delhi! *Chalo* Calcutta! And Gopal had stayed behind in Dacca.

Banerjee must carry on the work he had started, Gopal said. The old enemy still thrived and the Third World had need of Netaji's ideas to throw off their political and economic shackles. Banerjee should develop his movement, make it an international shrine to their fallen leader.

There had also been the question of the arms. Despite the processions and the speeches, the official welcomes and the visits to men of power, the new state of Bangladesh made it quite clear that the last thing they now wanted, was a continuing supply of illegal weaponry. There were also the Company's auditors who were beginning to ask embarrassing questions about payments for shipments of copra that never arrived and for which there were no vouchers.

Under the circumstances, Chiao Te had been a godsend. A spy for Chiang Kai-shek in Hong Kong, Chiao Te had been introduced to Banerjee by Mr. Datt. On behalf of the Nationalist Government of China, Chiao Te was prepared to buy all the arms that Banerjee could supply.

"I asked, what would you like to eat?" Banerjee came aware of Chiao Te's wife smiling at him, of a waiter standing by the table with pad and pencil poised.

"You order, please," Banerjee said forcing his thoughts to the present and the nagging question of Chiao Te's inability to pay.

Chiao Te ordered and his wife asked Banerjee if he'd had a good flight. These people were obsessed with good and bad flights. As far as Banerjee was concerned, all flights that got him where he wanted to go were good ones. This emphasis on comfort was a decadent British trait, unbecoming in a Chinese. However he did not say so.

Mrs. Chiao turned out to be a graduate of Taiwan University, a cheerful and vivacious person with a comforting capacity for small talk. Her polite questions allowed Banerjee to make suitably polite answers without taking his mind too far away from the question of credit.

The meal when it came, was superb. Despite his earlier lack of appetite, Banerjee ate with relish. *Gwah jee chong tong* — a soup of Chinese watercress and eggs, fried shrimp curls, pickled Shanghai cabbage with chicken, salted bamboo shoots braised with pork, noodles garnished with parsley and aubergines and strips of ham no larger than match sticks. The centre piece of the meal was five willow fish, a whole red snapper with ginger and sweet pickles and onions marinated in a sweet and sour sauce.

Banerjee decided that it was too late to stop the shipment now. He would have to negotiate the best terms he could. Whatever happened he would insist that their end of the transaction was guaranteed by a bank.

At last the meal finished and Banerjee felt he could start talking business. Mrs. Chiao filled his cup with more tea. It was, she told him, Win Mo Chaah from the Kiangsi province. It grew on mountains so high that monkeys were used to pick the leaves.

As if reading his mind, Chiao Te asked, "What about the shipment?"

Banerjee looked from Mrs. Chiao to him. "It left this morning," he said. "Your people checked it before it left." Chiao Te mumbled through the list of arms, FN automatic rifles, ammunition, flechettes, plastic, detonators, all coming to some 53,000 United States dollars.

"That is right," Banerjee said. "Have you had cable confirmation?"

Chiao Te nodded.

"Then," Banerjee said, anxious to get to what he thought was the problem, "I will have the money."

Chiao Te reached into the inside pocket of his jacket and brought out a huge, leather wallet. He took out a folded piece of paper and passed it across the table to Banerjee. Banerjee took it, smoothed it, laid it face up on the table and looked. It was a draft drawn on the Chartered Bank made out in favour of the Alor Setor Machinery Co. for the full value of Banerjee's final shipment, less ten per cent.

Banerjee said, "It is not the right amount."

Chiao Te nodded again, light dancing off his rimless glasses. "We have made a deduction," he said.

"But why? No deduction was agreed! You have not asked me! You must pay the full amount!"

Chiao Te placed a moist palm on Banerjee's wrist, and Banerjee realised he was shouting. "I have something for you," Chiao Te said. "Something worth more than $5,300."

Banerjee felt his mouth go dry. Deliberately he sipped some of the tea that had been picked by monkeys. "What?" he asked, fighting to keep his voice level.

"The matter we spoke of the last time. The plane crash." Chiao Te smiled, his cheeks dimpling. "My wife remembers it."

Banerjee turned to the even more broadly smiling Mrs. Chiao. "How can you remember such a thing? You must have been only a little girl at the time."

Mrs. Chiao smilingly acknowledged the fact. "I remember my parents speaking about it," she said softly. "It was shaming that such a great man should have been murdered."

Banerjee turned from husband to wife. This was what Banerjee had been determined to find out. Had Netaji been murdered or was the plane crash an accident? "Who murdered him? The British?" Remembering Raghavan had died suddenly too, in a British colony.

"We have no reason to suspect the British," Chiao Te said.

"My parents said the plane was sabotaged," piped Mrs. Chiao.

Of course everyone knew the plane had been sabotaged. The enquiry that had been held ten years after the incident was inconclusive. Reading it, Banerjee thought bitterly, one was left in doubt not only as to whether the plane had been sabotaged, but whether it had crashed at all. Typical British whitewash!

Chiao Te said, "The plane was fitted with radial engines. In those days, I would have been easily able to sabotage any radial engined plane without leaving a trace."

Banerjee shrugged. "That is not worth $5,300."

Mrs. Chiao said, "The man who organised that plane crash is now in Hong Kong. That is what we are charging you $5,300 for." She took out a thick envelope from her handbag and handed it to her husband. Ceremoniously Chiao Te handed the envelope to Banerjee.

Banerjee opened the envelope. Inside were a number of black and white photographs. They all depicted the same man, a thin, elderly, narrow faced Japanese, with a bristle of dark hair and eyes as expressionless as wells that had dried up twenty years ago. The topmost photograph showed the man coming out of the Hong Kong–Macau hydrofoil terminal, the next the man getting into a diesel engined Cedric taxi. There was a shot of the taxi taken through the windscreen of a following car, a shot of the man walking across a concrete path bordered by wire fences and what appeared to be a railway line. Banerjee looked at a rear view of the man climbing an interminably long flight of steps, of the man in the grounds of some public building, looked at a rather blurry print of the man in a temple. There was one very clear picture. Banerjee looked hard.

This photograph had also been taken in the temple. But there had been more light, or the photographer had got his exposure correct. It was a head and shoulders shot of the Japanese, peering intently at a statue. The statue was in the picture too. It gave off a dull sheen as if covered in gold paint and was of a Chinese man squatting in what Banerjee called the lotus position. A thin sliver of moustache half circled the mouth of the statue. The statue was not of any Buddhist saint that Banerjee recognised, but he felt his heart beating faster, his breath catch in his throat with excitement.

Chiao Te said, "The photographs were taken by my

chauffeur, Ah Au. The man in the photographs is Hiroshi Watanabe."

Banerjee kept his eyes fixed on the photographs. He felt he had come to the end of a long and weary road. The information and the photographs that Chiao Te had provided him with were worth far more than $5,300, hundreds of times more. He thought he could see a way to ensure that the movement was solvent for a long, long time and to repay the loans from the companies before the auditors found out.

Still, Banerjee knew he had to proceed carefully. He had to discover how much the Chiao Te's knew. He asked, "But I do not know this . . . Watanabe. Why should I have any interest in him?"

Chiao Te replied, "At the time of the crash, Watanabe was head of the 82nd Bureau in Taiwan."

Mrs. Chiao said, "It was said in Taiwan at the time that it was he who had arranged for the plane to crash."

Banerjee remembered. The 82nd Bureau had been the Japanese Intelligence Unit during the Second World War. "Why should the 82nd Bureau want to sabotage a plane carrying Japanese as well?" Banerjee knew full well it was the British who had put the Japanese up to it. They had been frightened of Netaji and the other Japanese leaders who had died in the crash.

Chiao Te's answer was surprising. He said nothing about British collaboration. "After eighty thousand people had been killed in a few seconds at Hiroshima, do you think ten extra lives mattered? Do you think those ten lives were important to a nation that believed in ritual suicide?"

Banerjee leaned forward, puzzled. "Tell me about Watanabe," he said.

"Hiroshi Watanabe worked with the Kuomintang for three years. I was the one who persuaded him to work for them, soon after the war, after I'd helped him escape from a temple in Shatin, where he was hiding."

"Was that the temple in the photograph?"

Chiao Te nodded. "Watanabe came of unknown parentage. He could have been an imperial bastard. Perhaps in compensation, he always thought of himself as a samurai. He could not accept the Japanese surrender. He was a friend of the imperial family." Chiao Te reached out for the photographs and picked one. His pale, half-moon nail pointed, "Look at the cufflinks he is wearing. Do you see the pattern of a fourteen petalled chrysanthemum. That is the symbol of a Japanese prince. Anyway, Watanabe could not accept the surrender, nor could he accept the fact that a traitor could benefit from his treachery."

"Traitor? Who was a traitor?"

"In Watanabe's eyes, your leader was. Let me try to show you how he thought. What date did the plane crash?"

The date was seared indelibly in Banerjee's consciousness. Were it not for chance or stratagem he was not sure which, that might have been the day that he, Suresh Banerjee, died. "August 18th, 1945."

"Four days after the Japanese surrender?"

Banerjee nodded. He remembered that night too.

"Where was the plane going?"

"To Manchuria. To the Russians."

Chiao Te nodded slowly. "To the Russians," he repeated, "The Russians who had been Japan's enemies for over forty years, who had declared war six days before Japan's surrender, in order to tear apart her war-worn carcass. Your friend was flying to *them* with everything he had learned in three years' collaboration with the Japanese. He must have been mad to think they'd let him."

Banerjee looked down at the table. He did not want them to see the excitement in his face. For him it was a private moment.

Mrs. Chiao said, "If it is revenge you seek, you must act now."

Slowly Banerjee looked up at Chiao Te and his wife. He knew that keeping information from the Russians was not the only reason why the plane had been sabotaged. Now there were certain things he had to do. Revenge could wait, but not for long. He said to Chiao Te, "I would like to go to this temple."

"It is not far from here. Come, I will instruct Ah Au to take you."

15

MONDAY DRAGGED ON for Richard Chan. More routine, more paper. Considerations of intracerebral haemorrhage and effects of expansile force, carbonaceous residue and rifling marks. In the late morning, a conference with brother officers on Kowloon side, lectures on the Use of Mobile Police Stations in the Help Fight Crime Campaign, discussions about a new poster campaign, a jovial mess-type lunch. Chan was anxious to get back to his patch, to get on with fighting his particular crime, the murder of an Indian with a museum piece of a pistol.

To work at all, the gun must have been carefully preserved, regularly oiled, fired occasionally over twenty-five years. Chan made a note to check the pistol clubs. Unlikely that the gun would be registered though. In any case, why a Nambu with so much modern weaponry readily available. Those youngsters who spent Saturday nights holding up jewellery stores used guns too. Bet a string of pennies they weren't using Nambus.

The cassette arrived from the lab in a sealed envelope, still containing traces of grey fingerprint powder. The attached report said parts of the tape were damaged, indecipherable. Chan took out Raghavan's dictaphone from his desk drawer. How did the damn thing work? Ah right, that had the cassette looped up. Plenty of power still available from the batteries. No, that was fast forward wind.

Now get the mike connected. That was better. He settled back in his chair and pressed the replay tab. Bloody hell, they were talking Japanese.

A half hour's delay till the interpreter came, a serious young man, unloading a heavy notebook on to Chan's desk, thick lensed spectacles and the way he spoke from the corner of his mouth, making him somehow look Japanese.

"How you like it? I make full notes and write translation or — ?"

"Give it to me section by section," Chan said. "I'll make the notes."

"All right. How you like."

The tape wound on, the voice on it old, wavering. Old age or perhaps a bad recording.

"He who is speaking," the interpreter said, "is Sergeant Kuranari, Gunnery Officer, Third Air Force Wing, Japanese National Air Force. It is noon of August 17th and their take off is being delayed because they are waiting for some ... *yando* ... Indian people."

Mr. Datt, thought Chan, and his President, Banerjee. They were the only Indians he knew, except Raghavan, and Raghavan was dead.

"They leave Saigon at 5.15 p.m. The speaker, Kuranari, is very frightened because the plane uses the whole runway." The interpreter switched off the tape. "They are, I think, overloaded. I did not hear something too clearly."

The interpreter smiled, nodded and got the tape going again. "They are flying to Tokyo through Touraine and Taihoku."

Where on earth was Taihoku, Chan wondered.

The voice faded, the tape filled with static and faint squeakings. A name, Shidei? Place? Person? Thing? It was like a childhood game, animal, vegetable, mineral.

The voice picked up again, faded. Quite definitely an old man, Chan decided.

The interpreter said the plane was in Touraine and there was an argument about guns. Guns, Chan leaned forward.

Nambus? No they were stripping guns off the plane and Kuranari had not liked it. He was not sure whether they should be flying anyway, and whether they would have a clear passage. They had unloaded twelve guns and established a weight saving of six hundred kilos.

After that, more static. The interpreter frowned at the tape recorder in annoyance. Something about Prince Kanin and a marquee tent, a lunch of sandwiches and bananas. The voice came clear again. The engine had been strained on take off from Touraine, run at 3100 rpm against a permissible limit of 2800. At approximately two o'clock they had taxied to the end of the runway in Taihoku. Major Takuzawa was in control.

"Once again, as in Touraine, I felt we would not unstick. I was more frightened than at Touraine because there was a cement factory at the end of the airfield, with tall chimneys. We were travelling very quickly and had nearly reached the end of the runway when the plane left the ground. We climbed sharply, the engines roaring in my ears. Then there was a sudden, sharp explosion and the plane veered to the right. I saw the right wing hit the ground and then the runway crashed through my canopy. That is all I remember."

And what, Chan thought, was all that about?

He was still thinking about it when Lau walked in, vibrantly batiked, and a face like an undertaker's. He'd just returned from the hospital. The bar girl, Heiki, had been taken there in the early hours of Monday morning with a knife wound.

"Didn't recognise me," Lau said, "Or pretended not to. Said she'd fallen down the stairs in the dark and stabbed herself."

"What do you think?"

"She's lying, chief. The doctor said it wasn't that kind of wound. She'd been held down and slashed across the belly."

Chan remembered the rough scar peeping over the waist

of the brown maxi, puckering the flesh of the smooth, flat stomach. Traditional punishment, he thought, for running away or talking to a cop. Punishment for talking about Raghavan.

"She won't make a complaint," Lau said. "There isn't much we can do."

"Isn't there?" Anger bubbled through Chan in boiling hot waves, blind, unreasoning anger, that had once made him pull a gun on Li-li's father. The knifing was more than a punishment. It was Wan Liu's answer to Chan's enquiry about Raghavan. You can't touch me, Wan Liu was saying, I am too rich, I have too many men and half the police force is in my pocket. My wealth and my power place me above the law. *You*, cannot touch me.

We'll see about that, Chan thought. We'll see about that, now. "Get Winston and meet me at my car," he snapped, wondering that he was clear enough to think of that shred of self-preservation. Wan Liu would be restrained in the presence of a European policeman, a humiliating thought, which only made Chan more angry.

He drove rapidly to North Point with much crunching of gears, sped along the shabby crowded alleys by the wharf. A dingy area of tailors and liquor stores, cafes and groceries crammed together untidily. A few hundred yards away the grisly brightness of flowers outside the Hong Kong Funeral Parlour. Very apposite.

He parked the Cortina untidily behind a tatty Datsun, loosed the gun in his waist clip and led Lau and Winston through a restaurant, up a flight of shabby stairs at the back. On the first floor the shabbiness disappeared, replaced with bright lighting, wall to wall carpets, gleaming furniture, pale wood and flamboyant lampshades.

A Chinese girl, made up like a film star, was seated behind a low desk, appropriate decoration for an executive suite. "Wan Liu in?" Chan asked. "Police."

The girl smiled, charmingly. "If you will please wait a

moment," looking towards a door at the further end of the room. Chan was already walking towards that door.

"Wait," the girl cried. "You can't — "

The whirr of a buzzer. The door at the end of the room opened. The two bodyguards from the Sun Sun Trade Association stood there, squashed into the narrow opening. They were at a disadvantage. They were standing still. Chan was moving forward.

His left streaked out, marvellously straight, beautiful release of tension, connected with a jarring of bone. The man's head rocked backwards, his body blocking his companion. Chan's right hook exploded into the man's middle, flesh folding around his fist, the man crumpling, a high pitched shriek, a blurring rush of bodies and Lau was chopping at the second man's gun hand, stabbing at his neck with the folded over fingers of his right hand.

Chan pushed past into the corridor beyond the door. Lau stooped down, took out the gun from his assailant's shoulder holster. It wasn't a Nambu, Lau grinned happily up at Chan. "What next, chief?"

Chan straightened his clothing, feeling immensely relieved, opened the door on the far side of the corridor and walked into Wan Liu's office. A large office, for such a small man, pale yellow carpeting and Scandinavian type bookshelves, neatly empty. Wan Liu half rising from his chair, sat down.

Chan sucked the back of his knuckles and said, "Police. Want to talk to you about a bar girl who was knifed early this morning."

Wan Liu forced his face into impassivity, looked slowly from Chan to Lau and to Winston. "There was no need to force your way in," he said. "I do not know any bar girls." He looked significantly at Chan. "I am a happily married man."

Lau waggled the gun in his palm. "That fountain of misery outside has a licence for this?"

"I do not know," Wan Liu said. "I do not ask him to carry a gun. He is only an employee."

"Okay," Chan snapped. "We'll check that later." Wan Liu was rattled. He was a man who instituted violence, too old now to participate in it. Now he was faced with three policemen who had burst into his office, breached his wall of security and made him lose face. "The girl worked in one of your bars," Chan said. "The Frisco."

"Don't know it, don't own any bars. Here I have a legitimate property business."

With bodyguards who carry guns, Chan reflected. There was the sound of retching behind him. One of the bodyguards stood in the doorway. Wan Liu dismissed him with a contemptuous wave of his hand. "Do you have a gun?" Chan asked.

"No."

"You wouldn't know anything about a Japanese gun called a Nambu?"

"I know nothing about firearms."

"What about cassettes? We're looking for a cassette that was stolen from a murdered man."

"No." Defensively.

"Tell me about the war. Tell me what you did at that time."

"Like everyone else, I was working. Import-export business. It is too long ago to remember very much."

Chan began to feel that the visit was a mistake. It assuaged his anger, shocked Wan Liu but little else. No wonder his superiors had reported he was too impetuous. Now Winston was there, to witness his failure. "You won't mind if we look around?"

"You have a search warrant?"

"What are you hiding? Cassettes? Guns?"

"No," Wan Liu said. "But you get a search warrant to search these offices."

"All right," Chan said. "That will take time. I'll go and get it. My friends will wait here."

Wan Liu contemplated a lost afternoon, seated in his office with two policemen. He gave in, impassively. "You can look if you do it quickly and tidily."

He hadn't even bothered to call his lawyer, Chan thought. Obviously the place was clean. People like Wan Liu were too experienced to keep incriminating evidence in their offices. They searched perfunctorily, files, papers, account books, all the trappings of a legitimate business. No Nambu pistol, no Philips cassettes.

Chan said, "We're still interested in the girl and what happened during the war."

Wan Liu's mouth stiffened into a smile. "You have your work to do." An inoffensive enough statement, but he made it sound like a threat.

"And we will keep on looking. I wanted you to know that." At least he had the satisfaction of seeing Wan Liu's smile freeze, an expression of concern flit over his dapper face.

Outside, walking to the car, Winston asked, "What the hell was all that about?"

"Delivering a message," Chan said. "Telling him there is no tree so tall that it cannot be felled by a woodman's axe."

Winston turned and stared at him. "Taking on the III K single handed," he said. "Jesus Christ! You must be mad!"

Chan shrugged. Wan Liu had lost face. So had Chan and there might be repercussions, but the amazement in Winston's expression was some compensation for that.

*   *   *

The anger and its consequences had purified Chan. He felt strong. Wan Liu had been made to feel afraid, made aware of his humanity. Perhaps now, someone would talk. Perhaps he would have to see the timorous Mr. Datt again.

In vastly improved humour, Chan listened to the constable who had followed Lin Yu the previous morning. He had stayed with him, the constable said, until he had started to work his taxi. Then he had abandoned surveillance. Chan listened calmly to Sergeant Yim telling him that so far they had no trace of the pimp, Yong Po. He even smiled when Pete Winston walked into his office.

"I must have more men," Winston said, "I've borrowed all I can from other stations. I must have at least seven from here."

"Ask Lau to let you have three. You can have all you like once we've solved this murder."

Winston snorted. "AC wants me to have more men than that."

"Even AC cannot increase the number of men available, overnight." Chan looked down at the file on his desk. He had been tidying up the details of a grain store robbery, deciding to worry about Raghavan later that evening, at home with the television turned on and the smell of Li-li's cooking wafting in his nostrils. The phone rang.

It sounded like someone who said he was calling from Taipei. He was a CID Inspector and had called earlier that day. Police Headquarters had suggested he speak to Senior Inspector Richard Chan. Was that Senior Inspector Chan?

Chan said it was. The Inspector from Taipei said the phone call had to do with a murder case he was investigating. He wanted someone put under surveillance in Hong Kong. An Indian gentleman, travelling on a Malayan passport, name of Debnath Raghavan.

Chan nearly dropped the phone. He shouted, "That isn't a problem. I know exactly where he is."

"That's good," the voice at the other end said. "Can you hold him till we get someone over?"

"He isn't going anywhere," Chan replied. "They've taken his guts out and he's begun to smell."

"I don't follow."

"He's dead," Chan said. "We've got him in the morgue."

"Oh," said the voice.

"Why did you want me to hold him?"

"It has to do with a witness we have. She thinks this

man Raghavan might have had something to do with the murder of her grand-uncle."

The absurdity of a murdered grand-uncle was only slightly more than finding someone who knew Raghavan at the end of a phone. "You've got someone who knows Raghavan?" Chan shouted.

"Yes."

"I'll be in Taipei tomorrow," Chan cried. "On the afternoon flight."

"You'll enjoy Taipei." Winston said. "It's all food and sex." Chan slammed down the phone.

*   *   *

"Taiwan," Hanson said. "Come off it, Richard. You're much too old to be running around the Far East chasing girls."

Chan allowed Hanson his little joke, sipped his departmental tea and explained politely that the girl in Taiwan was the best lead he'd got. Hanson stared anxiously at the cigarette smouldering down nicotine browned fingers and said he supposed it would be all right.

Sergeant Lau said it would be all right too. They would all love working eighteen hours a day so their chief could go island hopping across the China Sea. Meanwhile there were a few cases of robbery, arson, assault and fraud, to say nothing of a murder still to be solved. Chan, however wasn't to worry about such pedestrian matters. He was to have a good time and Sergeant Lau would take care of everything.

Li-li said, "I can't see why you have to go to Taiwan to meet this woman. Why can't you talk to her on the telephone?"

Chan explained that she was an important witness and he didn't think she was that kind of woman. Li-li said that she'd better not be and that police work was dangerous enough without Chan having to rush off to Taiwan to meet women. Chan had no business risking his life flying in an aeroplane. She'd flown once, when they had gone to Manila on their honeymoon and that had been enough. Aeroplanes were dangerous things; they travelled too fast and too high. Chan assured her that aeroplanes did not crash, certainly not with a Senior Chief Inspector on board. By then it was well past eight o'clock in the evening and he was much too exhausted to think constructively about Raghavan.

16

EIGHT O'CLOCK. WINSTON looked vexedly at the glow of his watch, deep sea green in the silvery blue light of the bar. Kate was late again, over involved in setting an example of the British Way of Life and spreading culture by the book load, encouraging slit-eyed bastards to improve themselves and become third-rate politicians.

Winston sipped his whisky sour and looked round the bar. Low tables, unobtrusive music, the rustle of low-keyed conversation, the discreet chink of ice against glass, symbols of a life style not necessarily ethically eximious although civilised, gentlemanly, decent, certainly worth preserving. Heaven alone knew it was changing, even in England, poisoned by a mixture of ignorance, envy and idealism.

This kind of life wouldn't last long in Hong Kong either, especially if the students had their way. The students didn't give a damn about Godber. The ramifications of *tam woo* were as natural to the Chinese as the County Cricket Championship to the British. No, the whole thing was a pretext to start trouble, a fuse to be ignited, a ploy to throw out the British. Pete Winston was certain of that. And if that pig-headed mother-fucker Richard Chan hadn't intervened, he would have had proof. Those whining pinkos would have talked. Wire them up to a hand held dynamo and they soon forgot about Lenin and Mao and all that crap. They talked, they screamed and cried and choked in their eagerness to tell all. Brotherhood of the people. Shit!

They were complainers, arrogant little sods abusing the privileges they had been given, using their puny minds and second-hand ideas to try and dictate terms to their elders and betters. A few years of bull and discipline was what they needed. They'd soon learn what was what and what it was like to work for a living. Then they could go back to Trotsky and Mao and Hegel and discover for themselves that Communism was all bunk.

Winston stared belligerently at the dragons lining the bar, beckoned one of the pert waitresses over and ordered a second whisky sour. The list of suspects that SB had given him was about as long as the Pearl River and just as unfamiliar. Winston's head bulged with strange names, his mind wrestled with the twin problems of men and surveillance. He'd spent most of that lousy day cajoling station superintendents into lending him men. He needed at least four men for every surveillee, he needed stand-by transport and access to phone taps. He was struggling with just two men for each suspect and all that Chan had made available was three junior constables who knew as much about tailing as they did about astrophysics. That was wrong. Wan Chai was his station, they should be giving him full support. Hanson was doing everything, but not Chan. Chan was obsessed with the question of Raghavan's death as if the death of one unknown Indian mattered when the whole Colony could go up like a lorry-load of nitroglycerine.

To listen to Chan talk you'd imagine that the students were public benefactors and that Godber, a member of the Japanese Police Force. Sometimes, Winston thought, Chan acted like a Commie.

He came aware of an elegant portly shadow looming over his table, looked up at Cameron Wah. "Whisky sour isn't it? Let me get you another one, dear boy."

Winston let him. He believed that from people like Cameron Wah, you took whatever was going and didn't stop to say thank you.

Wah snapped his trouser creases and sat down. His face looked liverish in that light and there was something conspiratorial in his attitude as he leaned sideways across the table towards Winston.

"What happened this afternoon wasn't very nice. Not nice at all."

The waitress arrived and he ordered Winston's drink and a Campari soda for himself.

"Wan Liu was very upset. He was made to lose face."

"I was only the back-up guy," Winston said. "Only carrying out orders."

Wah wagged a finger in his face. "That's no defence, you know. No defence at all. That's what all the Germans said at Nuremburg. Acting under orders. It wasn't good enough. Every man has a duty to ask himself if the orders he is given are legal."

Fine philosophy if you had time to think or the courage to ask. Only a liberal blowhard who had never even served in a Boy Scout Troop would dream that it was practical.

"Forcible entry, assault, illegal search. Wouldn't look good if Wan Liu brought charges."

"If," Winston said, pointedly.

"He doesn't want unnecessary problems," Wah said. "You know the score as well as I do. Cheers." He made a wry mouth at the bitterness of the Campari and went on, "Here in Hong Kong, we work together, you and us. We each keep to our side of the boundary, we co-operate as much as we can. We don't give unnecessary aggravation."

Winston lit a cigarette. To some extent, that was true. For example, the triads controlled vice and gambling. They ran clean places without trouble. If a tourist got gypped it was usually non-union. It didn't happen too often or for too much. The triads valued their control and soon sorted out trouble makers, because like everyone else in Hong Kong, they believed that trouble was bad for business.

"What was the point of this afternoon's fracas?" Wah asked. "I don't understand it at all."

Winston shrugged. "Something about a girl who was knifed."

"Ridiculous! You don't think Wan Liu messes about with pinchbeck stuff like that."

"I don't think. I only carry out orders."

Cameron Wah leaned back, as if blown aside by the rebuff. He sipped his drink, brought out a flat silver cigarette case and offered it across the table. Winston extinguished his own cigarette and waited for Wah to get his silver Dunhill going.

"Chan's interested in a murder," Wah said.

"That's right. An Indian called Raghavan. Good cigarettes these, hand-rolled Turkish."

Wah studied the smoke curling up between them. "I don't see what Wan Liu has to do with it."

Winston grinned. "I don't either. It isn't my case."

"I see," Wah said and frowned. He remained frowning until he had smoked halfway down his cigarette. Then he rested his elbows on the table with sudden decision. "We don't want a repetition of this afternoon's unpleasantness," he said. "Next time we won't be so forgiving."

"That sounds as if you are threatening a police officer?" Winston smiled to show it wasn't meant.

Wah patted Winston's arm with a palm like wet dough. "We don't hold you responsible, old boy," he said. "Not you personally. You couldn't help being there this afternoon."

Dead right too. If Winston had known that Chan was going to burst into the III K offices, slap their heavies around like naughty schoolboys and treat their leader like a two-bit ponce, Winston would have made sure he'd had something very important and very urgent to do in the furthest part of the New Territories. Treating triads like that made for a short if eventful life. Chan must have been mad. Fearless as a whole pride of lions, but mad.

When Winston had seen Chan go for the first bodyguard, he'd taken out his gun. He remembered the sick sensation of fear that had dried his mouth and how his gun had stuck in its holster. Winston couldn't help admiring courage, even though it was Chan, even though Chan was being unreasonably truculent over the surveillance operation.

"We know," Cameron Wah was saying soothingly, "that it was Richard Chan. I've known Chan a long time. We were in school together." Wah sighed. "He's still the same, I'm afraid, too ready to think with his fists simply because he's good with them."

That wasn't true either. Chan was a good cop, single minded perhaps, but still good. Not only was he courageous enough to take on Wan Liu and the III K, but his plan, whatever it was, was working. Wan Liu was undoubtedly worried. He'd got Chan's message and sent Cameron Wah to try and put the bits together.

"What is it about this murder that involves Wan Liu?" Wah asked.

"Doesn't Wan Liu know?"

"He hasn't the faintest idea, old boy, and that's gospel. He's told me so and I can rely on his word."

"You'd better tell Chan that," Winston said, "your old school friend. He'd like to take Wan Liu's word too."

Wah scratched his chin and looked thoughtful. "I wonder if that would do any good."

"Try it. What have you got to lose?"

"I suppose Richard Chan wants a solution to this murder," still thoughtful.

"That before anything else." Chan had his murder, Winston had his arms plot. They were both cops and they both wanted solutions. In that at least, they were together. Winston felt good about that and was about to tell Cameron Wah so when he saw Kate walk in, peering hesitantly around the bar.

"I've got to go now," Winston said getting to his feet. "Thanks for the drink."

"My pleasure old boy," Wah murmured, "my pleasure,"

and casually picked up all the tabs that were lying on the table.

*   *   *

Winston slipped the parking attendant $10 and eased his burbling Triumph sports car into the traffic, cutting off Kate's lengthy apology with, "I've got to see a man on Kowloon side."

"But darling, I thought we were having dinner. I'm starving!"

Then you should have come three drinks earlier, Winston thought, whipping past a faltering Nissan, accelerating hard up to the next set of traffic lights. Without even listening, he knew why she had been late. They were rehearsing *Major Barbara* and there was this divine director who'd worked at the National Theatre and —

"I can't see this man after dinner," Winston explained, relenting. "It will be too late."

Kate gave a small sigh of irritation, took off her glasses and tucked them away in her handbag. "Go on," she said tiredly. "I suppose it is important."

Winston squealed away from the traffic lights, managing to slip her a fast grin as he did so. "It's very important," he said driving quickly towards the Cross Harbour Tunnel.

He'd first met Kate at ex-DC Thompson's. Since he'd retired from the police, Thompson had moved in with the Diplomatic and British Council crowd. Mrs. Thompson was one of Hong Kong's best known literati. Kate and Mrs. T had been making arrangements for an actor to come out from England and read Wilde soliloquies to the Chinese masses and that evening she had brought Kate home to dinner at the same time as Thompson had invited Winston home for a drink.

Kate had been in Hong Kong ten months then, a tall, light-eyed blonde, with heavy glasses, ungainly brown slacks and a bulky cardigan that was protection against the

Thompson's arctic air conditioning and the remote possibility of an onslaught upon her chastity.

They had disliked each other at first sight, and the antipathy had grown over drinks and later, over dinner. Kate Farleigh was one of those compulsive do-gooders who had come out to Hong Kong to help liberate the Chinese. She had little parties of students to tea, gave her *amah* three weeks' holiday a year which undoubtedly bored the poor old woman to tears, organised poetry readings and prescribed reading lists. She was furious at the high price of books in Hong Kong and at the popular taste its book shops catered to. She was furious at the way she felt the Chinese were being exploited and had no hesitation in saying so.

She thought Pete Winston was an archetypal ex-pat. Smug, narrow minded, arrogant and sex mad. That evening when he dropped her back at her flat, she'd moved stiffly away before he could attempt to fondle her, and she'd said she was going to be extremely busy over the next few days and didn't think she would have time to see him again.

Four months later, almost to the day, Winston had put his boat in at Stanley. He'd been testing a conversion to his inboard diesel engine. It had been a searing afternoon. The beach had been quiet, a few Chinese diving off the buoy, a covey of ex-pat wives spread evenly over the golden sand. At the furthest curve of the beach which he had to pass on his way back to the boat carrying the cartons of beer he'd stopped for, was Kate.

She was reading Lin Yutang's *My Country and My People*, her skin a gorgeous oily brown, the heavy sunglasses creating an impression of mystery and allure. She had the longest and loveliest legs that Pete Winston had ever seen.

She could read just as well on the boat, Winston had said. Better. She might even succeed in educating him. Later that evening when both of them, slightly drunk, had made love in Winston's bed, she'd abandoned what was left of her school-marmy disguise with the rest of her clothes, revealing a wild, sensuous, animalism that had made Winston explode with a frequency and ferocity that was mind blowing.

"You can come inside and wait in the lobby," Winston said, parking illegally outside the Peninsula, pulling down his sun visor with *Police Vehicle on Emergency Duty* written on it. That notice was good for any zealous UB man, though once he'd come back and found the valve removed from his nearside rear tyre.

"Thank you very much," Kate said. "Are you sure it won't interfere with this highly important arrest or whatever you're going to do?"

"Not if you wait in the lobby," Winston said. Sometimes he wondered why he kept on seeing Kate. "I'll be as quick as I can."

They went up the regal flight of steps, past gigantic frescos and the hotel's fleet of black Rolls Royces, into the towering lobby with its gilt ceiling and marble floors. Vast areas of carpet were covered with comfortable chairs and arrangements of tables. Waiters scurried around serving coffee and drinks. Winston left Kate at a table moodily sipping coffee and took the lift to the eighth floor.

Watanabe's room was extravagantly spacious. Two single beds with heads of comfortable leather separated by a console which controlled the radio television and room service, a pale green three-piece suite, prints on the walls that were numbered and signed and a bathroom large enough to sleep four in. One lived well at the Peninsula as ex-DC Thompson knew by now.

There were two young men with Watanabe, neatly dressed, impeccably groomed. They bowed courteously to Winston when Watanabe introduced him, then sat down side by side on the sofa and gazed politely at Winston with unwinking eyes.

"Sons of my fallen comrades," Watanabe explained. "They're helping me with my work."

There were papers scattered on the table between them,

technical drawings of a skeleton-like structure which Winston could have sworn was the air frame of an early First World War plane.

"A new toy," Watanabe explained, giving the boys a friendly smile. Two pairs of button eyes looked back at him with filial piety. "They're building a model aeroplane with which to amuse themselves. It is quite interesting."

Winston remembered the Hong Kong toy shops crammed with racing cars, tanks, aeroplanes, Japanese do-it-yourself kits of extraordinary realism and attention to detail. Those plans on the table looked exactly like the real thing.

"Will it fly?" he asked.

"With the right engine, yes. It is radio controlled."

Another side to Watanabe's character, Winston thought. The family man. The model plane enthusiast. The old man was as excited as a child with a new pair of roller skates. Still, enough cosiness. There was business to do and he was aware of Kate waiting irritatedly downstairs, growing hungrier by the second. "I wanted to show you this," Winston said, handing Watanabe a typewritten list of the SB files. "Do you know any of these people?"

Watanabe took the list, adjusted his spectacles, looked intent. His lips moved as he silently read the names. "I am sorry," he said giving the list back, "I do not know these people."

"They are agitators," Winston said. "They must be concerned with the smuggling of arms?"

Watanabe waved his head in gentle motion. "I am sorry. I do not know."

"Is there anything else you can tell me about these arms?" Winston asked. "Anything at all."

"The arms left Thailand today. They will be here in time for the rally. That is all I know."

"How are they being transported?"

"By ship or plane. They are the only ways."

"Can you find out more?"

"I will try. But I am not hopeful."

"We must know," Winston said. "We have half our men tied up shadowing these customers." He tapped the list.

Watanabe looked impassive. "You have news for me?"

"Not yet. Your samples are still being processed in London. I will let you know as soon as I hear anything. Are you comfortable?" It was a rhetorical question.

Watanabe accompanied Winston to the leather-framed, mirrored entrance area. The two young men stood together in the bedroom and bowed.

"I will speak to you if I learn anything more," Watanabe promised, shaking Winston's hand limply.

"Thanks," Winston said and hurried along thick carpets to the lift aware not only of Kate's hunger and impatience, but also of another severe problem. If he didn't get more men by tomorrow, the whole operation could be blown sky high.

THE NEXT MORNING, Tuesday, was consumed with the messy details of foreign travel. Chan had to get tickets and make hotel reservations, he had to pose for his photograph, glowering ferociously in the curtained enclave of the automatic machine at the Macau Ferry Terminal. He exchanged Hong Kong dollars for wads of compact Taiwanese currency bearing the picture of a militant Chiang Kai-Shek and had to queue at the Shinwa Travel Agency which, because Taiwan had no diplomatic representation in Hong Kong, issued visas. By the time he got home, packed, ate, changed and made sure his revolver was locked away, he was running late. There was only time for a brief embrace of the children, a tight hug and a kiss for Li-li and then he was rushing madly to Kai Tak, urgency anaesthetising the pang of departure. Consequently Chan knew nothing about the double murder. That became Pete Winston's problem.

Two men in a shabby tenement room off Johnston Road, green paint peeling off the walls, ramshackle furniture, an unmade bed, a table scattered over with playing cards, glasses, bottles and over two thousand Hong Kong dollars, smells of alcohol, cordite and death.

The men were lying on the cement floor stained brackish brown with dried blood. A thin man and a fat man, like two comedians, the fat one lying on his arse, a wound the size of a tennis ball gouged high up on his chest, his vivid sports jacket patterned with blood and the tiny black holes burned by shotgun pellets. He'd got two shots off at his thin assailant before he'd died. He still clutched a Nambu 8 mm pistol in his chubby fist and he was wearing the most tasteless, two-toned shoes Winston had ever seen.

The shotgun lay underneath the table, a lethal Winchester pump type, the trailing fingers of the thin man caressing its butt. More by bad luck than design he'd been shot between the eyes, the little blood-rimmed puncture at the top of the nose blossoming out at the back of his head in a mess of bone and silvery grey brain matter. He'd been about thirty, with close cropped hair, yellow protruding teeth, a small Cantonese body. Winston thought this was going to take even more men away from the surveillance operation.

He commandeered an adjoining room and began to write his report. With Sergeant Yim helping him with the more obscure Cantonese intonations, he interviewed the eight witnesses. The room had been rented to the fat man and the men had been part of a noisy party that had begun the previous night. There had been drinking and there had been gambling. Throughout the night there had been people coming and going, much shouting and laughter. In the early part of the morning, things had grown quiet. The losers had gone leaving these two with everything to play for. After a long period of silence there had been shouting. Then shots. It was only two hours ago that someone had dared to come up and see what had happened. That was when the police had been called.

An open and shut case, Winston thought with relief. He could have it wrapped up by late afternoon. Then, Sergeant Yim, going through the dead men's possessions handed him the passport. It was wrapped in a red plastic cover and had been issued in Malaya three years previously. It had belonged to Debnath Raghavan. Winston uttered a long, low whistle and started to grin happily.

Back at the station he called for the Raghavan file, studied it rapidly. It was obvious what had happened. Those two comedians had kidnapped Raghavan, beaten him up, stolen his money and shot him. Three nights later they had met again, gambled, quarrelled and shot each other. It was poetic justice, of a kind to be found in the sort of books Kate Farleigh read. Fine, it saved the state the expense of a trial and Pete Winston a great deal of inconvenience.

He completed his report and marked the Raghavan file closed. As Pete Winston recorded it, Raghavan had been murdered by a pimp called Yong Po and a taxi driver named Lin Yu.

*   *   *

The Detective Inspector was at the airport to greet Chan, an angelic, choirboy of a policeman, hardly more than twenty-five, wearing a fashionably wide-shouldered, broad-lapelled jacket in pastel blue and white stripes, with a pronounced waist and a blue silk choker of a tie. His shoes shone, his hair gleamed and his skin was as smooth as a baby's. He wasn't quite the sort of person Chan had visualised from their telephone conversation.

The boy Inspector said he'd never met a policeman from abroad before. There was a cool awareness in his manner that was mildly disturbing. Even more disturbing, his Cantonese was better than Chan's halting Mandarin. He insisted they should examine the old man's body at once. Not only good, but a goer, Chan thought, must be brilliant to be a Detective Inspector at twenty-five. *Haw sik!* Why couldn't he have someone like that at Wan Chai instead of that miserable Pete Winston.

The murdered man looked about ninety-two, a frail patriarchal figure with a wispy grey straggle of beard and trailing moustaches. His hands were placed on his chest, steepled over the rough brown stitching of the thoracic dissection. The body was mottling, and looked quite peace-

145

ful and content except for the blood-stained wadding on which the head rested, and the curious foreshortened effect of the back of the skull. Chan pressed fingers against cold flesh, lifted and looked. The back of the man's head had been shot off, leaving a gaping, empty hole like the inside of a dried egg.

Chan asked, "What did they use? Cannon?"

The boy Inspector considered his words carefully. "The doctor says it is a freak wound. The man's skull was brittle, easily smashed by the bullet."

"What kind of gun?"

"Japanese. 8 mm Nambu."

Chan felt a stirring of excitement. He pulled the sheet over the corpse. "That's what they used in Hong Kong too," he said. "On Raghavan."

The boy Inspector stared at him over the sheeted mound. The old man had been killed early on Sunday morning, the body found underneath a railway bridge on Changshun Road, facing eastwards. Except for the difference in location it was a carbon copy of Raghavan's killing.

The boy gave the coincidence much consideration. Finally he said, "Knights of Bushido. The Order of the Rising Sun. We do not execute at sunset but at sunrise."

Chan looked at him in surprise. Not only good and a goer, but a theorist too. He liked that. They were in Chan's hotel room, a comfortable single, with lacquered furniture and fretwork decorations. It looked very Thai. The boy had planted himself at attention in a chair, neat hands clasped loosely between his thighs.

"That was thirty years ago," Chan said. "You weren't even born then. How do you know that?"

"Taiwan was Japanese for nearly fifty years. 1895 to 1945. We know something of their traditions."

1945, Chan thought. The boy Inspector was much too young to remember what that was like. But not Raghavan or the old man. Could they have been killed for something they had done to the Japanese during the war? Nonsense.

146

That war was long over. The Japanese had surrendered unconditionally, for the first time in their long history, tasting defeat. A revenge killing after all this time was absurd.

Absurd? Could a Japanese forget and forgive? Weren't they like the Chinese in that respect? Chan remembered one of his first murder cases. A business man in Mongkok who had been poisoned. Eight years before his death, it had been during the Korean war, when CCO's had been necessary, he had broken his word over the delivery of some textiles. Someone had lost money and more important, lost face. If eight years later there was enough hatred to kill, what was twenty-five years if lives had already been lost and a cause betrayed.

Chan stripped off thoughtfully and showered. Taipei was just as humid as Hong Kong. It was a steamy day, the sun struggling through low clouds, muggy. The boy Inspector shouted exhortations from his chair. "Don't drink the water!" "Use beer to brush your teeth!"

He studied Chan carefully when he emerged from the bathroom, a white towel wrapped around his barrel-like middle, muscular arms whipping a second towel rapidly across his back. The boy Inspector noted the slope of the shoulders and the tilt of the head, the rubbery layers of fat over hard muscle. "When did you stop boxing?"

"When I got married," Chan grinned. "I was Police middleweight champion, when I was your age. After a while you slow down and you can't work out hard enough. Things start getting to you."

Not to me, the gleam in the boy Inspector's eyes said. He was going to conquer the world. It would be nice to be twenty-five again, Chan thought, especially if he could use all the experience he now had.

The old man's name was Saito Chu. He had been found at nine o'clock on Sunday morning. His family knew nothing except that two men had called for him late the previous night. They were Japanese and had promised the old man work as adviser on a film they were making about the Second World War.

The boy Inspector shrugged. "We have over a hundred thousand Japanese tourists a year. There had been four flights to Tokyo before we realised what had happened."

And at least that many to and from Hong Kong, Chan thought. He picked up the phone and sent a cable to Lau, asking him to obtain lists of Japanese arriving and leaving Hong Kong during the two days before and the two days after Raghavan's death. It would be a mammoth task and it would undoubtedly impede Winston's surveillance operation. So what! Chan grinned, and resumed dressing. "What about this woman?" he asked.

"It is best you meet her yourself. Unfortunately, she is working now. She will not be free until later tonight. Is that all right?"

"That's fine," Chan said. He ran a comb through his spiky hair, docile now with damp from the shower.

"Till then, let us forget about murder and have a good dinner."

Chan smiled acquiescence.

They ate at a restaurant called The Genghis Khan, a reminder to Chan that Northern China had once been Mongol country. The food, not unsurprisingly, was a Mongolian barbecue, a mixture of paper thin slices of wild boar, venison, beef, pork and other meats, a selection of onions, peppers, tomatoes and cabbage.

Chan ate with great appetite and the boy Inspector said he was considering whether to accept a training course in America.

"The Americans are not friends of ours any more," the boy Inspector said, seriously. "They saved us from Communism and now they want to trade with Mao."

Chan speculated how long it would be before Hong Kong became part of Mao's China. The lease of the New Territories expired in 1998, but Communism need not wait till then. They could walk into Hong Kong any time they liked, and the British armed presence on the island was worth as much as spit in the wind. Chan realised it could happen in his own lifetime.

But even under Communism there would be a need for cops. There would still be murder and theft and woundings and fraud. Communism did even less for the soul of man than Capitalism. Besides, under Mao there would be a whole series of new crimes, the need for policemen would be even greater.

Chan decided he wouldn't like to be a Communist cop. One either had to be ten times as security obsessed as Pete Winston or ten times as brutal as the worst criminals he had come across.

Chan said, "I think you should go to America. I think you should try to live there."

"Would you?"

Chan thought of Tony and of Blossom, of a grey egalitarian Maoist future. "I think I might," he said. "If they'll let me."

Afterwards Chan refused the boy Inspector's offer of a visit to a nightclub or what he called, a place of entertainment. They went to a movie, a Shaw Studios historical epic, which Li-li would have much enjoyed. Then still having time on their hands, they went to the Golden Dragon Pavilion at the Grand Hotel. It was half past one when they got back to Chan's room. The woman came nearly an hour later.

*   *   *

She was a bloated, ugly creature, breasts the size of boxing gloves, a belly rigid with crimpled fat. She was about thirty-nine with heavily shadowed eyes and vividly crimsoned mouth. Her hair was dark and smooth though and she had remarkably beautiful hands. She looked challengingly at Chan and said her name was Sylvia.

Chan offered her whisky in a tooth glass and watched her spread her ample bottom on a chair. She was different to Heiki, this one. Much shrewder, more experienced, harder. Raghavan seemed to have liked his women in all shapes and sizes, a Hindu with catholic tastes, Chan reflected, smiling. Then he remembered Heiki saying that Raghavan had spoken of his girlfriend in Taiwan. Could this gross tart be what he'd meant?

The boy Inspector said, "This is a senior police officer from Hong Kong. He wants to talk to you about the Indian."

The woman gulped at her whisky, took out a powder-stained packet of cigarettes from her handbag and offered them round. "The Indian, he is in Hong Kong?"

"He is dead," Chan said. "Murdered."

She inhaled deeply, holding the cigarette between the lower joints of her fingers and sucking at it with pendulous lips, a gesture of crude sexuality. Chan wondered if Raghavan had found that attractive. He asked, "You met the Indian here, in Taipei?"

The woman nodded.

"When?"

She wrinkled her eyes against the cigarette smoke. "Last Monday, one week ago."

"How did you meet him?" the boy Inspector asked.

The woman hesitated. "In the hotel, here."

Nice touch that, booking him into the same hotel as Raghavan. Chan looked round the room. More expensive than the Harbour. What had made Raghavan lower his standard of living so dramatically?

"Where did you meet him?" the boy Inspector was asking. "In the bar? In the lobby?"

The woman hesitated again. "Why do you want to know that?" she asked, "I told you I met him in the hotel and took him to see my grand-uncle. That is enough?"

"That is not enough," Chan snapped. "Not with two people dead."

"Everything is important," the boy Inspector added.

The woman drew deeply at the cigarette. "How was the

Indian killed?" She finished the tumbler of scotch and set it down on the table with a ringing noise.

"He was shot," Chan said. "In the same way as your grand-uncle." He reached out and re-filled her glass.

The woman drank it neat, licked her lips to take away the burn of the raw spirit. Chan wondered why she was back on the game so soon after a death in the family, the body not buried yet. Did she need the money so badly? Or was it simply habit? Would he cease to behave like a cop when he left the police force?

"I have arrangements with some boys in the hotel," the woman said. "The Indian, he sent for me."

"And then?"

"What do you mean then?" She gave Chan a flirtatious smile, lips parting to show uneven, stained teeth, eyes turned modestly downwards. "I gave him good time. I stay with him till he go."

'Three days," Chan said. "What did you talk about?"

"Talk?"

"What did you do apart from having a good time?"

"I go with him. Touring."

"Where?"

"Just touring. Lungshan Temple, the Palace Museum, we go everywhere in Taipei. Most of all we go to the *fei-ji-chang*."

"The airport?"

"Yes. Four times we go there and look. Debi, that is what I call him, he says to me, he wants to find out about an air crash."

"What air crash?"

"Long ago air crash. During the war. An aeroplane that crashed at Taipei."

"It was called Taihoku then," the boy Inspector explained.

Now, Chan thought, he knew what the tape recording was all about.

"I told him I saw the wreckage of the crash," the woman said.

It had happened nearly thirty years ago. She had been at Taipei Girls School, and the Japanese had come and taken them away in three buses to the airfield. There had been about a hundred of them organised into squads of ten. They had been made to change into track suits and the Japanese had forced them to remove the elastic from their knickers and then made them dig up the sand about the scene of the crash.

"It was very difficult to work like that," the woman said. "With one hand holding up your panties. It was hot too and we collected the sand into boxes. The Japanese, they sifted the sand through sieves. They were looking for valuables. I didn't find anything but another girl found a sapphire brooch."

"What did she do with it?"

The woman laughed harshly. "Gave it back to the Japanese. She did not want her head cut off."

"Do you remember who the girl was?"

"Yes. She went to Canada, a long time ago."

"Do you remember exactly when this happened?"

The woman shrugged. "It was during the war. Near the end."

"And Debi?" Chan flinched at the unfamiliar intimacy, "was interested in all this?"

"Yes. He gave me one thousand Taiwan dollars for telling him about the crash. He promise me more if I could have him meet the people who knew about the accident. I took him to see my grand-uncle, Saito Chu. My grand-uncle was working at the airfield then."

"And . . ."

"Debi spoke Japanese with my uncle and gave him five thousand Taiwan dollars. He said he would come back in one month and give him more and he was not to talk to anybody about it. Not even to me."

Five thousand Taiwan dollars are six hundred and

twenty-five Hong Kong dollars; one hundred and twenty-five American. Chan took out his wallet and slipped out a thousand Taiwan dollar bill. "But you talked to your uncle. He told you what he had already told Debi." He took out another thousand dollar bill.

"He liked to drink wine," the woman said with her eyes fixed on the money. "Even at his age. Debi left him a bottle of whisky."

"What did he say?" There was three thousand Taiwan dollars in Chan's fingers.

"They spoke about the war."

"What did your grand-uncle do in the war?"

"He drove a . . . a . . . *camion*?"

Chan turned to the boy Inspector for help. There was a rapid crossfire of Mandarin and the boy Inspector said, "He was responsible for petrol supplies. He drove a petrol tanker."

"He had refuelled the plane that crashed," the woman continued, taking five thousand dollars from Chan. "And he had some trouble. Some men came up and took things away from the plane because they said it wouldn't fly and it had to be made lighter. My grand-uncle was puzzled because it was the second time they had done that while the plane had been standing at Taipei.

"This second lot of men, they told him to go away. But Saito Chu, he refused, because metering the fuel was his responsibility. Then their boss man came. He was the Security Chief of Formosa and he called my uncle an interfering old fool and told the men to unload the plane anyway, that my grand-uncle was not important."

"Is that all?"

"No." She looked expectantly at Chan's hand, as if she wanted to nuzzle it. A thousand dollars changed hands.

"The next day, the Security Chief came with a pilot and ordered my uncle to fuel a plane for them. My uncle refused and then the Security Chief put a gun to his head. So he did what they wanted. The plane, my grand-uncle

said, was a Tenzan torpedo bomber. He never saw either of
the men again."

"Is that what Raghavan wanted to know?"

"That's all my grand-uncle told him," the woman said.

They stared uncomfortably at each other in silence.
Then the woman said, "I'll tell you something more."

Chan was right out of thousand dollars bills. He tried
five hundred.

"There is a friend of Debi's in Taipei. I speak to him
yesterday. He asked me when Debi and I go to Europe.
He does not know that Debi is dead. He works for JAL.
Debi spoke to him too." She folded the bill away and told
him the man's name. It was Tadamato Higachi and he
had been working in Taiwan for six months.

"We will see him tomorrow," the boy Inspector
promised.

Afterwards, Chan sat cross-legged on his bed and
thought. He read his notes of the Kuranari tape-recording.
There had been Indians aboard that plane. He thought
of Raghavan and the ever so self-effacing Mr. Datt. Whatever had happened here in Taiwan thirty years ago, whatever had happened in Hong Kong four nights ago, the
Delhi Foundation were involved.

He went over to his suitcase and took out the pamphlet
Datt had given him. Subhas Chandra Bose's moon-face
stared imperiously at him from the cover. He was seated
in the classic pose of a writer, facing the camera over a
blank sheet of paper holding a delicately tapering pen,
looking as if he was about to sign the Magna Carta.

Chan started to read, and was immediately sickened by
the unctuous prose. The author believed that in Bose were
combined the intellect of Einstein, the courage of Captain
Scott, the military genius of Eisenhower, and the political
shrewdness of Roosevelt. The facts were somewhat less
flattering.

Bose had been born into a middle-class, politically-
oriented Bengali family. His anti-British sentiments were

demonstrated at an early age. At nineteen he had organised the thrashing of an English university lecturer who had made disparaging remarks about Indians. At twenty-four, he had passed the Indian Civil Service Examinations and immediately afterwards resigned, refusing to serve an alien king in someone else's country. He had plunged into politics, growing rapidly in political stature. An equal of Gandhi and Nehru, he had become President of Congress — the highest political office any Indian could aspire to — in 1939. He had been repeatedly jailed by the British.

Soon after the outbreak of war, a war which Bose declared unjust because no Imperial Government had the right to declare war on behalf of 350 million of its un-represented subjects, Bose had escaped from British custody. He had travelled to Germany where he had asked Adolf Hitler's assistance in liberating the Indian people. Hitler had been less than enthusiastic. In 1942, Bose had been summoned to Japan. He met with Premier Tojo and helped reorganise the Indian Independence League and the Indian National Army which was ready to fight side by side with the Japanese in Burma, Thailand and Malaya.

Four days after Japan's surrender, Bose was in an airplane which crashed on take-off from Taipei aerodrome. He died that same night, August 18th, 1945.

18

OVER A *congee* breakfast later that morning, Chan abandoned his theory that Raghavan had been blackmailing someone. That theory did not allow for the facts. Specifically, it did not allow for the crash of an airplane loaded with treasure at the end of the Second World War. Raghavan had been killed because he knew where that treasure was. He had been captured, tortured till he gave up his secret, then murdered. That theory made more sense. Money was of considerable interest to the III K.

But why had the killings of Raghavan and the old man been ritual, executions at sunrise with the bodies facing eastwards? There was more than coincidence in that. There was deliberate planning and another organisation involved, not Wan Liu's. Wan Liu's influence did not extend beyond Hong Kong. If that was so, then whose?

The boy Inspector eased into a chair opposite Chan. A pearl-grey suit today, in the same bootlegger style, hair gleaming like black ice, eyes clear as an infant's, no sign of having been up till past three that morning or drinking the greater part of a bottle of Johnny Walker. He'd been working since then, too.

"I've got a lead," the boy Inspector announced. "I've found someone whom Raghavan talked to."

She was Mrs. Meiwa, the headmistress of the local school, a fierce looking woman in her sixties with grey hair pulled to the back of her head in a tight knot, circular, steel-rimmed glasses and large, splayed teeth. She sat behind a tiny square desk in an airy room decorated with children's drawings and looked keenly from one to the other of them. The thin screaming of children at play seeped into the room.

"I thought there would be trouble with that Indian," Mrs. Meiwa said. "He had such funny eyes. Shifty." She studied the faces of Chan and the boy Inspector while she spoke, satisfying herself there was no shiftiness in either of them. "The Indian spoke to me of my brother."

Chan repressed the question that rose to his lips. This formidable woman made him think of his own school days, waiting outside the headmaster's office for the ritual six cuts with a rattan cane, listening to lectures on how impolite it was to interrupt one's elders.

"My brother was a fool," Mrs. Meiwa went on. "That is why he died. He had no business mixing with spies or politics." Her face twisted in momentary anguish, brief recollections of a life wasted. "My brother was a trained pilot. For two weeks before the end of the war he had prepared himself for *kamikaze* missions. He was never called."

He must have been a good deal younger than her, Chan thought, a baby brother. By the end of the war, Japan had lost the best of her fighter pilots. Most of the *kamikazes* were boys, hurriedly trained, knowing just enough to take-off and keep airborne. Landing was not expected to be a problem.

"My brother could not believe that Japan had been defeated. All the time we had been told that the Americans and the Australians were being pushed out of the Pacific, that our navy and our airforce were winning great victories. We did not know of Hiroshima and Nagasaki till long afterwards. So when we heard the voice of our Emperor saying that Japan had surrendered, it was a grievous shock.

157

Many of our troops refused to believe it. Prince Kanin had to convince them it was true. He even came here."

Mrs. Meiwa paused and looked directly at Chan. "You can see now why he allowed himself to be led by this older man. He had to keep fighting the war. Samurai never surrendered. He wouldn't listen to me. I was too old he said and didn't understand the warriors' code. I didn't have to be a warrior to know when someone was being foolish, when someone was being used. My brother was not the material from which governments in exile are created. He was too high spirited, too boyish. He was also too full of pride, too stubborn. He wouldn't listen." Her voice was flat with too much telling, the eyes distorted behind the thick lenses, dry. "He said he would write to me and left. He promised he would come back for me. He left in his Tenzan bomber, Heavenly Mountain they used to call it. I remember that day very well. It was August 19th, 1945."

*   *   *

Tadamato Higachi was a different kind of Japanese. An extremely fit-looking man in his mid-fifties, well-dressed in a pale blue lightweight suit, with black eyes that danced inquisitively in a square head, close-cropped hair still black, a solid fleshy face. He was a man strong in himself, one who had made the transition from the age of Emperor-worship to that of the Economic Miracle without trauma.

He welcomed Chan and the boy Inspector into his air-conditioned office, where modernity and tradition blended in Japanese-made Scandinavian-style furniture, where large scale views of Tokyo and Kyoto blended with close-ups of brilliantly costumed Kabuki performers. On the spotless desk in front of him there was a model of a Boeing 747. Modernity and tradition, an uneasy combination, but Higachi faced that problem lightly.

When he had asked for the appointment the boy Inspector had told Higachi of Raghavan's murder. Now

Higachi wasted no time on exclamations of surprise or pointless enquiries.

"I met Raghavan in Tokyo, about a year ago," he said, speaking in Cantonese for Chan's benefit. "He was working for the *Asian Clarion*, writing about the Japanese style of life." His smile asked how any *gaijin* could write truthfully about the Japanese. "Raghavan was very interested in Toyota motor cars and progress."

Also wife-beating and sumo wrestling, Chan recalled.

"Our public relations people wanted me to talk to him about expansion. I had just returned from the other China where I had been discussing landing rights with them."

The boy Inspector coloured. "If you trade with them, you will not be allowed to fly here."

"Let us see." Pacifically. "Time changes all perspective. After the interview was over, Raghavan talked to me about the last war. He had been a press-officer in the Indian National Army. You know about that?"

"I know about the Indian National Army." Chan said. "I didn't know Raghavan was in it."

"He was. I saw him again, a week ago, here in Taipei. This time he talked only about the war and he recorded what I told him." Higachi leaned forward and ran a stubby finger over the hump of the 747. "I was a member of Japanese intelligence during the war. Specifically, I worked for the 82nd Bureau. For a time I was stationed here in Taiwan."

The 82nd Bureau. Chan wondered where he'd heard of that department before. "Tell us what you told Raghavan," Chan said. "What he recorded."

"You do not have the recordings, then?"

"They were stolen. We expect to recover them shortly."

"Without doubt," Higachi said. "Raghavan was interested in the attitude of the 82nd Bureau to Subhas Chandra Bose, the Indian leader. You know about Bose?"

"A little," Chan said." A collab — he fought with the Japanese in the last war."

Higachi looked at Chan with amusement. "Yes," he said. "Initially the 82nd Bureau approved of Bose. We arranged for him to be transported by submarine from Germany. We required him to fulfil four functions. One, to ensure that the Indians in Nippon dominated territory were happy. Two, to provide economic and political information about India in order to ease their absorption into the South-East Asian Co-Prosperity Sphere. Three, and this was very unimportant mind you, provide agents for infiltration into India. We Japanese would have looked even more ridiculous wearing *dhotis*."

Chan smiled politely.

"Four, maintain an efficient propaganda service. Only this last function was properly carried out. Bose was an impossible man. He was responsible to the Hikkari Kikkan and they were too indulgent. There was all this nonsense about Bose being the head of an independent state, of his controlling an independent army. He raced about Malaya in a big car, the flag of a springing tiger fluttering from the bonnet. For some time he even had his own airplane called the Azad Hind. From a practical point of view it was ridiculous. The Indians in South-East Asia were a conquered people or they were not. The compromises achieved between Bose and the Hikkari Kikkan were madness."

Higachi paused to draw breath, offered them green tea. When it had been brought, he went on. "You realise that all this is an impression of a long time ago. In wartime, intelligence departments do not have such things as public policies. This is what I felt at the time, what I heard discussed. I only got directly involved with Bose at the end.

"Bose fielded a few divisions of the INA in Burma. They were not good fighters. Captured people never are. They whined and moaned and deserted in large numbers. But still, even after the defeats in Burma and Thailand he persuaded the Hikkari Kikkan to let him carry on, refusing to amalgamate his soldiers with those of the Japanese army which would have been the sensible thing to do. The trouble was that Bose fancied himself as a great military commander. He was, as our American friends would say, on a gigantic ego trip. His only military experience was a few months as a schoolboy in the cadet corps.

"In July 1945 he had retreated with the remnants of his army to Singapore. From there he negotiated the loan of one hundred million rupees. This was at a time, mind you, when people in Tokyo were starving. This was after the Americans had taken Iwo Jima and Okinawa, and Super Fortresses had razed Yokohama to the ground. And some fools lent an even greater fool one hundred million rupees!

"We knew that Bose had not been able to use this money by August 1945. It was lying in the Southern Development Bank in Singapore. We planned to get it. In the middle of August, I flew to Singapore. Before I could get our scheme into operation, Japan had surrendered, and Bose had cleared the money out of the bank, together with all the gold and valuables he had deposited there."

"What did you do then?"

"What could I do. I telegraphed my superiors in Taiwan and that was the end of it. When the British came, I surrendered to them."

"What about the treasure?"

"The 82nd Bureau never had it."

"Was it with Bose when he crashed?"

"That is right. The treasure was collected here in Taiwan and transferred to Japan. Some ten years after the war, it was handed over to the Indian Government. You will find that this is officially recorded."

If that was so, then why had Raghavan been killed? "To whom did you send that telegram?" Chan asked.

"To the head of the 82nd Bureau." Higachi smiled. "I do not know if he ever received it. Everything was disorganised at the time."

"Who was the head of the Bureau?"

161

Higachi's smile grew wider. Slowly he shook his head. "It was a very flexible unit," he said. "Also, it was a very long time ago."

Afterwards it was too late for Chan to get a plane back to Hong Kong. He went shopping with the boy Inspector, bargaining avidly, buying a classically dressed Chinese doll for Blossom, a puppet for Tony, a windstone bracelet and turquoise comb for Li-li.

Over dinner he told the boy Inspector about Bose and the foundation in Hong Kong. The answer was there, Chan said, impatient to return, wishing he could take the boy Inspector with him to resolve the mystery.

19

RAIN WAS WHIRLING across the runway at Kai Tak when Chan landed, whipping up from the sea in great whirling squalls. Chan drove directly to the offices of the Delhi Foundation, rain spattering the roof of the taxi like pebbles. Typhoon weather, Chan thought, peering anxiously up at the buildings perched precariously on the murky green hillsides, landslides, a vision of men toiling hopelessly amongst rubble and liquid red mud. Not this year, he hoped, not again.

Clutching his suitcase and Blossom's doll he went down the dismal corridor. He should have seen Datt two days ago. The door with its panes of frosted glass and stencilled lettering was unlocked. Chan opened it. Cluttered reception area bereft of middle-aged, myopic typist. The silk-skinned sareed girl on the calendar smiled at him from the wall, the date for Sunday week was still ringed in red.

Dragging the heavy suitcase, Chan went up to the door of Datt's office, knocked on it twice with his head. He hadn't known how long he would be away in Taiwan, but Li-li had packed enough for two years. The door opened and Datt peeked up at him, surprise and alarm changing to a quick-silver effusiveness, pulling the door back and rushing out to Chan, hand stretched forward for shaking.

"Inspector Chan hello, hello, how are you? You have come to see me? Please come in, come in."

Chan didn't have a free hand. He put the suitcase down by the door and went in after Datt's backward-stepping figure, still clutching the doll. Someone had opened the windows and let out the smell of joss-sticks and seed oil. Dusted the place too, and put away the files which had cluttered Datt's desk. Datt was not alone.

A burly Indian sat in Datt's grease-stained chair, leaning away from the desk, comfortable and assured. A handsome man, gleaming brown skin, thick curly hair and an expression of polite irritation. He was wearing a suit of dazzling white cotton that matched his teeth.

"This is our President," Datt was bobbing between them as if he was walking a rope bridge. "Mr. Banerjee."

Banerjee's hand stretched across the desk, pudgy and short-fingered, a grip that was elaborately brisk.

"Sit down, sit down, Inspector." The hand withdrew, waved in a grand flourish towards the decrepit chairs.

Chan sat, wondered about the bugs and what to do with the doll. He perched it on his lap.

"I wanted to talk to you but you have been away. You are the fellow who has been dealing with our rally, no?"

He must look ridiculous, Chan thought, sitting with a classically attired doll on his lap. More like a pouf than a policeman. "I processed the application."

"What are you going to do to help us? We have made tremendous preparations. There are people coming from all over Asia for this rally. We have booked hotels, taken advertisements. We have hired loudspeakers also," as if that settled the matter.

Chan sighed, stroked the doll's hair, realised what that must look like, stopped. "I have already explained to Mr. Datt. There is another rally on the same day."

"That is right, that is right," Datt piped. "He has told me."

"That I know already," Banerjee snapped, cutting off Datt's joyous confirmation. "But Hong Kong is a big city.

There must be other places where we can hold our rally."

"We have no men to spare," Chan said.

"What for policemen? You think we are troublemakers, ah! That we will create revolution and havoc and bloodshed and general public disturbance?"

Chan repressed a smile. No one was less likely to cause a revolution, havoc and general public disturbance than the timorous Mr. Datt and his grandiosely theatrical president.

"It isn't bloodshed we are worried about," he said quietly. "Any kind of rally causes disruption, crowds, traffic. Policemen are needed to deal with that. We haven't got the men to spare."

"Whitewash," Banerjee spat out contemptuously. "You are saying one thing to my face, another thing to my backside." He plumped his elbows on the desk. "You are a policeman. Tell me the truth. You have orders to stop our rally."

"Why?" Chan asked.

"Because the cowardly British are frightened of us. They know that we stand for freedom and that we will spread our ideas and you Chinese will rise up and kick them into the sea."

This time Chan had to smile.

"What they are doing is illegal," Banerjee went on. "I am telling you that. Illegal. They are stopping us from making free speech. That is against the constitution. But we will speak and we will kick them out of Hong Kong like we kicked those bloody Pakistanis out of Bangladesh."

Chan had an uneasy feeling that Banerjee's words were not being addressed to him alone. Somewhere behind him, was a crowd of invisible rabid anti-imperialists, on the verge of breaking into a thundering ovation. "Non-availability of venue is the only reason," Chan said firmly.

"Propaganda!" Banerjee snorted. "But we will beat them. I'll tell you what we will do." His fist crashed on the desk. "We will pledge solidarity with the students. That is it. The Delhi Foundation will pledge solidarity with the students. We will stand together with them and fight with them, shoulder to shoulder. Hong Kong will vibrate to our war cry. *Inquilab zindabad!*"

The cry echoed round the room. Banerjee sat erect in his chair, pulled his stomach in and looked steadfastly across the desk at Chan. "That is what we will do," he announced.

Chan remained impassive. The man was a raving nutcase. His pledge of solidarity would give Pete Winston a few more problems. That was all. There was no threat to security, here. These two were no more than tin cans banging in the wind. A phrase he had heard when he was at the training school in Hendon came back to him. "I wish you the best of British luck," Chan said.

It was like a match to kerosene. "You are with us Inspector, I am glad. You are a man, you will cast away the chains of slavery. You will march with us under the flag of the springing tiger. Datt, Datt, call the *Hong Kong Standard*. Call all the newspapers. Tell them I will give a press conference to announce solidarity with the students."

Chan said, "I will march with you but only to control the crowds."

"Press conference," Banerjee went on, "4.30 this afternoon. Tell them I will speak. Good idea, isn't it Inspector."

"I have come," Chan said, "to talk about Mr. Raghavan."

Datt reaching for the phone gave a little squeal and started to shimmy. Chan fixed him with a baleful glare and went on. "You said he was not a member of this Foundation. Let me see the membership list, please."

Datt broke into a little dance.

From behind the desk, Banerjee said, "If that bloody pan-wallah said that he lied to you."

Datt gave another little scream and went still.

"Debnath Raghavan was a member of the Delhi

Foundation," Banerjee continued. "He was working for the Foundation when he was killed."

Chan turned to Banerjee. Datt crept around slowly and sat on the other chair. Datt's lie had been nothing more than the desire of a frightened man to escape. Banerjee's frankness was something else. "What kind of work was he doing for you?" Chan asked.

"He was investigating a murder," Banerjee said.

Chan found he was stroking the doll's hair again and put it down beside the chair. "Whose murder?"

"A murder that happened thirty years ago. The murder of Netaji Subhas Chandra Bose, our leader and founder, the greatest man who ever lived."

Chan looked up at the photograph above Banerjee's head. The garland was still dusty. Bose looked down at them, still po-faced. "Bose died in an air crash, in Taiwan," Chan said, wondering if there was more to it than Banerjee's apparent madness.

"Plane crash, how? Only a simple accident? That is what everyone says. But we know more than that. Raghavan had proof that Bose was murdered."

"The plane was overloaded," Chan said, not asking the obvious question, deciding that if forced to justify his theory Banerjee would blurt out more of the truth.

Banerjee was looking at him with an air of surprise. "Propaganda," he said. "Not proof."

"I have listened to a tape recording by a man named Kuranari," Chan said. "He was the gunnery officer on the flight."

"Tragic flight," Datt murmured.

"He said the plane was overloaded. They had unloaded guns before they got to Taiwan."

"You have heard only that tape recording?" Banerjee asked.

Chan nodded.

"What happened to the others?"

"They were stolen."

"They had the proof," Banerjee said, sadly. "Raghavan spoke to me two or three times from Tokyo. He told me something of what he had learned. Bose was killed by British Intelligence."

Chan wondered if Banerjee's insanity was contagious. "Bose died in Taiwan," he said, "in a country that was controlled by the Japanese. How could the British have had anything to do with it?"

"Collaboration," Banerjee replied. "The British knew they could never try Bose. The Indian people would not have allowed it. See what happened at the INA trials in Delhi. Everyone went free. What would India have not done for Netaji! They would have burned the country to a cinder before they let the British hang him!"

"And what about the Japanese?" Chan asked. "Why would they participate in such an act?"

"Look at the Japanese now. They are friends with the British, yes. They are friends with the Americans, yes. They are friends with everybody, yes. They are selling good cameras, good motor cars, good everything, yes, and there are people in Japan who saw that this would happen. They saw that they would have to be friends with everybody. So they are doing favours for the British, no. Raghavan had proof of all this. That is why he was killed."

"By British Intelligence?" Chan asked scornfully.

"That is right. Do you think he was killed by some *goondas* who only wanted to rob him?"

"Of course not."

"Then why the hell are you bloody police not investigating this murder?"

"I am investigating this murder," Chan said tightly. "That is why I am here."

Banerjee whipped open a desk drawer, took out a newspaper cutting, pushed it across to Chan. "Explain that to me," he demanded.

Chan looked and read. DOUBLE MURDER SOLVES SINGLE, screamed the headline. It was poetic justice, Inspector Pete

Winston was quoted as saying, I wish all murder cases ended this way.

"Whitewash," Banerjee said.

Dead fucking right, Chan thought rushing to the door. He was going to break Winston into a million little pieces and spread him all over the China Sea.

*　　*　　*

The squad room was deserted, only Reserve hovering anxiously by the phone amongst scattered files and abandoned desks. There was an atmosphere of disaster being fought at a distance. Perhaps there had been a landslide after all.

"Where the hell is everybody?" Chan demanded.

"Out," Reserve said.

"I've got eyes, haven't I. I can see that. Out where?"

"Surveilling. Big emergency."

"It bloody well better be," Chan said and stomped back to his office. He dumped his case on the floor and kicked it to one side. Just routine correspondence on his desk, no list of Japanese passengers. He yanked open his filing cabinet and looked. There was a gap like a missing tooth, where Raghavan's file had been.

He heard Lau's voice and shouted to him to come in. Lau stood in the doorway, soberly clad for once, smiling, saying, "Welcome back, chief."

"Where the hell is that list I asked you to make and where is Raghavan's file?"

The smile disappeared from Lau's face. "The case is over, chief. Closed. Raghavan was killed by Yong Po and — "

"Where the bloody hell is Pete Winston?" If that bloody Lau didn't get out of his way, Chan was going to walk through him.

Lau stood there, immovably solid. "Cool it, chief," he said. His arms gripped Chan's shoulders. "I know what you are going to do. It isn't worth it. Don't go looking for fish by climbing trees."

His fingers twisted into Chan's flesh, the grip was like a vice. "Damn you," Chan muttered, "damn you," and waited for the anger to seep out of him, for the throbbing in his head to stop.

*　　*　　*

He got Winston twenty minutes later, on the way to the canteen, feeling the anger mounting again, forcing himself to remain calm till they were back in Winston's room.

"The Raghavan murder," Chan said.

Winston flung his hands up from his waist in a gesture of compliance. "All over," he said. "Finished. An open and shut case."

"It's still open," Chan snapped. "And I want everyone back on it, now."

Winston looked away, down at the floor, smiling secretly to himself. He allowed his gaze to wander around the room, finally come back to Chan. "Can't do that. I am afraid. They are all on surveillance — "

"Fuck surveillance! I want them back — "

"AC's direct order, I am afraid." Winston said "A matter of national emergency."

*　　*　　*

The Assistant Commissioner was a big, meaty man of forty-five, ruddy faced, protuberant eyed, walrus moustached. Chan knew he had spent fifteen years in the Force, all of them in administration. Now he turned away from the window, where he had been staring down into the courtyard, looking at the row of police vehicles neatly parked between diagonal white lines. "I am afraid I must ask you to be reasonable, Inspector," he said to Chan. "The smuggling of arms, the possibility of riots in this colony must take precedence over the murder of someone, who after all, was a stranger to our shores."

170

"Besides," the Assistant Commissioner added, "it isn't as if the matter hasn't been resolved already. You are only theorising, Inspector. Quite right too. But just at this moment we do not have the men to spare."

"Raghavan wasn't murdered by Yong Po and Lin Yu," Chan said stubbornly.

"Even if he wasn't," the Assistant Commissioner said, "and I am not endorsing that view, mind you, it is of considerably less significance than a repetition of '67. I have no need to remind both of you what happened here then."

"In 1967," Winston said smoothly, "I was a copper in Melton Mowbray."

"Ah pies!" the Assistant Commissioner said with enthusiasm. "I was once stationed in Wigston." He recovered hastily and gave Winston a long suffering look. "We had riots in '67. Bombs exploding all over the place, confusion everywhere, total disorganisation, utter chaos."

Chaos in administration was nothing like chaos in the streets, Chan thought bitterly, knowing that the Assistant Commissioner had never baton-charged a violent crowd.

"As a result we formed the Police Tactical Unit, the Blue Berets." The Assistant Commissioner smiled modestly. "It was partly my idea."

Chan supposed that the banning of fireworks since 1967 must also have been the Assistant Commissioner's idea.

"Congratulations, sir," Winston said. "The PTU is the best riot control squad I have seen."

"I am glad you think so," the Assistant Commissioner said enthusiastically. "But even so, we can't afford a repetition of '67."

"No sir," Pete Winston said piously.

The Assistant Commissioner turned back to Chan, feeling he had drawn the heat from the dispute. "So Inspector Chan," he said smiling, "we will concentrate on first things first. Get this damn students' rally out of the way and then you can have all the men you need to substantiate your theory. Meanwhile, I will make a personal request of you.

Please co-operate with Inspector Winston, here. What he has to do is very important."

"No," Chan snapped, modifying his tone at the shock on the Assistant Commissioner's face. "Let him play tag with as many men as he wants. I'll remain at Wan Chai and look after all the other crimes."

"Good idea," the Assistant Commissioner said. "Someone has to mind the shop," but Chan was aware the Assistant Commissioner hadn't really meant that.

20

GLOOM AND BITTER frustration, the funereal prospect of routine after the high excitement of murder. Chan went home angry, the joy of welcome doing nothing to ease the feeling of helplessness. All evening he stared peevishly at the television, ate his dinner in silence, gloom and frustration turning to dark suspicion. Perhaps Banerjee was not so mad after all. Perhaps there had been a plot to kill Bose and then Raghavan. Perhaps British Intelligence had persuaded the triads to help them to make the Raghavan killing look like a ritual Japanese execution. Or could Wan Liu have got at the AC? Everything was possible. Nothing was possible.

The next morning the station was unbearably quiet, everyone out on surveillance. Chan hoped they'd start following each other and drop Winston right in it. He pored over the robbery of the grainstore, the problems of unlicensed dentists. Open and shut cases, Winston would have said. Why the hell couldn't he deal with them, then.

There was the jewellery store robbery of two weeks ago. Sergeant Yim had not made much progress there. Too busy tapping telephones, Chan thought as he walked down a steamy Lockhart Road, any excuse to get away from the station with its air of hopeless lethargy. The Wei Lo Jewellery store was a large room that opened on to the covered pavement, its sides and rear lined with waist-high glass cases containing rings, ear-studs and brooches. Those in front were mostly jade, set in brash ten carat Hong Kong gold, the more expensive pieces at the rear, set in fourteen carat, and stones, diamonds from South Africa, rubies from Burma, sapphires from Thailand and Ceylon. The case the robbers had smashed was already repaired, the stock already replenished. Even robbery was not allowed to interfere with business.

The proprietor was a fat Cantonese, with gold-rimmed glasses and gold teeth, suffering from a deep need to advertise his profession. He wore a dark grey suit to emphasise the difference between his status and that of his shirt-sleeved employees. He repeated the details of the robbery enthusiastically, flattered that a senior Chief Inspector was looking after the case, and agreed with Chan that this kind of thing was a result of too much television. The proprietor also had a theory. He had been robbed because he had never paid protection and smiled disbelievingly when Chan told him it was foolish thought.

By lunchtime, Chan couldn't stand it any more, the emptiness in the squad room, the emptiness within. He made a few phone calls and drove over to the Excelsior.

As he had promised, Banerjee was in the coffee-lounge, that towering terrace suspended two floors above the vast lobby. It was not, Chan realised with a sinking heart, going to be a discreet meeting. Banerjee was conspicuously dressed in a knee-length, high collared black tunic with splendid gold buttons and what looked like jodhpurs, made of thin white cotton. He was surrounded by that morning's newspapers, his photograph prominently featured in the front pages in an enfant terrible pose, hair wild, eyes popping, arms akimbo. It had been a highly successful press conference.

"You see, you see, Inspector *babu*, we have made a great hit. All of Hong Kong knows we are marching with the students, and soon many others will join us. Already the cowardly British have begun to shiver in their boots."

Not only all Hong Kong, but everyone in the coffee-lounge was aware of Banerjee, and now, of Chan. Banerjee's voice rang round the open area as if amplified by the loudspeakers he had hired. Heads turned inquisitively in their direction, masked by discreet Chinese smiles. They knew well enough to leave the mad alone, unlike Winston's rubber-heels. It was only a question of time, Chan thought, despondently, before the news of his meeting leaked back. He pushed the thought from his mind. What he did in his lunch hour was his own damn business, nothing to do with the AC or Pete Winston.

Banerjee was already launching into what seemed to be a rehearsal for the rally, a portly Indian Don Quixote tilting at imaginary British windmills. With Chief Inspector Sancho Chan in attendance, Chan thought, wishing that Banerjee would lower his voice.

"I will kill the filthy British lie that Netaji was a traitor, that he would have sold India to the Japanese. Netaji was a patriot!"

No way of interrupting the man now. Chan looked down at the lobby where droves of visitors trooped across the vast area beneath them in a rustle of leather and low voices, a cluster of suits and tropical dresses, uniformed aircrew too. The hotel was partly owned by British Airways, Chan remembered, a suitable preying ground for Winston no doubt, with his fondness for air-hostesses. Chan should have arranged the meeting in the dining-room. All he was having was coffee, and he'd heard the Excelsior served the best buffet lunch in Hong Kong.

Banerjee's voice washed over him. Let him expend himself and who knew, he might let something significant slip. He was talking of Bose arriving in Singapore, visions of a tall, steadfast man, standing in the back of an open car, surrounded by adoring crowds, even the Japanese bowing low. Scenes of adulation in the packed Cathay cinema, a magnificent revue of INA troups on the *maidan* opposite

175

the town hall, standing shoulder to shoulder with Prime Minister Tojo himself.

"He looked like a young god," Banerjee was saying, lost in reverie, his voice thankfully lower. "It was a splendid show. He was Head of State and everywhere he went the people cheered him. *Subhas Chandra Bose Ki Jai! Subhas Babu Ki Jai!*"

Chan winced at the sudden increase in loudness, tried to ignore the turning heads. Bose must have been a remarkable man to have inspired loyalties that remained so steadfast after thirty years.

"What he gave us Indians was pride and dignity. When he was our leader, to fight the British was not treachery. It was a war of independence and only Netaji made it that."

Banerjee must have been an adolescent at the time, highly impressionable. That might account for some of the passion, but there were the others, Datt, Raghavan and still others, spread through Asia.

"Were you part of his movement?" Chan asked.

"Yes, yes of course I was. I could not be a soldier. Since I was a boy, I have had asthma. But I worked. I joined the IIL. At first in the Manpower Ministry, then Finance."

Chan realised his coffee cup was empty. Banerjee ordered more, clapping his hands and shouting *"Foki, foki!"* There were no heroes like childhood heroes, Chan reflected, no heroes bigger, purer, better, more beautiful. His kind of heroes had been sportsmen, cricketers, boxers, people he now avoided because they were old and human. Banerjee had had Bose. It was fortunate for him, that Bose was dead.

"You are still investigating?" Banerjee asked.

Had Banerjee heard, or was he simply curious. "Why else am I here?"

"You will investigate, Inspector *babu*, whatever happens? Even if the Governor General himself tries to stop you?"

176

A tall order, that. Chan didn't know how he would react to that kind of pressure. Yet, "I will," Chan promised, as if it were his wedding day.

"And you will tell me, also, what you have found out." There was a beseeching look in the dark eyes, an unusual humility in Banerjee's tone.

"Why?" Chan asked.

"For my speech on Sunday. On Sunday I will tell how the British killed Netaji and stole his treasure. You will help me to tell how the British killed Raghavan."

"I don't think — "

Abruptly, the humility vanished. "Absolute condition," Banerjee said. "Total." His dark hands flashed over the coffee cups. "Unless you promise, I will not tell any more."

Chan thought carefully, weighing the advantage of information against his oath of secrecy. "I cannot give you such a promise," he said. "I'm a policeman, I have certain responsibilities. But I will promise you this. I will not allow any cover up, by the British authorities or anyone else. If you trust me, I will find out who killed Raghavan. His murderers will be brought to justice and the facts will be made public."

"Before Sunday?" Banerjee asked.

"If it is possible."

Banerjee drank his coffee. "You are a strong man, Inspector *babu*. You are brave," as if that was a quality he much admired because it was the one he most lacked.

Chan said, "You said the British stole Bose's treasure. How?"

"That I am still investigating. That I will reveal on Sunday."

"But the treasure was taken to Japan and returned to India. That is a matter of official record."

"Record? Whose record? British records? Whitewash! Have you seen the Netaji Subhas Chandra Bose treasure at the Rashtrapati Bhavan?"

Chan shook his head.

177

"Everything is there," Banerjee said, "that was taken by the Japanese to Tokyo. One lakh of rupees worth of jewellery and bric-a-brac. One hundred thousand Hong Kong dollars worth, about £8,000."

Chan remembered Higachi's mention of the loan of 100 million rupees. How much would that be worth?

Banerjee said, "There was more than £8,000. I know. I was there."

Chan listened as Banerjee went on speaking, his voice growing softer as memories crowded in. Bose's movement had been financed by the Indians. Whatever they had taken from the Japanese was loans. Banerjee knew. He had worked in the Ministry of Finance. He spoke of a tax structure, a system of voluntary contributions, of collections at public meetings. Names and dates rolled forth. October 22nd, 1943, at a public meeting declaring war on America, a collection of thirteen million Malay dollars. Rangoon, January 1944, the assets of the Zeyawaddy Sugar Estate were handed over to the movement. May 1944, another public meeting, a collection of five million rupees. January 23rd, 1945, Bose's birthday. The assets of the British Indian Corporation were transferred to the movement, over twenty million rupees in cash was collected and Bose had been given his weight in gold!

A hell of a lot more than £8,000 there, Chan thought, trying to calculate, trying to estimate Bose's weight from the photographs he had see. 170 pounds, 180. Sixteen ounces to the pound. That was . . .

Banerjee was talking about August 10th, 1945. Bose had been in Seramban, without his shortwave radio. They had to inform him that the Russians had declared war on Japan and has been forced to make the trunk call through Kuala Lumpur.

"The next day we could not even do this. All the lines had been sabotaged. The BBC had announced that Japan had surrendered and we had to inform Netaji. But how to? No telephone, no telegrams. We drove to Seramban.

"It was a terrible journey. The roads were all full of potholes and there were Communist guerrillas all over the place. We reached the Guest House in Seramban at two o'clock the following morning.

"Netaji was about to go to bed. He was still wearing his breeches and top-boots and had taken off his tunic. We were taken to him immediately. He listened carefully to what we had to say and his face was like a rock. Even then, he was not afraid. He was frightened of nothing, Netaji. When we finished he said 'So that is that, what now?' That is what he said, when he had lost everything. He even made a joke. 'We are the only people who have not surrendered,' he said, and that is true, we have not surrendered, even yet.

"The next day we drove back to Singapore. Singapore was in total collapse. Wild bazaar rumours had gone round the place saying the British would shoot every single one of us. Many of our people had thrown away their uniforms and were wearing civilian clothing. It was disaster. No one knew what to do or anything.

"But there were some of us who stayed with Netaji. There was still a lot to do. Official confirmation of Japanese surrender to be obtained, payments to our soldiers and workers, instructions to be sent to our other branches. We worked all day and all night right up to the 15th. For three days, I tell you, I hardly slept a wink.

"On the 15th we heard news of the Japanese surrender, direct from Tokyo. Then I knew it was all over. I went straight to the bank with some other officials and cleared the account completely. We took everything, what was left of the loan Netaji had got from Japan, all the valuables, and the gold.

"We did not know what Netaji was going to do, if he would surrender to the British or if he would form a government in exile. We went to Netaji's bungalow and I had charge of the gold. It was in two suitcases and I stayed there because I could not bear to leave Netaji. There was also nowhere for me to go. My father's business was very small then and, as he had supported us too, I thought he too would be killed and his business confiscated by the British. I sat in the verandah and waited all that day and that night, knowing that Netaji would know what to do.

"Early the next morning, that was August 16th, Netaji asked me, 'And what about you, young man? Will you come with us or stay?' He turned to the members of his cabinet with whom he had been discussing things all night. 'We need young people too.'

"I went.

"We left Singapore at about ten o'clock that morning in a Japanese bomber and flew straight to Bangkok. We stayed the night there and took some other officials from Bangkok with us in two planes to Saigon. At Saigon the British plot began to work.

"We had landed about noon and were taken to the IIL headquarters. Hardly had we arrived there when a Japanese officer came up and said that Netaji must get back to the airport at once where there was a plane waiting to take him alone to another destination. Netaji refused. Everyone began discussing the situation and we all said, 'Netaji, how can you go alone? Who will administer to your needs? For God's sake, persuade the Japanese to let you take at least one of us with you.'

"Netaji spoke to the Japanese and finally they agreed that one other person could go with him. Lieutenant-Colonel Habib-Ur-Rehman was selected and the Japanese promised to fly the rest of us to join Netaji as soon as possible. They were in a great hurry to get us to the airport, because a senior Japanese officer, Lieutenant-General Shidei of the Burma Army Command, was being held up by Netaji's refusal to travel alone.

"We were rushed in two cars to the airport. I was in the second with the two suitcases of gold. Our driver was an incompetent fellow. He lost his way and we got to the airport about an hour after Netaji. Netaji was standing on the tarmac outside the plane, talking to Lieutenant-General Shidei. He had refused to fly without the suitcases. The cases were rushed aboard and then Netaji came up to me and said 'Thank you very much.' He shook my hand and went briskly up the steps, walking like a king.

"I could hardly speak and my eyes were filled with tears, and I swore that I would join him soon. That was the last time I saw Netaji Subhas Chandra Bose."

170 pounds of gold, Chan thought, nearly half a million US dollars. "And the gold?" he asked. "What happened to that?"

Banerjee smiled, still sad. "It was lost," he said, "but now, it has been found again. It is here in Hong Kong, where the British took it."

"But, but—"

Banerjee shook his hand in front of his chest. "You go and find those who killed Raghavan," he said, "and come to the rally on Sunday. Then I will tell all."

21

CHAN WENT BACK to the station. By some weird administrative quirk, the passenger lists were lying fatly on his
desk. Things would be twice as confused when they got
computers, he thought happily, sitting down, studying the
list.

There were thousands of names, spreading over six
pages, an impossible research task even if he had the men.
But it was good to be back on the case again, whether the
AC approved or not. He would find Raghavan's killer and
show them. Show up that arrogant *kwei lo* Winston too.
Revolutionary students, *wai*!

A name catapulted out of the list, vivid as if it had been
typed in dayglo. Hiroshi Watanabe, passenger from Macau.
Hurriedly Chan scanned through the departures, reaching
for his notebook and the telephone. There was no listing of
Watanabe's leaving Hong Kong. He opened his notebook
and checked the references on the Raghavan articles for
the *Asian Clarion*. Then he called Hotels.

Hotels came back impossibly quickly. It must be because
Winston had so many men out on surveillance, Hotels had
not enough work to do. Still, it was a good omen. Chan
stuffed Raghavan's photograph into his wallet, thinking
his luck was changing at last. All the way to the Peninsula
he had that exciting gut feeling that the case was about to
break.

"Police," Chan called in answer to Watanabe's shouted question, chotto mattayed while the door was opened, followed Watanabe's spare figure into the room. The man had a large head, an enquiring tilt to it, half-framed glasses, a dash of moustache, a face that was both intelligent and rapacious, a straight mouth, determined, cruel. Watanabe walked with the splay legged gait of an old man.

"What do you want?" returning Chan's warrant card, filing the details away in a card-index mind.

"A few questions. Just routine." Heavens, it was a large room, probably cost more in a week than he earned in a month. Strangely bare though, no guidebooks, no gaily coloured pamphlets from the Hong Kong Tourist Association. There was a novel by Yukio Mishima lying face down on the low table. Interesting that. Wasn't Mishima the Japanese writer who had seized an army headquarters in Tokyo and committed *hara kiri* when the soldiers refused to join him in a right wing *coup d'etat*. Never mind, Li-li would know. Li-li read a lot.

Watanabe was waiting for his questions, alarmed and controlling it well. Chan took out his notebook. "You arrived in Hong Kong, when?"

Watanabe told him.

"You are here on business?"

"Yes."

Chan faithfully wrote that down. "What kind of business?" He wasn't doing this too well. He had been too excited at the prospect of resuming the enquiry to plan his interrogation of this man.

"Journalism."

"For what paper?"

"*Asahi Shimbun.*"

No matter. Chan could soon check that. He snapped the notebook shut. "What did you do in the war?"

They had been standing in the centre of the room, both of them uncertain how long the interview would last. Now Watanabe sat down. "What is the purpose —"

"You must have done something in the war. You are old enough." Old enough to have commanded the Fifth Army and massacred the villagers of Shansi.

"What is the purpose of your enquiries?"

"Who was the head of the 82nd Bureau in Taiwan on August 18th, 1945?"

Watanabe pursed his lips primly, his face taking on the fastidious appearance of an old lady who had heard a distasteful word. "I cannot answer your questions."

"Do you know this man?" Chan thrust Raghavan's much-creased photograph uncomfortably close to Watanabe's face. Watanabe had to look, had to twist his head away.

"No."

"Ever heard of someone called Saito Chu in Taiwan? He used to be in charge of fuelling operations at the airport."

"No."

"What about Subhas Chandra Bose? Ever heard of him?"

"I will not talk about the war. I am not obliged to."

"Let's try it another way. Let's talk of now. Are you a member of *Ao Arashi* — the Blue Storm?"

"Yes."

"Are you its head?"

"I am a member. Why are the Hong Kong police interested in a Japanese political organisation?"

"So you are a politician, not a journalist?"

"I told you I was a journalist. That is enough."

"As a journalist, have you ever met a man here in Hong Kong called Wan Liu, the head of the III K Society?"

Pause for thought. Subtle weighing up of alternatives. "Yes. I have met him."

"How many times?"

"I don't remember exactly. Twice, three times."

"What did you talk about?"

"Triads, organised crime. I was interviewing him."

"May I see the article?"

"It was not published. What he had to say was not interesting enough."

"How long do you plan to stay in Hong Kong?"

"A few weeks more. Why?"

"Do you have your passport?"

Watanabe got up, walked over to the bed, took out a passport from a slim attache case with a combination lock. He handed the passport to Chan.

"I intend to hold your passport," Chan said. "I'm also putting you on a stop list at Kai Tak."

"Why?"

"Because I want to talk to you again and I don't want you disappearing before that. I think you could give me information about a murder — two murders."

Watanabe stared at him blank-faced, took the receipt that Chan gave him and tucked it away in his wallet.

"If you're not leaving for a few weeks, you won't be inconvenienced," Chan said.

Watanabe didn't say anything.

*   *   *

All he needed was proof, Chan thought joyously, proof that would connect Saito Chu's story of Bose's plane being unloaded with Watanabe's presence in Taiwan at the time. He had already asked the boy Inspector to check that, and had found out from Li-li's father that someone called Watanabe had been a Japanese commander in Hong Kong in 1942. What he had to do now was establish the link between Watanabe and Wan Liu, the link between Watanabe and the treasure. If Banerjee could produce it at the rally that should clinch it, motive, evidence, everything. Pity he couldn't press Banerjee, but never mind. Watanabe wasn't going anywhere yet,

That night to celebrate, he took Li-li to the pictures, hiring a baby-sitter at $8 an hour. Afterwards they went to dinner and Li-li told him he was right about Yukio

Mishima. She also confessed that while he'd been in Taiwan, she'd been to see the acupuncturist and that her arm was completely cured.

That was something else to celebrate, so in a fit of happy spontaneity they went for a drive. Because Hong Kong was such a small place, it would take him three months to run his car in properly. In any case, it was a beautiful night, the moon nearly full, heralding the festival in three days time when Yin and Yang would meet. The roads were marvellously empty and they were away a long time, which was why Pete Winston couldn't speak to Chan before the AC left for Macau. Not that Chan would have wanted to speak to Pete Winston or hear what he had to say.

*　　*　　*

Pete Winston had had a lousy day. First there had been that jumped-up gook from SB insisting that the files he had brought were Special Branch property and couldn't be left at any old police station. Then had followed the sickening realisation that Chan could well be right. The files showed that these people were not as heavily politically orientated as say, students in London. The last big agitation had been over the secession of some uninhabited islands to Japan and that had been peaceful enough, with only a few bloody noses to show for it.

He thought desperately about the map in his office, covered with red pins like porcupine quills. The surveillance had provided much interesting gossip about personal relationships, but so far, nothing to do with arms or revolution. The whole operation was costing a packet. It could not go on indefinitely and so far had produced nothing.

If this failed, Winston thought, he was out. All his carefully built up connections, all his studied politeness to the wives of senior officers at the club, all his excellence at rugby and squash would avail him nothing. No one would remember the Whampoa Docks Affair. No one would remember the Korean Spy Ring. All they would remember was that he had cocked up the uprising following the Godber Rally.

What would he do if promotion was barred, if he was condemned to failure? Resign? And do what? Returning to England was unthinkable. It was too full of damned pinkos dragging the country down with their usual combination of misplaced idealism and ignorance. Go back to the SAS and Ireland? No thank you. Jesus Christ, he had to get this one right.

It was difficult enough without that bastard Chan interfering.

"What's the matter darling?" Kate asked, her long body stretched out beside him. "Can't you get to sleep?"

"That bloody flied lice Charlie Chan," Winston said, "Chan had no business seeing Watanabe. Even less crowding him." Jesus, if he lost Watanabe the Department would have his guts for garters.

Kate said, "That's no way to talk about any Chinese, however much you may dislike him."

"Fucking flied lice gook," Winston said slowly and deliberately. It didn't make him feel any better. Chan had disappeared and the AC had left for Macau. There was nothing he could do about stopping Chan till Monday. Taking it higher up in the AC's absence was no solution. The AC was on his side, someone else might not be. Superior officers were so unpredictable. It looked like Watanabe would have to do without his passport for a few days more. Unfortunate, but inevitable. When the AC returned, he, Pete Winston, would personally see to Richard Chan.

"Darling what's wrong?" Kate asked, her hand moving lazily between his legs, stroking him gently. "You want me to relax you?"

"It's this bloody case," Winston said staring up at the dark ceiling.

Kate laughed softly. "The students?"

"The bloody students."

"You have found nothing so far, I take it."

"Not yet."

His breath was catching at the back of his throat and he could feel himself growing hard.

"I told you, you would find nothing," Kate said. "They're only kids. They aren't old enough to know anything about politics."

That was true, Winston thought, arching his back. The oldest were no more than twenty, middle-class kids playing with ideas, testing their strength, not the kind from which revolutionaries were made.

"If there is a plot," Kate said, "there must be older people involved. People who remember '67."

Winston felt he would burst. He flung away her teasing hand and threw himself upon her, thrusting deep into her warm moistness, barely hearing her yelp of pleased surprise. Someone who remembered '67, moving quickly, feeling her body smooth and spread out beneath him, an older person. Her mouth was a cool wet cave, softly opened, names reeled through his brain like leaderstrip on film. It made such sense, fantastic, fantastic sense, fantastic, fantastic sensation, clutching her to him, feeling her nipples sprouting hard against his naked chest, hands roving hungrily over her smooth flanks, fantastic, fantastic, feeling her twist slowly, slowly, throbbing, fantastic, he was vibrating like a plucked string, fantastic, Jesus Christ it was — And in that moment of shuddering climax Pete Winston knew exactly what he had to do.

*   *   *

The *Flying Dragon* had been at sea nearly a week now, a high-sided, flat-bottomed junk with curved bow and high, raked back stern, its sides strung with old tyres. It rowed in the water, the bright red water-line submerged by the waves, tossing on the sea with none of the majesty

188

and elegant height it would show when moving through shallower waters.

Three days more, thought the master of the *Flying Dragon*, and it would all be over. He sat squatting in the stern of the junk, gazing out to sea, an old wrinkled man with the face and figure of a monkey. He was hoping it would all go well.

*　　*　　*

Twenty minutes later Pete Winston got out of bed and began to dress.

"What's the matter? Where are you going?" Kate asked.

"Out," Winston said. "I'll see you in the morning."

He tiptoed out of the door. It was an awkward hour but he was going to get a search warrant to explore the offices of Steven Koo and those of the *Free China Truth*.

22

IN THE BITTER grey light of morning, Steven Koo, editor of the *Free China Truth*, was barely given time to dress before being bundled into the back of an unmarked Hillman and taken to his office. Pete Winston was already there, his Triumph sports car parked arrogantly across the kerb, its downturned sun visor bearing the card that said it was a police vehicle on emergency duty.

Koo was a northerner, bigger than the policemen who walked on either side of him, up the steps of the building where his office was. "You could have done this at a more civilised hour," he snapped at Winston.

Pete Winston smiled. His year in the Leicestershire Constabulary had taught him the practicality of politeness. "We didn't want to upset your staff," he explained.

He moved aside to let Koo open the door of the building and the six of them marched across the empty lobby and up two flights of cement stairs with hollowly echoing footsteps. The offices of the *Free China Truth* consisted of a large communal area with open desks and typewriters bordered by a reception counter, three small partitioned rooms for senior staff and a larger room for Koo, at the front of the building, overlooking the street.

Winston went with Koo into his own office and allowed him to sit in his own chair. He shut the door to eliminate the steady tramp of feet, the sound of drawers being flung open and furniture moved. He leant back and studied Koo. A chubby man with straight black hair, worn longer than usual for a Chinese in an uncharacteristic trendy executive style, just covering his ears. His head was large and cocked aggressively, the full lower jaw thrust forward, the big mouth pursed and the eyes behind the horn-rimmed glasses intent and hostile.

Winston reached into his vest pocket for his cigarettes. He knew that Koo had been educated in America, and that he was a well-known figure on the diplomatic cocktail party circuit. He knew that Koo had to be handled with a certain tenderness. He noticed the large gold ring on the fourth finger of his left hand and that Koo had dressed too hurriedly to put on his watch. It seemed he had forgotten his cigarettes too.

Winston gave him one and put the packet away. Koo lit his from a desk lighter. Winston had never read a single copy of the *Free China Truth*. All he had read was the SB file on Koo. Koo had been on the fringe of an arms smuggling incident which had occurred four years ago. Winston hoped to hell that would be enough.

"Your paper's full of shit," Winston said, conversationally.

"So's the police force," Koo replied equably. "What difference does that make?" His accent was curious, the Chinese lilt overlaid by a slow American drawl.

"You've been writing that students should be more politically active, that they should be demanding Hong Kong for the Chinese."

"If you are going to adopt a political posture, Inspector," Koo said, "You really must learn to read." He paused deliberately before adding, "More carefully."

"You have not written that students should be more politically active, then?"

"I have advocated that students should be more politically active, yes. I have forecast that Hong Kong will one day belong to the Chinese. What I have always urged is that it should belong to the Hong Kong Chinese and that its present rulers should take steps to ensure that end." He paused to give Winston the benefit of a sneer. "We may all look alike but, believe me, we really are different."

Patronising bastard, Winston thought and hoped that his men would make a mess of the office. "You think Hong Kong should have closer ties with Taiwan?"

"With Nationalist China, yes. I also think that Hong Kong should sever all connections with Maoist China. There is nothing seditious in that."

"Do you think that the students should militate openly against colonial rule?"

"Of course I do. There are four million of us, less than a hundred thousand of you. Every Chinese must do what he can to bring such an unfair disposition of power to an end. But they must be correctly channelled."

"Channelled how?"

"By exhortation and advice, by proper leadership. By reading the *Free China Truth*." He paused to smile at his flippancy. "They must be taught to use democratic methods and in order to do that, they must be given democratic powers."

"You sound like a Communist," Winston said.

"On the contrary, Inspector, my published works show that I am totally opposed to Communism."

Winston decided to change his angle of attack. "You believe that violence is sometimes necessary?"

"Of course I do. I believe that if the people are oppressed, they have a duty to rise up and overthrow their oppressors."

"And do you feel that such people have a right to arm themselves?"

"They have a right to fight oppression in any way possible."

"Even if it means overthrowing the lawful government of this colony?"

"That will come in time," Koo replied. "An uprising

now will cause a power vacuum that the Communists will fill. Besides there are more important battles to be fought."

"Such as . . ."

"Inspector, I thought you were an avid reader of my paper. You must know that our primary objective is to return to China. China is our home. From there we can deal with the problems of Hong Kong."

"Would you then give arms to the Chinese in Hong Kong to throw out the British?"

"We will do then, whatever we think necessary."

"Four years ago," Pete Winston said, "there was an attempt to smuggle arms into the colony. Tell me about that."

"At the time I made certain statements to the police. Read them. I also wrote certain articles in my newspaper. Back numbers are available by calling at the reception desk during office hours."

Winston asked, "What do you feel about the demonstration next Sunday?"

"On that topic, I have already expressed my opinions in print. I think that a demonstration against police corruption is a meritorious one. Police corruption is a perfect example of the exploitation of the Chinese in Hong Kong by their rulers. What I feel such a demonstration lacks is the broader platform of Chinese unity. The Chinese are one people and they should stand by each other. They should protest at the way their brothers in Taiwan have been exploited and abandoned by the United States of America, just as Taiwan should protest at the connivance that allowed Godber to escape."

"Should they fight for Chinese unity, do you think?"

"If they have to."

"On Sunday?"

Koo smiled. "Inspector, you're trying to put words into my mouth. I think I will now cease answering your questions."

193

"But tell me, how do you feel about a violent demonstration in favour of Chinese unity on Sunday?"

"I must remind you that I am here voluntarily, to assist you in the exercise of your lawful duty — searching my office. I am not under arrest and even if I were, I needn't answer your questions. Isn't that the law?"

"I'm only interested in your — "

"I know. But you too are bound by the law. Let's talk about something else, shall we?"

There was nothing else Pete Winston wanted to talk about. He wished he could have half an hour alone with Koo in the basement cell of a lonely police station. But Koo was too important a figure for that kind of treatment. Within seconds he'd have a team of lawyers round showering writs like there was no tomorrow. No, Winston had to find another way.

Deliberately he took out another cigarette and lit it, watching Koo's face go blank as he restrained the impulse to ask for one, too. There wasn't much point in cross-examining Koo further. He was an experienced debater and Winston would need more time than he had available to wear the man down.

For want of something better to do, he ran through his questions again, probing Koo on his attitudes to violence and rebellion. Koo answered as blandly as he had done before and Winston felt that not only was he getting nowhere, but that he was at a minus advantage.

Desperately he tried to think of a way to break the deadlock. He thought about arms smuggling. Arms smuggling needed a vehicle, a boat or a plane to land the arms, legally or illegally in Hong Kong. The operation needed people to man the vehicle, a person or persons to buy the arms from. Above all, such an operation would need money.

"I'd like to have a look at your accounts," Pete Winston said.

Koo stopped clicking the desk lighter and looked

thoughtfully at Winston. "They're in the next office," he said. Winston went with him to get them.

Winston decided to concentrate on the cash book, on monies received and paid out by the magazine. If he was to find anything quickly, it would be there. He pored over rows of figures. There were columns for cash receipts from distributors, from casual sales, from subscriptions. There were also occasional round sum receipts anonymously marked "Contributions".

"That's no secret," Koo said. "Everyone knows we get financial support from the Nationalist Government."

The payments out seemed even more routine. Contributors, rent, salaries, telephone hire, travelling. The largest regular amounts were paid to the printers, the Pak Luan Printing Co., once a fortnight. Nothing there, Winston thought with disappointment except, why had the last payment to the Pak Luan Co. been for nearly three hundred thousand Hong Kong dollars.

"Simple economics," Koo explained. "Paper prices are going up. We bought forward stocks."

Maybe so, maybe not. This could easily be checked.

Traffic noises from the street outside filled the room. It was eight thirty and the rush hour was at its peak. Pete Winston still hadn't found a damn thing.

He went out and spoke to the men. One of them showed him an article published six weeks ago that might have been treasonable. Winston decided that if it had been, the Attorney General's Department would have picked it up. For Winston to draw their attention to it now, would look like dredging the bottom of a very small barrel.

Another man had scheduled out the past three months telex messages. They seemed to conform to a pattern, he said, rising to a peak on copy day, falling below normal on the three intervening days, and rising again on the day of publication. Winston asked him to take the copy telexes back.

Koo came out of his office and scrounged a cigarette off

a policeman. Blowing smoke luxuriously he asked, "Everything in order?"

"We think so," Winston said. "If there is anything else, we'll be back."

"Don't hurry," Koo said. "The next time I shall be considering proceedings for harassment."

* * *

Pete Winston flung himself behind his desk and concluded that the search of Steven Koo's offices had been a waste of precious time. All he'd got from it was a possibility that the $300,000 was dodgy and the telexes. The telexes were being checked over at Special Branch, now. Despondently he called them and asked if they had anything on the Pak Luan Printing Co.

They had. Its proprietor, Chiao Te, was suspected of being a Nationalist agent. No proof, just suspicion. There was nothing else on the file. That could mean anything, Winston thought bitterly, that the man was lying or had simply once subscribed to the *Free China Truth*.

He pulled yesterday's surveillance reports and began to read. That bloody Chan was every bloody where. What the hell had he been doing in the Excelsior chatting up Banerjee? Winston had enough problems with that man and his charming press conference without Chan standing on the side lines giving advice. He'd sort that schwartzer out too, when the AC returned. There was no way anyone in the Delhi Foundation was going to march with the students.

Winston was still poring over his files and wondering what to do when the Anti-Corruption Office telephoned. They'd had an anonymous tip-off and were investigating a customs officer who'd had $15,000 more in his bank account than he could explain away. The customs officer was saying it was money paid to him to let through a shipment of three crates consigned to the Pak Luan Printing

Co., arriving the following Monday evening on a British Airways flight from Bangkok.

*   *   *

Later that morning Pete Winston sat in his second best lightweight mohair suit, looked frankly across at the bank manager and agreed that the request he had made was highly irregular. But, he explained, it was a matter of national emergency.

The bank manager was unimpressed. The bank had its rules, rules that had evolved out of the customs and traditions of medieval Florentine bankers. He sounded as if he was their sole custodian.

Winston said he realised that in the normal course of events he should have obtained a court order. But the whole matter was so secret and so important that they couldn't risk alerting the suspects by the publicity that an application to the court might receive. Besides there wasn't any time.

The bank manager said, "Hrrumph! But rules are rules, dear boy. You come back with a court order and I'll tell you everything I know about the Pak Luan Printing Co."

Winston suggested that instead, the bank manager should speak to ex-DC Thompson. Yes, the very same Jack Thompson with whom he played bridge every Wednesday evening at the Craigengower Cricket Club. Because it was his friend, Jack Thompson, the bank manager agreed to phone, though he warned Winston that he could no more break rules for a friend than for anyone else.

The conversation wasn't a long one. The bank manager's protests diminished rapidly as Thompson told him what they were trying to prevent. The bank manager agreed that if there was going to be an armed uprising, he would not want it put about that the bank's intransigence had contributed materially to its success. That would do the bank more damage than passing over information about what after all was a small and possibly criminal account.

"My God!" he said, putting the phone down and glaring down his nose at Winston. "You should have told me. My God! It'll be '67 over again. We had to get the army out then, you know."

Winston said, "All this is highly confidential."

"I appreciate that," the bank manager said. "Of course, I do." He had served his National Service in Intelligence, checking Russian telephone directories at Aldershot. He pressed a button and asked a boy to bring him the ledger cards on the Pak Luan Printing Co. account.

Winston looked at the ledger cards. The three hundred thousand Hong Kong dollars received from the *Free China Truth* magazine had been converted immediately into United States dollars and a bankers draft for $47,700 drawn against it, endorsed over to one Suresh C. Banerjee.

Winston thanked the bank manager profusely and left. He had no doubt as to what would be in the three crates being flown in from Bangkok on Monday. He had no doubt that Chiao Te had paid for them, Banerjee had shipped them, and Koo had acted as an intermediary. By Monday evening he would have them bang to rights, except for that loud-mouthed Banerjee. He would take Banerjee tomorrow, the day before the arms landed, and totally confuse the opposition.

Winston hurried back to the station to call off the surveillance operation.

23

SATURDAY NIGHT. BRILLIANT neon smouldered over Hong Kong. Its pavements rang with the gay susurration of leather on stone, echoed with the brittle cadences of spirantal voices. The thrum of traffic burbled along the packed streets with strident urgency. Tall ferry boats and tiny *wallah-wallahs* darted ceaselessly across the harbour in frantic haste. It was Saturday night. Fun night. People were going places to be happy.

In the Peak and around Mid-level, groups of six or eight were gathering in company-subsidised flats, talking of their last furlough and how high prices were, about police corruption and new boats, of whether the rains would come. At Gaddi's, at Jimmy's Kitchen, at the Four Seasons the triple layered conversations assumed the constant roar of a waterfall, punctuated by the tambourine clink of cutlery, the occasional whoosh of flame and the sizzle of meat as dishes were cooked before the customer's eyes. Saturday night. Happy night.

They were crammed on to the dance floor at the Eagles Nest, hips twisting, fingers snapping, arms akimbo, having-a-good-time, happy, alive only to the music and swinging on a Saturday night.

Below the dancers the lights of Hong Kong blistered. Happy Hong Kong night. Crowds swarmed up the steep step-laddered streets, prowled amongst jade and vases and bellicose Buddhas. They milled about the markets, washed by the greasy yellow light of pressure lamps, thronged around the fortune tellers and medicine men, the story tellers and soap box gamblers playing "fish, crab and prawn", with six-sided dice. Saturday night. The big night of the week.

Hydrofoils whipped through the ruffled sea to Macau, where the casinos at the Lisboa and the Estoril were already packed, where hearts and eyes were locked on to turning card and tumbling ball. In the walled city of Kowloon, which is neither walled nor a city, but a group of suppurating alleys surrounded by shops and markets, there were crowded into a dingy room, a number of middle-aged men carrying transistor radios, and betting vociferously on the dogs running at the Canidrome in Macau. In another part of the city, in a room protected by burly men with spiky hair and wearing loose black shorts, people crowded round a black jack table playing *fan-tan*, *tin-kau, pai-kau*, and Russian poker. And all over Hong Kong it was mahjong night, Saturday night, the pieces rustling like cascading stones. Saturday night was someone's lucky night.

Someone's? Whose? In a room lined with dirt and soot an old man fitted an opium pellet into his pipe, his eyes already turned inward peering towards a mind long past its tether. A mainliner crouched in a darkened doorway and yanked hard on the rag twisted round his arm, searching for a vein in which to pump sweeter dreams. Happy, wretched Saturday. A young prostitute expertly unzipped her clothes and splayed herself naked on a still warm bed. Her eyes were shuttered, gliding impersonally over the body of her customer and fixing themselves on a predestined spot on the ceiling. Saturday night was fun night. By the jetty, *sampan muis* offered boat rides around the lanes of the typhoon shelters and visits to the flower boats, offered to procure twelve-year-old girls who would beat cymbals in time to your rutting. It was Saturday night, the happiest, biggest, most fun full night of the week.

The dance halls were full. The girlie bars were crowded. Hostesses raced from telephone to table, drinking tea, eating pistachio nuts. The beauty parlours were full of steam and soiled towels, and everybody, buddy, was having a good, good time. Everybody was trying to be happy.

Even in Tzn Wan Chan, where the sky was not orange and the buildings were tall and dilapidated, with crumpled papers and used cigarette packets littering the bare cement stairs. Here also it was Saturday night and youths stood around in gangs, in the shadows of playgrounds, on street corners, talking, looking, wondering what the hell to do on the happiest night of the week. Here the streets were the only refuge from over-crowded apartments and even more over-crowded dormitories. Here you owned what you could store on your bed and only on Saturday night did you have the time to stand and stare and wonder why. They stood around waiting for something to happen, a rich stranger to pass, a fight, or someone's sister to sell.

The girl was seventeen years old and she had been working late because she was saving extra money to put down on a flat, together with her fiance. She would be married when she was twenty. She was a pleasant-looking girl, not beautiful, slim-waisted, slender-legged, with a tight little bosom. She had come down from the twelfth floor to the refuse room, as she had done every alternate night for two years. She was carrying a plastic bag full of food scraps, empty tins and sauce bottles. As she went into the room, she was thinking that tomorrow she could sleep a little longer. She did not see the man till it was too late.

A hand went round her startled mouth, coarse and salty. Her bag was snatched from her, as other hands grasped her and bore her to the ground. She struggled but the hands were too strong and the fingers seemed to brand her flesh. She writhed on the floor smelling sweat and decaying food, choking, trying to curve her body sideways.

She gasped against the stifling hand as her arms were pulled above her head. Then the hands were everywhere, crawling over her like huge insects, pulling away her skirt, forcing her legs apart. They ripped off her panties and stuffed them in her mouth. She fought soundlessly, trying to force her body upright against the unyielding pressure of those hands. They held her taut as the first man thrust himself into her. She shuddered at the weight of him and the sharp pain that threatened to tear her apart. Tears started from her fast shut eyes and she began to beat her head against the floor.

It was Saturday night. Happy night. Fun night. Even in Tzn Wan Chan.

*   *   *

The man staring at the catfish outside the restaurant must have known it was Saturday night. Why else would he be wearing a false moustache? The restaurant was called the Wong Kee and it had a cardboard sign on the door that said it was air-conditioned. Beside the door were three fish tanks filled with crab, cuttlefish, eel and catfish. The man stared fascinated at their ordered movements, and at the stream of air bubbles that rose upward and burst.

He was still staring at the fish when a black Ford Zephyr clouted the kerb behind him. He turned. The car bounced on the pavement and stopped, two wheels high, doors dangling open like wings.

The man by the restaurant ran towards the car. As he ran he tucked a hand into his pocket and took out a snub-nosed gun. He reached the car and jumped away from it, on to the step of the open fronted jewellery store. The man landed on the top step with a yell, and reversing the gun in his hand, he smashed the nearest showcase. Two other men from the car with stockinged faces scooped the contents of the case into canvas bags. Then all three ran back to the car.

The car squealed away from the kerb, doors slamming.

It straightened and shot directly for the intersection. The lights were just changing as it streaked through, with blaring horn and blinding lights. As it passed, a Thames pick-up and an open sided truck moved across the lights and met. The crash completely blocked the intersection.

*   *   *

On any night, especially on Saturday night, the Public Square in Yau Ma Tei is crowded. There are stalls hawking cooked food, dog meat and snake soup, coffee bars, street peddlers selling cloth by the yard, carved ivory, kitchen utensils, scrolls, silk ties, watches, wigs, pre-recorded tapes. Around the edges of the square, touts display pornographic snapshots and issue discreet invitations to even more pornographic movies. Groups of blind musicians play incessant Mandarin variations and the crowds come, to watch, to buy, to meet, to eat, on their way to and from the cinemas that surround the area, moving in a turbulent swarm around the illuminated showcases under the giant neon ideograms.

The four youths in the dented grey Toyota were barely noticeable amongst the crowd and the traffic along the periphery of the streets surrounding the square. They were all in their early twenties, were smartly dressed, and unusually keen-eyed, with the scouring gaze of policemen on the watch.

The driver was called Chi-Wah. He had come out of prison ten months ago. Seated beside him in the front passenger seat was Ah Au, Chiao Te's chauffeur. Ah Au revered Chi-Wah. Chi-Wah was only one year older than Ah Au and lived with a dance hostess, who let him borrow her car whenever he wanted to. Chi-Wah had been to jail and knew the right men. It was he who had organised them into a triad, with blood curdling oaths of secrecy and the ritual decapitation of a cockerel to exemplify the treatment that would be meted out to traitors. Chi-Wah had shown them how to extort money from the coffee stalls by creating disturbances, and how to get free passes to the best seats in the cinemas by threatening the managers. Best of all, Chi-Wah had shown them how to earn real money. In this last week Ah Au had made more than he had done in three months driving Chiao Te's Audi.

Ah Au knew that soon he would be rich. Chi-Wah had promised him the better jobs, and to introduce him to the hierarchy in the triad. Soon Ah Au would be both powerful and rich. Then he would not have to hand his pay packet to his father, every Friday. He would be able to go to the cinema every night and buy the most expensive hostesses in the dance halls, those who did not sleep with every man. People would be afraid of him and give him respect and for all those things that were about to happen, Ah Au gave Chi-Wah humble thanks.

Chi-Wah stopped the car abruptly and looked over his shoulder. Ah Au followed his gaze, thrilling with admiration. Chi-Wah had such sharp eye-sight. He had spotted the boy with the football before any of them. And he had been driving too! Chi-Wah touched Ah Au's shoulder and nodded. Ah Au extinguished his cigarette and as the boy drew level with the rear of the car, he got out.

The boy with the football would have made a good winger. He was lightly built, with strong legs, whose long muscles were clearly defined and rippled as he played with his football. He was wearing the top half of a blue track suit, dark blue shorts, blue and yellow hose and plimsolls. He was completely absorbed in his private game.

Ah Au tapped the ball. The boy looked up in pleased surprise. Instinctively he made to move the ball away. Then he recognised Ah Au and froze. Ah Au hit him once in the solar plexus. The boy gasped and bent forward. As he doubled up, the two men who had got out of the rear of the Toyota, grabbed him round the body and swung him choking into the car.

They didn't drive far. A few streets away there was a deserted space where a building had been demolished.

Chi-Wah bounced the car over the pavement through a gap in the fencing and bumped carelessly over the scattered mounds of brick and stone. In the centre of the yard, he stopped.

The only light came from the widely spaced street lamps and the dim reflections from the columns of apartments. It made the youths look like lighter shadows against the greater darkness. Chi-Wah walked to a two-foot high remnant of wall and stood. The others pulled the terrified boy out of the car. They had tied his hands behind him and they dragged him roughly over the broken ground to where Chi-Wah waited, and flung him forward on to his knees in front of their leader.

Chi-Wah said, "You've been brought here to be punished."

The boy cried out, "No. Please, no. I have done nothing."

"You have refused to work with us."

"That is because I knew I could not be useful. Please. I have no mind for the sort of things you do."

Chi-Wah's voice went dangerously quiet. "What kind of things do we do?"

The boy hesitated. "I don't know — but please — I only want to play football — I'm no good at anything else. I don't want to — "

Chi-Wah slapped him. "What things?" he repeated. "What have you heard about us?"

The boy cried, "Nothing, nothing. Please believe me. Please let me go."

Chi-Wah kicked him in the stomach. The boy gasped, knifed over and felt a hard, brutal pain as Ah Au's shoe exploded on the side of his face. The boy sprawled sideways, struggling like a trapped crab. A foot caught him in the back and turned him over on to his face. Shod feet crashed against his arms and ribs and shoulders. He rolled over trying to escape the pounding blows. The feet thudded into him mercilessly. He opened his mouth to scream and

205

a leathered foot crashed across his front teeth, filling his mouth with tangy blood and the feel of pebbles. Someone cried, "Better than football." Ah Au screamed, "We'll teach you football." Then there was a cry of, "Police!" Above their heavy panting and the terrified sobbing of their victim, they heard the rising wail of a siren.

For a moment Chi-Wah stood still, staring at the rectangular pattern of lights from the apartment above. Some day, no one would dare inform on him. Some day, the police would not even dare to come. The lamentation of the siren was shriller now, accompanied by a screaming gear change. Chi-Wah began to run.

The patrol car slithered into the yard, siren dying, spot lights blazing, the blue light on its roof blinking furiously. Ah Au running, looked back in fear, caught his foot on a pile of rubble and fell. Frantically he clawed himself upright, ignoring the stinging of his palms and knees. The others were already crowding around the the the car. Doors slammed. Ah Au heard the boy cry out, and he ran madly across the uneven ground.

There was a puff of smoke from the Toyota's exhaust, a keening clamour from its engine. Ah Au heard the clatter of flying stones as it spun its wheels. "Wait for me," he shouted. "Wait you bastards," hurling himself after the car. The Toyota skidded across the yard, smashed through the fencing and bounded out on to the road. Like a man possessed, Ah Au ran towards the gap with sobbing lungs.

There was a fleeing wall of metal rushing past his elbow, an ear splitting screech from a siren. Brake lights flared as the police car paused in the centre of the gap and skidded across the road. Ah Au heard stumbling footsteps behind him and forced himself to move faster. He was still running when the policeman's baton slammed against his head. There was a vivid ribbon of pain, then his legs collapsed under him like dynamited chocks.

After that there was only darkness and an ending to Saturday night.

24

Hot, lazy Sunday afternoon, crowded beaches, crowded roads. Chan stayed home in air-conditioned comfort, fretting at the enforced inactivity, but still happy. The Raghavan case was practically over. All he had to do was wait to hear from the boy Inspector, wait till next Sunday when Banerjee made his revelations.

So he played with the children, helped them build their kites and ate hugely. Tomorrow night was the Moon Festival, the fifteenth night of the eighth moon. At midnight, the sun and moon, Yin and Yang would meet, and Yeng O, that curious wife who swallowed her husband's pill of immortality would be united with Hou Yih, sometime wizard and extinguisher of the nine suns. Tomorrow, all Hong Kong would be blazing with lanterns and illuminated kites, tomorrow night all Chinese would seek to walk on high ground.

The phone shrilled. Not another body in a taxi, Chan thought jovially, putting the finishing touches to Tony's fantailed dragon. Li-li shouted that it was Father Loyola.

"Richard Thomas, you haven't been avoiding us, have you?"

Chan felt the same fear-ridden guilt as he had done that day many years ago when Father Loyola had discovered him enjoying a Capstan cigarette in the privacy of the school lavatory.

"No, Father. I have been busy. Truly."

"I wouldn't expect anything but the truth from you, Richard. How is Catherine? And Anthony and Maria?" Father Loyola only referred to Chan's family by their baptismal names as if that were some kind of protection against the heathen hordes surrounding them.

"They are well, Father. Li — Catherine had some trouble with her arm, but she has been to see an acupuncturist and she is now better."

"And you, my son?"

"Overworked. I've been in Taiwan on a murder case which is why I haven't been to see you or phoned you before."

"You must come by and see us, Richard Thomas. Only the other day, Father Joseph was remarking what a stranger you have become."

"I am pleased he remembered me," Chan murmured. "I will come and see you soon."

"There is someone who needs your help, Richard." Father Loyola said.

"But of course," Chan murmured.

"He is presently in police custody. A boy from a good family."

Chan wondered what a boy from a good family was doing in police custody in the first place. "There are limits to what I can do," he warned.

"I realise that, Richard. The family are greatly distressed and I have spoken with the young man. He will not reveal what is concerning him, but it seems that he would like to talk to you. He has some idea of . . . doing a deal?"

"We don't do deals, Father."

"You must use your own judgment, my son. The boy's mother is deeply concerned. You must at least meet with the boy before you make a decision."

"Of course, I will see him."

"I don't think you will recognise him. He must have

208

been very junior to you in school. But he remembers you. We all do."

"I can't hold out too much hope," Chan said. "What is his name?"

"Ah Au," Father Loyola said. "He is being held at Yau Ma Tei police station on charges of assault and robbery."

*　　*　　*

The interview room at Yau Ma Tei was smaller than the one Chan was used to at Wan Chai, furnished with two bare, green tables and a few upright wooden chairs. A notice board on the wall held a yellowing advertisement for last year's Police Sports Meet.

Ah Au turned out to be a stocky fellow with thick greasy hair that looked in need of care. His patterned shirt was grubby and his trousers had lost the pristine elegance that the knife-edge creases had once given them. The belt with the ornamental buckle that should have completed the outfit had been taken away, and his shoes were scuffed and stained with earth. Chan did not remember ever having seen him before.

"When were you in college?" Chan asked.

Ah Au told him. It was four years after Chan himself had left. "They were still talking about you," Ah Au said. "You were the school's first national boxing champion. We used to come and watch you fight for the police."

Chan felt flattered and more than slightly embarrassed. "You told Father Loyola you wanted to see me? Why me?"

"I wanted someone who could help me. I don't know any policemen and I thought . . ."

"Because we were at the same school?"

Ah Au nodded.

"I can't promise much. Now, what do you want to say to me?"

Ah Au looked very hesitant. "I would like a cigarette," he said and while Chan sent out for them, he looked down

209

14—TBI * *

at the desk and fidgeted. The Richard Chan that sat opposite him was not the Richard Chan he had cheered in the
boxing ring. He was bigger, fatter, older and his face had
that look of mean toughness that was common to every
policeman Ah Au had ever known.

He lit up and sucked quickly at the cigarette. Father
Loyola could obviously influence Chan, and his mother's
piety could influence Father Loyola. There could be some
margin in talking to Chan. He was likely to be more help-
ful than a stranger, and in any case, Ah Au did not know
any other policemen, even at third hand. Talking to Chan
would bring him more benefit than not talking and he
didn't see why he should be punished for what Chi-Wah
had done.

"I want to do a deal with you," Ah Au said.

"That's not how it's worked," Chan replied. "You're
here for assaulting one of your friends and for being in
possession of stolen jewellery — jewellery that was taken
by men with guns from two jewellery stores. You could
get ten for that."

"What will happen if I talk?"

"I can't make promises, I've told you that. All I can
say is that if you help us, we'll help you. We'll recommend
clemency but whether you get it or not is up to the judge."

"What do you think I will get if I co-operate?"

"If you co-operate and we say that it is a first offence
and that you have shown signs of reform, you could get
five years. With remission for good behaviour that'll probably work out at three, three and a half."

"I don't want to go to jail," Ah Au said.

"You should have thought about that before."

"Will I go to the same jail as the others?"

"No, we can prevent that."

Ah Au stared at the floor, smoking furiously and thinking. "What happens if I tell you about something else?"

"That depends on how useful it is."

"How much less will it be? Six months, a year?"

"I can't tell you," Chan said. "All I can say is that we will do our best to get it down as much as we can. We'll do more for you than the friends who left you and ran away."

Ah Au lit a fresh cigarette. Smoking furiously, he told Chan all about Chi-Wah and the jewellery robberies, about the dance hostess and the coffee stall owners. He hoped he would not die for breaking his oath.

Three years, thought Chan, even three months surrounded by hardened criminals would be too much for the boy. Ah Au would come out of prison, tougher, more cunning, concerned not about keeping the law but about not getting caught. Once he went inside Ah Au would be scarred. He would not be able to get a job easily and in this case prison was only the confirmation of a life of crime. Chan believed he knew now how Father Loyola felt when he saw a soul plunge into eternal damnation. Then he reminded himself that his duty was not to reform the prison system, but to bring criminals before the court. What society did with its wrong-doers wasn't Chan's problem, or so he told himself. He still felt uneasy when he finished writing and pushed the completed statement across to Ah Au to sign.

Ah Au took the pen from his grasp and signed it. "Don't you want to read it first?" Chan asked.

Ah Au shook his head. "I'll trust you."

"I'll do what I can," Chan said. For a moment their eyes locked and Chan's heart went out to the boy. When one was young, one had so many alternatives and so little knowledge with which to choose between them.

Ah Au asked, "Can you get back the things they took from me when I was arrested?"

"If they aren't illegal or weapons, yes."

Chan asked a constable to bring Ah Au's jacket and the packet that had been in its pocket. Ah Au took the packet and opened it. "I used to work as a chauffeur for a man called Chiao Te," he said, "the owner of the Pak

Luan Printing Co. When my mother told him about my arrest, he would not even give an advance on my salary for bail."

"Is that why you are telling me this?"

Ah Au shrugged. "Perhaps." A strange expression crossed his face, as if for the first time he realised he was all alone. "Chiao Te had me take these photographs and follow one of these men."

With that Ah Au handed Chan the photograph of Hiroshi Watanabe peering closely at a gilt statue, whose wispy moustache drooped like wet string.

"Why did Chiao Te have you follow this man?"

"I don't know. All I know is what Chiao Te had me do. Then he had me show the photographs to this other man."

He gave Chan a second photograph. It had been taken in the same place as the first, and there peering closely at the statue was Suresh Banerjee, President of the Delhi Foundation.

"Where were these pictures taken?"

"The Shatin Temple. The one with the ten thousand Buddhas."

Shatin wasn't too far away, Chan thought, but if he went there, he'd probably miss evening mass. He grinned. Father Loyola had an obligation to forgive him that.

25

SHATIN WAS NOT far away, except for the Sunday traffic. There were long, grating, shiny queues everywhere, sunshine and the holiday feel of a long weekend driving everyone on to the roads, like wood lice from a burning spar. Crowds in Shatin too, come to eat roast pigeon and play mah-jong. It was a devil's own job, parking.

Opposite the townlet with its four streets, the gaudy three-storey confection of Shatin's floating restaurant, hardly moving on the placid brown waters of Tide Cove. People were still aboard the restaurant, enjoying late lunches, too sensible to spend Sundays looking at statues, or worrying about unsolved murders. Junks and sampans scudded lazily by, a conglomeration of furled masts crowding against the sky delineating the typhoon shelter, getting more crowded as boats returned for tomorrow's Moon Festival. Opposite Tide Cove the dark green mound of Shatin Heights, dotted with white houses and airy roofed pagodas, earth partitions neatly separating the rice fields on the lower slopes. Not for nothing was Shatin once known as the Emperor's rice bowl. Chan had to go above the rice fields, past the pink pagoda to the summit of Shatin Heights. What a way to spend a sunny, Sunday afternoon.

He set off along a concrete embankment, bordered by a railway line and rows of houses. Dogs rushed up to fences and barked at him, trains shuffed past, he began to sweat. At the end of the path, a complex of souvenir shops and restaurants, fish tanks full of crabs and prawns and eel and grouper. Touts too, offering statues and carved bowls, seats in their restaurants, seducing tourists and locals alike.

Beyond the shopping area, cement steps cut into the green hillside, gushing drains and dark huts set well back. A fairground, shrill screams of children, tinny wail of cassettes, a merry-go-round of gigantic fish and ducks and rabbits, truncated elephants, gigantic mice, whirling its treadmill round to the clatter of an old diesel engine. Blossom and Tony would have enjoyed that.

Chan went on, the serious part of the climb still before him. The steps became steeper, the dingy huts more isolated. Water from a broken drain flowed sluggishly green over the worn steps. Gradually the people and the houses were left behind. A few pilgrims or sightseers only in this kind of weather. He climbed steadily, accompanied by the sound of his deep breathing and the scrape of his feet against the cement. His calves began to hurt and there were shooting pains in the front of his thighs, the constant repetitive motion bringing on a dullness of muscle and mind. There was a time when he used to do six miles of road work a day, when these steps would have been no more than a test of fitness. Now it was something more than that. He willed himself not to stop and sit at the shady stalls along the way, which sold soft drinks.

Banerjee and Watanabe had climbed the self-same path, to look at this statue, and it wasn't because they shared the same religious belief. Had their pilgrimage something to do with the war? Had Bose once sought sanctuary in this place? And what of Chiao Te? Why was he helping Banerjee? And why had Banerjee not told Chan about this visit?

Questions, always questions. That's what investigating this murder had been about. Why couldn't he have a simple case, an open and shut one, with clear evidence, plenty of witnesses and one suspect? That would at least have saved him shoe leather, tramping up mountains in this heat. But where was the excitement in that?

He laboured on, past a house cordoned off from the steps by wire netting, its garden overgrown, windows shuttered, crumbling walls stained with dirt. Strange it should still be empty. Too arduous for the squatters to get to, he supposed.

The climb became slightly less steep, the steps branching out in alternative looping routes. Through the trees above he could see the red roofs of the buildings, look horizontally across at the pink pagoda. Not far to go, he would make it in one. At the top he stopped and leant against the balustrade panting, clothes clutching at him in a cold embrace, feeling there was life in the old muscles yet, still able to take on a challenge, though he felt like a wrung-out rag. Voices of fit and foolhardy pilgrims floated up to him as his pulse pounded steadily in his head and he looked about the temple grounds.

There were three temples built on the flat of the summit, modern brick constructions with tiled roofs. They were connected by a broad footpath, fringed with trees, muddy where the sun had not yet reached it. To the left of the summit a row of steps, an open soft drinks stall, a large platform of earth cut out of the hillside. Where the platform jutted out over the sloping hillside, the pagoda.

Chan went down and looked. Opposite the pagoda a large brick building, a refrigerated Coke machine in the entrance, a gigantic golden Buddha in the middle and its walls lined from floor to ceiling with row upon row of foot high seated Buddhas. All gold, all glistening, all valuable. Chan bought himself a Coke and thought it must be a very practical religion that did not allow business to interfere with it.

The area between the pagoda and the temple was a courtyard lined with outhouses, whose tiled roofs and brick pillars sheltered gigantic statues, blue pop-eyed dogs, white elephants, rows of sages playing with animals or wrestling with bears. In the centre an immense statue of a Chinese woman, all in white seated on a throne and mounted on a pedestal decorated with artichoke leaves.

The pilgrims in the courtyard and wandering through the Shrine of the 10,000 Buddhas were informal, laughing, talking, taking pictures. A happy religion, Chan thought.

The statue he was looking for was not amongst the 10,000 Buddhas, nor was it in the pagoda. He went into the first of the temples on the summit, a rectangular room dominated by gigantic gilt statues seated in front of the altar and standing upright, like guards, on the sides. An old man sold joss-sticks by the entrance while devotees burnt these at a separate table before the seated giants.

The second temple was much the same. The same result too.

It was in the third and topmost temple that Chan found what he was looking for. There, on a stand beside the altar, dwarfed by the gigantic idols around it, was the statue of the man with the wispy moustache. It was life size, seated in a contemplative position. With horrifying shock, Chan realised that the hair of the moustache was real. Bose? But then he didn't have a moustache and he looked different. Chan reached out and touched the statue. It felt solid and it had that peculiar dull sheen about it that evidenced pure gold.

What was so significant about the statue? Chan turned to the black garbed man selling joss-sticks and showed him the photographs of Banerjee and Watanabe. The man did not recognise them. There were so many visitors and he not only had to sell joss-sticks, he had to see that visitors didn't make the place untidy.

"The statue? Who is it?"

The man made obeisance and said, "That is a former superior of the temple. He died five years ago."

And what had he to do with Bose and Watanabe and Banerjee, and treasure that had been hijacked at the end of the Second World War. Chan placed a ten dollar bill in the man's collection box and started to walk down the hill. Mr. Banerjee, he felt, owed him a detailed explanation.

*　　*　　*

A lengthy, sweaty drive to Hong Kong side, another five dollars to use the cross-harbour tunnel. Too many cars, Chan thought, too many people, that was the trouble with Hong Kong. One day, everything would jam up solid. Not today though, looking for a parking place.

He locked the car and walked quickly past the squad of Mercedes under the hotel porch, past the blue-uniformed Sikh doormen with their magnificent turbans, through the tall doors into the vast lobby.

The Chinese girl behind the avenue-long reception desk repeated Banerjee's name to herself, checked it on the guest list and said Banerjee occupied room 637. She threw a fast glance at the row of pigeon holes behind her and said he was probably in his room. Chan said that was fine and made for the lift.

Leaping bell boy, humming doors, the smooth rush of ascent and he stepped on to a dim landing opposite gleaming shop windows advertising perfume and clothes. He strode down a dim passageway, blue and red lighting. Room 637 was four doors from the ice container.

Chan knocked twice, loudly. Silence. He knocked again. Still silence. Banerjee was either asleep or out. Chan brought out his ring of skeleton keys. He owed Banerjee something for not telling him about the statue.

Behind the easily opened door a short corridor, an open recess with coat hangers to the right, bathroom on the left, the room decorated in rich blue, widening out beyond the corridor to take two beds and a fitted dressing table. Beyond the beds a small alcove and a picture window, a view of a large terrace and the back of a block of flats, balconies decorated with the day's washing.

A nice room, a comfortable room. Only one thing wrong with it, though. There was no sign of Banerjee. There were no clothes, no suitcases, no toothpaste in the bathroom, no slippers under the bed. A single stubbed out Stuyevesant in the ashtray, room service slips, a Sunday paper and a brochure from Hong Kong Air in the waste basket. Chan took out the brochure, looked at the figures scrawled in red biro along the margin. Flight times and prices, hurried answers to a telephone call, perhaps nothing to do with Hong Kong anyway.

He crumpled the brochure into his pocket and went down to the lobby. The receptionist was definite, Mr. Banerjee was in room 637. She turned the guest list round so that he could see it. Chan stared at it puzzling, became aware of a figure sidling along the counter towards him.

A European about Chan's height, blue eyes, a zapata moustache, black jacket and striped trousers, good for weddings, births and funerals. Good for an assistant manager too. "Can I help you, sir?"

The girl blurted out that Chan was looking for Mr. Banerjee and that his room was empty.

The assistant manager eased him away from the counter towards the centre of the lobby. "You are a friend of his, sir?"

"No," Chan said. "Police."

The manager looked at him, thoughtfully. "You must be aware then, sir, that Mr. Banerjee was arrested an hour ago."

"Why?" Chan blurted it out before he realised his stupidity. He turned quickly and rushed out of the lobby, climbed into his car and drove to Lockhart Road.

The offices of the Delhi Foundation were unusually busy for a Sunday. Five men under the command of a strange sergeant were searching it as if they expected to find emeralds under the lino. They were looking for seditious literature the sergeant said, returning Chan's warrant card. Everyone was under arrest. Mr. Datt, too. Inspector Winston was in command of the operation.

Chan heard Winston's voice as he stepped out of the lift, marched straight up to Winston's office, flung open the door.

"Talk of the devil," the AC said from behind Winston's desk. "The very man we wanted to see." He was in a nasty mood, having been pulled away from the tables in Macau when his luck was running well. Pete Winston was slouched sideways across a chair, opposite the AC, looking at Chan over his shoulder.

"Inspector Chan, I thought I asked you to leave that murder investigation alone till after the rally?"

"I thought it was a request, sir," realising how feeble that sounded, Winston smiling at it too.

"It was an expression of my wishes, man, a polite order. Surely you know we haven't the time or the men to spare worrying about dead Indians."

Murdering Indians was still a crime, Chan thought. A policeman's job was to find criminals not spy on students.

"I understand you saw Mr. Hiroshi Watanabe in connection with this so-called investigation of yours. You confiscated his passport."

"He surrendered it voluntarily, sir." Chan hated the sheepishness in his tone, the cheekiness of Winston's grin. "There were new leads in the murder case — I was following them — "

"And in the process nearly blew the whole operation. You must know Inspector Winston and his team have been working hard, working patiently over the past few days to prevent a catastrophe in this Colony. And you nearly blew it." The AC's moustache twitched irritably. He stared angrily at Chan and went on, "Mr. Watnabe is staying at the Peninsula as a guest of the British Government. He is the most important source of information we have as to this whole arms business. You nearly sent him back to Japan. Do you realise what that would have meant?" The AC turned to Winston. "Tell him."

Winston wiped the smile from his face, looked serious and responsible. "It would have been an end to the operations," he said. "We would never have been able to find out that the arms are being landed tomorrow, how they were going to be brought in or anything. If not for Watanabe, next Sunday we would have had riots."

"Many more people would have been killed than your precious Indian," the AC pointed out. "And it would have all been your fault."

"I didn't realise — "

"You must understand, Inspector, that this arms thing is very important. Not only are we now able to prevent a revolution, but we can stop that confounded rally. At one stroke, an insurgent movement and goodbye bring back Godber."

Goodbye embarrassment to the police department and exposure of corruption too, Chan thought. All this because Godber was European. If he had been Chinese they would all be shaking heads over their whisky-sodas saying, what could you expect.

"I want to make this very clear, Inspector Chan, on no account, and I repeat on no account, will you see, talk or concern yourself in anyway with Mr. Watanabe. That is a direct order. You will also cease this so-called investigation of yours forthwith. That also is a direct order. Do you understand?"

Chan nodded, not trusting himself to speak. He understood the words all right. The AC had been got at, by or through Winston, by Wan Liu or Watanabe or British Intelligence. It looked like Banerjee had been right after all, though what the hell did it matter now. He was being reprimanded, prevented from doing his job.

"I will have no hesitation," the AC was saying, "In having you up on a disciplinary charge if you so much as think of seeing Watanabe or proceeding with this lunatic investigation."

Chan drew himself up to attention, tight lipped.

"I have had Watanabe's passport returned to him," the AC said. He brushed a hand across his eyes, wearily, then smiled to show that he had only been doing his job. That he had been fair.

Sometimes the police force was like being back at school. Chan remembered school masters like that, they walloped you and told you it hurt them more than it hurt you.

The AC asked, "Now what is it you wanted to see Inspector Winston about?"

"About Banerjee." Chan turned to Winston. "You've arrested him?"

"That's right," making an effort to be serious, making a great show of taking the smile from his face.

"On what charge?"

"Arms smuggling."

"On what evidence?"

Winston's attitude showed that he could afford to be kind. "Come on Richard, we all know you can't make an arrest without evidence."

Except you, you bastard, Chan thought. If you didn't have the evidence, you'd plant it. "Where is Banerjee?"

"Pokfulam."

Chan knew the place, it was called the Victoria Detention Centre, undoubtedly a building of which that old Queen would have approved. "I'd like to see him."

"Sorry old boy, I know he's a friend of yours and all that, but no can do. He's being held under a DAO." DAO, Deportation of Aliens Order, Ch.240, an act under which non-British residents could be held and deported without trial.

"No visitors," Winston continued. "He's going to be telling us a lot about arms smuggling."

Fuck you, Chan thought, fuck the lot of you, rushing out of the office, going down the steps, tears of rage and frustration and most of all shame stinging his eyes.

26

THE NEXT DAY, the day of the Moon Festival was gorgeous, a brilliantly white sun, silvery blue sky, you couldn't tell it was the beginning of autumn. Chan looked at the sun-covered Peak and wondered what to do. He didn't have to work today. Correction, he didn't have any work he wanted to do. The memory of the previous afternoon still filled him with shame.

Li-li was in the kitchen, baking honey-sweet moon cakes that would dribble on the tongue, and stick to the teeth. Tony's kite was assembled, holding pride of place by the front door, ready for flying on the Peak that night. Chan wondered about the brochure from Hong Kong Air that he had found in Banerjee's room. What was Banerjee doing with helicopters? The man had been to Hong Kong before. He was working, arranging solidarity with the students, holding press conferences, hiring loudspeakers. No time for idle helicopter tours. Perhaps it was something to do with arms smuggling and Chiao Te. Banerjee an arms smuggler? A frustrated childhood there, a raving idealism. It was not impossible.

Chiao Te? Not a nice man, refusing bail for Ah Au, but then Ah Au wasn't very pretty either. He should see Chiao Te. He shouldn't see Chiao Te. He shouldn't even think about this lunatic investigation. That was what the AC had said.

Chan considered the alternatives. They, the faceless ones, they were stronger than he was, the police department, the triads, Wan Liu, Watanabe, British Intelligence for God's sake, perhaps even the CIA. If Chan saw Chiao Te and was found out he would be on a disciplinary charge, followed by interdiction, probably expulsion. He couldn't imagine life without a police station to go to, without police business to do. What did an ex-CID Inspector do for a living? A European like Thompson could become Head of Security at a bank. But for Chan, guard duty outside a jewellery store, night watchman; much worse than being a constable.

Besides, what about Li-li and the children? He had a duty to them, too. The consequence of free will was the problem of choice. Even with a gun pointed at your head you could choose to live or die. Some choice. He must ask Father Loyola about that, sometime.

Last night Lau had been consoling, Hanson embarrassed. Li-li had said, "You do what you think right. That's what you do."

Surely it wasn't as simple as that. Life couldn't be that simple. Unless not living made it so. There were always consequences, memories of an incense-filled college chapel dyed blue and yellow from the cheap stained-glass windows, and somewhere behind the altar, hell and punishment.

"You have to live free," Li-li had said. "Better to starve in the stomach than in the heart." *Ei ya!* He was over dramatising everything. He wasn't going to do anything about Raghavan's murder. Nothing, nothing at all, except maybe slip down to Harcourt Road and talk to Hong Kong Air.

They were very busy at Hong Kong Air. It was a holiday and all the scheduled tours were fully booked. They didn't have much time to talk with a policeman about an Indian. Chan waited in the refreshment bar, watching the helicopters fluttering over the concrete pads like giant insects. After about an hour, the pilot who had flown Banerjee came in, a clear-eyed smiling Chinese, totally unworried by the rush or about talking to a policeman. He had half an hour before his next flight, he said. Chan bought him coffee and asked about Banerjee.

The pilot remembered Banerjee, even without the photograph. There weren't that many Indians in Hong Kong, not that many people who chartered a chopper three times a week. The first time, Banerjee had been flown by someone else, a lengthy trip over every single one of Hong Kong's two hundred and thirty-six islands. The second time, they had gone together in the Alouette. He had taken Banerjee to East Ninepin Island. Last Thursday, Banerjee had come with a friend, another Indian, a tiny, nervous man with spaniel eyes and they had flown again to East Ninepin Island. Banerjee and his companion had remained there all afternoon, asking to be picked up just before dark. It was a strange place for a picnic, the pilot said, but then everyone knew that to be very rich, you had to be crazy.

You had to be crazy to be a policeman too. Chan spoke to the Marine Police about lending him a launch to get to East Ninepin. Policemen couldn't afford helicopters at 240 US dollars an hour. The Marine Police were reluctant. A launch wasn't due to East Ninepin till next Thursday, but when Chan told them it had to do with the alert on arms smuggling, they agreed to take him as far as Lam Tong and let him hire his own transport from there.

* * *

The island was an uninhabited hill, covered with trees and undergrowth, surrounded by a narrow ring of beach. Chan felt unutterably lonely as the launch churned away, leaving him with the indentations on the sand, made by the Alouette. The cry of birds and the rustling of small creatures in the thicket worried him. Chan was a city person, and nature was strange and frightening. He drew his gun and followed the line of scuffed footprints into the trees.

Away from the beach the land rose steeply, with lush

undergrowth and thick trees blocking out the sun. Chan wished he had worn something more practical than an every-day office suit, and that he had brought a *kukri* to hack his way up the hill. He tried to follow the path Banerjee and Datt had taken, but after a while his early boy scout training deserted him and he had to plunge on, knee deep in creepers, sweating profusely, cut off from light and enveloped in steamy air.

Fortunately he did not have far to go. The island was small and the hill was steep. The plane had barely cleared the top of the hill before it had smashed into the trees, tearing off a stubby wing and slithering through the undergrowth on its belly to stop with its single propellor flattened against the earth.

The plane looked part of the jungle now, coloured a uniform grey-green and trees had grown up close around it, protecting it from view except directly from above. The canopy had been ripped open and the seating had rotted away. Chan looked at the buckled controls, the trailing belts, at the layers of leaves and earth that filled the cockpit and felt an eerie thrill of horror, alone in this mausoleum of trees where years ago, a plane had crashed and men had died.

He stifled the impulse to run back to the beach, away from the spirits of the dead. From the tail-high angle at which it had landed, and the fact that apart from the torn wing and the twisted fuselage, it was still pretty much in one piece, Chan deduced that the plane had been losing height sharply and had been travelling slow. It had been coming from the east, from the direction of Taiwan. He walked round to the raised tail and looked closely at the holes in the fabric, evenly spaced as if they had been drilled there by a mechanical punch. Only it hadn't been a punch but a .50 mm machine gun that had shot away the rudder controls. Lost, probably low on fuel, out of control and losing height rapidly, the plane had just cleared the summit of the hill and crashed.

It had been a single engined aircraft, stocky looking, its under-carriage retracted, as if the pilot had been hoping for a belly flop in the sea. Chan reached up to the fuselage and rubbed. Gradually, the dirt and the sticky deposit of leaves came away and the markings showed through, not the blood red sun of Japan, but the green cross and white background that was the emblem of surrender.

Chan found himself remembering a colouring book that he had once had, soon after the war. It was a time when children's books were scarce and it had been found by his father in a second-hand stall. The book had been in Japanese and contained pictures of Japanese aeroplanes, the famous Zero-Sen, the G3 M2 Mitsubishi bomber that had sunk the *Prince of Wales* and the *Repulse*, the Ki 43 Hayabusa and the Hayate dive bomber. There had been a plane like this in the book too. It was known as the Heavenly Mountain, the Nakajima B6 M2 Tenzan, and it had been used extensively in kamikaze attacks at the end of the war. He remembered Kate Meiwa too. The plane was a three-seater torpedo bomber and if when it had crashed it had been flying with a full complement, what had happened to the crew.

The canopy was open and there were no skeletons strapped to the seats. Chan remembered that Banerjee had spent a long time on the island, and left the plane and walked. In a short while he came across the path that Banerjee and Datt had taken to the graves. The earth looked freshly turned and there were only two of them.

*   *   *

One person had walked away from that crash, Chan reflected, sitting on the unyielding bench of the fishing launch, wind whipping at his clothes, covering his face with salt. Someone had killed and walked away. Watanabe, flying from Taiwan with Bose's treasure on board. He could see how it all fitted together. Saito Chu had told Raghavan about the unloading of the plane, Mrs.

Meiwa had told Raghavan of the flight. Raghavan had identified Watanabe and Watanabe had had him killed, called upon Wan Liu's assistance to do that. Killed the old man too and Wan Liu, under pressure had made a sacrificial offering of two bodies, which that fool Winston had accepted.

Only one thing to find out now, what had happened to the treasure? Banerjee could tell him, but he couldn't see Banerjee. Couldn't see Watanabe either. Couldn't? Who would know if he did.

Chan got back to Kowloon that afternoon and drove straight to the Peninsula. No enquiring at the desk, this time he marched straight through the lobby and into the lift, went up to the eighth floor. His hand was raised to knock on Watanabe's door when slim fingers coiled around his wrist. A Chinese, about his height and weight, crew cut hair, bush shirt, slacks and sandals.

"No visitors," the Chinese said, his grip tightening around Chan's wrist.

"Police," Chan said.

"I know," the man replied. "I recognise you, Inspector Chan. Mr. Winston said we should expect you. My name is Ling, Special Branch. I will thank you to come with me."

*　　*　　*

The meeting with the AC was short and brutal. There was no defence for disobeying a direct order, no explanations for using a police launch for apparently private purposes.

"You are interdicted as from now," the AC said. "You will leave your gun and your warrant card at Wan Chai Station and remain on paid leave till the hearing. I will see that you have a copy of the charges as soon as possible."

And that was it. A lifetime of police work blown, because of stubbornness and insatiable curiosity and a dead Indian.

27

So MUCH FOR doing what one had to do. So much for honesty and devotion to duty. Chan slunk out of the police station grateful there was no one there to speak to, because of the holiday.

It was a good thing, Li-li said. He needed a rest. Lately he had been tense and grouchy as an old bear. At the hearing everyone would know that he had done right, they would acquit him, with commendation, wasn't that the word they used. Chan couldn't help smiling. Li-li's belief in the ultimate triumph of good was touching. Tonight, Li-li said was the Moon Festival. He was to cheer up and come to the Peak with them and not worry about a thing.

Chan couldn't face going out with Li-li and her family, pretending nothing was wrong, side-stepping questions about his murder case, wondering if they knew and if he should tell them. He drove Li-li and the children over to his father-in-law's and returned home. That wasn't such a good idea. He missed Li-li's presence, the constant clatter of the children. His thoughts in the empty flat were grim, stained with depression and defeat. If they contented themselves with knocking him back to sergeant, he would be lucky. They'd lose the flat though, lose all hope of a superintendent's car.

At precisely ten minutes past six, his new car, the auspiciously yellow Ford Cortina, bought with a two-year loan from the Special Police Fund, exploded in a searing yellow ball of flame, making a noise that made the whole building tremble and shattered the windows of the flats on the first and second floors.

Chan looked in disbelief, then in anger. If it had been a normal working day, that was the time at which he would have left the station. Today, he might have been taking Li-li and the children somewhere.

He raced down the stairs, ignoring the people gaping at the smouldering car, ran past the wreck, down the hill. They weren't satisfied with taking his job away from him, they weren't going to stop till they'd killed him and his family too. Well he'd see about that. Let other people call the police. Let the car become a police problem. Watanabe and Wan Liu were his.

He found a taxi and went to the Peninsula, fretting furiously at the traffic, impatient at the delays in the tunnel. At the hotel, he jumped out while the taxi was still moving, ran past the surprised doorman, across the lobby and into the lift. Now that he had nothing to lose, he was prepared for the SB man, for Winston, even the AC. He raced along deep carpet, didn't bother to knock. The skeleton keys rasped in and out of the lock. The door opened and he stepped inside.

Watanabe was not there.

He went back again to the lobby, thinking more clearly now. He had an urgent message for Mr. Watanabe from the Commissioner of Police. If that was so, would he be so kind and leave it. Chan said he couldn't do that. The message had to be delivered personally. Then would he please wait. Mr. Watanabe was out, but he would come back soon. Mr. Watanabe was leaving Hong Kong that night.

Interesting information, but where was Watanabe now? Someone must have seen him leave.

Someone had. The doorman had seen Watanabe go out an hour ago. He had been driven away in a new Mercedes

229

limousine. The doorman remembered the special number plates, too. WL1. Mr. Wan Liu's new motor car.

Chan used the phone in the lobby, pretended he was a police informer. Ten of Wan Liu's places were going to be hit tonight, and he had missed a meet with Wan Liu at the Peninsula. It was vital he should speak to Wan Liu now. Yes, he knew everything had been paid, but there was this Inspector Chan, who was determined to break Wan Liu. The voice at the other end of the line said Wan Liu would either be at the Sun Sun Trade Association or at the warehouse. What warehouse? Oh yes, he'd try both places and if he missed them, he'd try to see Wan Liu at home.

The warehouse was near the Shell oil depot in Kwan Tong. Chan hailed a taxi, sped rapidly away from the brightly lit, touristy atmosphere of Nathan Road, past resettlement areas and housing estates, past factories and partly demolished buildings, past cranes silhouetted against the skyline. Already, the lanterns were beginning to glow.

The warehouse was an ugly, square building, eight stories high, crowding by the waterfront. High walls around it, high gates, a watchman who believed that it wasn't what went in that mattered, but what came out.

Chan paid off the taxi by Wan Liu's Mercedes, walked up to the narrow entrance on the left of the building. Narrow doorway, narrow corridor, narrow stairs leading to offices on the upper floors. There was the sound of hammering from the warehouse on the ground floor. Chan slid open the heavy wooden doors and looked. Two young men in spotless white overalls working on something that looked like a cross-section of a bridge. Only it had seats and they seemed to be mounting an engine on it. Inventors or motor enthusiasts, preparing for the Macau Grand Prix.

The men turned and looked at him, smiling.

"Security," Chan said. "Just checking. Please carry on."

He went up the stairs to the first floor. Narrow corridors, hardboard partitions, an air of grimy abandonment. Wan Liu and Watanabe were seated in an office at the end, slightly larger than the rest, a metal table between them with an empty bottle of Coke and a wad of money. Behind them, a grimy window looked out across the darkening harbour.

Watanabe was nearest to him. Chan seized him by the front of his jacket, lifted him out of his chair, slapped him viciously across the face, twice. Watanabe's head whipped sideways, his glasses flew across the room and Chan dropped him back in the chair watching him reach for a handkerchief, wipe the blood that trickled out of the corner of his mouth.

"Now let's talk about murder," Chan said.

Wan Liu had remained impassive. He wasn't the kind of man who carried his own gun. Looking cautiously at Chan he bent down and gave Watanabe his glasses, miraculously intact. "I thought the question of the Indian's murder was over," he said quietly.

"No," Chan said. "Nor is the question of the murder of the other Indian." He looked back at Watanabe. "Tell me about Subhas Chandra Bose," he said. "Tell me how you sabotaged his plane and stole his treasure. Tell me how you flew to East Ninepin Island and how you killed your companions. Tell me where the treasure is now."

"One of them died in the crash," Watanabe said. "The other would not have lived."

Wan Liu bared his gold teeth. "If it is money, Inspector . . ."

Chan ignored him. "You couldn't have Raghavan tell the truth about you, could you?" he asked. "There were Japanese aboard that plane. Lieutenant-Colonel Shidei, head of the Burma Army Command. He died too. You couldn't have your people know, even thirty years after, that you'd killed your own for money."

"It wasn't the money," Watanabe said softly, "it was the principle. You would not understand." He exchanged glances with Wan Liu. Then he continued speaking, softly. "It was a very different time. The gold, the money did not belong to Bose. It was ours, and it was my job to get it back. I am a soldier, a samurai. I had a duty to keep on fighting. The money was needed for a government in exile. It belongs to Japan. The new Japan that will replace the brothel that it is now, that will bring back the old values, the lasting ones."

He was staring intently at Chan. Chan stared back, waiting for the old man to continue. Staring, he felt a cool fanning of air behind his head, turned. He glimpsed a politely smiling figure in spotless white overalls. Then the butt of the gun crashed against his head. There was nothing polite about that.

Chan felt his knees go like snapped elastic. He'd felt like that once before, when he had been knocked out in the ring. There had been the same explosion of sound, the same flash of light, the same sudden blackness.

*   *   *

The master of the *Flying Dragon* saw the first fishing boats, their great spars extended sideways like birds in frozen flight, shut off his diesel engine and raised the square, battened sails. He shouted to his son to see that everyone was packed and that they had got everything. He also asked him to see that the small boy had finished pasting up the decals.

At the same time the *Misty Dragon* picked its way through the teeming traffic of Hong Kong Harbour, its sails furled, its propellers churning out a thin stream of white. It rode high, the ensign fluttering from its mast as it hooted opposite the customs point, slowing down momentarily and acknowledging permission with a wave.

*   *   *

Pete Winston walked tiredly into the station and took the stairs up to the first floor. He moved slowly, with shoulders bowed, head sunk on his chest, avoiding contact with people, a fugitive from the frenzied streets outside.

The British Airways flight had established nothing. Every passenger had been body searched, their luggage minutely examined. The crew had been made to wait while every item of air-freighted cargo was examined and checked to the plane's manifest. The plane itself had been vigorously searched and the steward compelled to open his stores of liquor and duty-free cigarettes. There had been nothing that even remotely looked like a crate of the right size, nothing that remotely looked like a weapon.

He sat behind his desk and looked at the day's messages. He was in charge of Wan Chai CID now. Everything that should have come to Chan had come to him, including a telex from an Inspector in Taiwan. Hiroshi Watanabe, it said, had been Head of Security in Taiwan on August 18th, 1945. He had disappeared on the 19th and had not returned to Japan till 1952. In the interim, he had spent four years working with the Kuomintang in Mainland China.

Ridiculous message, Winston thought. What had Watanabe to do with Raghavan's murder. Besides the case was over. He had closed it. His case was over too, except he would have many lengthy explanations to make. He let his eyes wander over the message, before pushing it aside. If Chan wanted more information about Watanabe's past, the message concluded, he should talk to Chiao Te of the Pak Luan Printing Co.

Winston put the message away and got to his feet. Chiao Te was someone he had to speak to as well, for a completely different reason.

*   *   *

His head was tight as a drum, full to bursting, a pain down its centre like a red hot knife. He opened his eyes, stared unbelievingly, shut them again, feeling the sickness fill the back of his throat, threaten to clog his nostrils. With an effort he swallowed. He opened his mouth, breathed, opened his eyes again and looked.

Stars glistened whitely against the black velvet of the sky, clouds raced across the moon. He saw ships bathed in light surrounded by tugs and lighters, *wallah-wallahs* bouncing cheekily on ruffled water, huge black and white, two-tiered ferries churning majestically towards North Point. He could see Central, a blaze of light and unwinking neon signs, and the Peak, a fairyland of lanterns. He could see them all clearly, though it was all far away, far below and upside down.

Fear quickening in spasms Chan realised he was suspended by his feet along the side of a high building. Slowly he brought his gaze nearer, looked out of the top of his head, a hundred and fifty chilling feet at a wharf the size of a cricket pitch, trucks and trains like children's toys, the sheer straight walls of the building stretching endlessly along empty air to the toy pavement below.

He folded his head into his chest, looked up at his bound feet, twelve inches of grimy wall below the windowsill. Darkened windows like sightless eyes, a flat roof and a mast topped with a red light. His head was pulsing fit to split and a cool breeze tugged at his sweat damp body. God alone knew how long he'd been there. Much longer and the engorged blood vessels in his brain would burst.

He filled his lungs and screamed, his body bumping against the wall, dropping. He was pulled up with a sharp jerk. Screamed again. Another drop, definite now, his back scraping the wall. He stopped screaming. He tried to stop moving. If he remained still he was all right. His feet and whatever was holding him up were joined by a series of slip knots. Each time he moved a knot parted, threatening to free him from the whole contraption and send him hurtling to the pavement a hundred and fifty feet below.

He remained still, trying to fight the gentle breeze, the steady force that pulled his body downwards. Oblivion! Death! If they wanted to kill him why hadn't they thrown him out of the window while he was unconscious? That could only mean they wanted to teach him a lesson, that they would be back to free him. But if they intended that, they wouldn't have used the slip knots. Hanging head downwards a hundred and fifty feet above the ground was torture enough.

Chan knew they meant him to die, meant his death to look like suicide. Most of all they meant him to suffer the awful torture of enforced paralysis till he gave up, broke free and died.

Winston would call it an open and shut case. The area around warehouses was filled with scattered bits of rope and Chan had attended enough coroners inquests to know they wouldn't look beyond the obvious. He'd been in serious trouble with his job, he'd been worried and depressed when his family had left him, he had taken his life while temporarily insane, no one asking why he had jumped off the eighth floor of a warehouse building in Kwan Tong when he could have done it just as easily from the balcony of his flat.

He opened his eyes. They were fiery, feeling as if they were being pushed out of his head by red hot pokers. He could see the Peak. Li-li and the children were there, amongst those fairy lanterns. He should have gone with them, left the Raghavan case alone, been less curious, much less involved. That way he would have had a job now, he wouldn't be hanging out of a window too frightened to move. It would have been a different kind of a life, but better that than being a dead cop.

His very helplessness made him angry. It would have been easier to bear if he had been trussed tight, able to vent his fury against his bonds. The freedom to move and the fear of moving was a hideous, subtle torture draining away his courage, his confidence, his will to live. He was so frustrated he could scream and his anger combined with his unnatural posture sent the blood pounding through his head forcing him to shut his eyes, go nearly unconscious. Chan gagged, feeling the vomit run out of his mouth and up his nostrils, over his forehead.

He forced himself to remain still, to try to think clearly, to form a plan. No good planning if he didn't dare move. Perhaps someone would see him. No he must be realistic. There was little chance of that, not till daylight anyway and by then he would be killed by a burst blood vessel or by crashing to the pavement below. Shouting only threatened to unleash him quicker, not that anyone on a boat could hear him over the clatter of the diesels or that there was anyone on the wharf. He had a sudden horrifying vision of his freed body wheeling past darkened windows, down the tall side of the building, smashing on to the unyielding concrete below, his skull cracking like an egg. He looked at the Peak again, gay with the lights of the festival. At least like every other Chinese he was on high ground, he thought wryly and settled down to think.

If he moved gently, unwound the knots one at a time, perhaps he could lower himself slowly to the ground. No, they wouldn't have left him a hundred and fifty feet of rope. *They meant him to die.* He repeated that slowly to himself. They meant him to die. Another thought. There was nothing he could do about it.

He looked down. A glowing white of a neon sign twenty feet below, a window ledge, much closer, but still an impossible distance away. If he could only get his hands on that window ledge he might be able to manoeuvre his body into the building. He looked down again at the Lilliputian world below. The window ledge was about ten feet away from his straining fingertips.

He coughed. Nothing happened. Coughed louder and swung himself away from the wall. That worked. His back slapped against the wall, his head slipped six inches down-wards. Fine. Another cough, another swing, eyes fixed on his fingertips, feet pressed together, clammy sweat breaking out all over his body, running over his palms. He tried not to think of the awful emptiness below his head, of the solidity of earth below. He moved, swung out again, coughed, felt his shoulders scrape the wall, his body drop.

236

The throbbing in his head increased, his face felt flushed and swollen, the Harbour and the Peak blurred before his tearing eyes.

He swung out again, bang, dropped. He was getting better at it. Again. Again. He was dropping just the right amount each time. Fine. Fine. Ten, twenty more times and he'd reach the ledge — if the rope held out, if the knots held. His fingers were tingling, his head bursting, he brushed his damp palms against the wall. Bump, jerk, sag, hold. He was going to do it! He was going to do it! Once more. Bump, jerk —

His legs sprung free. His body wheeled. He had a whirling vision of stars and rippling water, of fairy lights and blackened windows, the light glowing red above the mast.

Chan screamed as he fell.

28

THE JUNKS SHOWED no lights, clung together like mating spiders, dark shadows against the moon-rippled sea. The Captain of the *Flying Dragon* carried his youngest grandson over the creeking gap between the boats. The only sounds were those of slapping water and low pitched voices as the crews were exchanged.

A few minutes later the *Misty Dragon* pulled away with a stammering clatter from its diesels. It travelled half a mile before its navigation lights blinked on and by then it was wallowing heavily in the open sea.

The *Flying Dragon* turned in a wide arc and headed diagonally away from the meeting place, towards Macau. Only it wasn't called the *Flying Dragon* any more. It looked like and was to all intents and purposes, the *Misty Dragon*, the junk that had slipped out of Hong Kong a few hours before and was so innocuously familiar to the Customs authorities in Macau.

*   *   *

Chiao Te came into Winston's office walking very upright between two policemen. He was neatly dressed in a dark suit and gleaming shoes, making the policemen look like escorts rather than captors. Winston waved the policemen away and beckoned Chiao Te to sit. Chiao Te did so, carefully.

A careful, assured man this, despite the softness of his dimpled cheeks and the flat hair style that made him look like an unsuccessful bank clerk. Winston shook out a cigarette from the pack on his desk and lit it. Immediately Chiao Te fingered a gun-metal case, flicked a Ronson, not asking permission, behaving as if he were making a social call.

The bastard knew his rights, Winston thought, a very different can of beans to Banerjee. Chiao Te wasn't going to scream if he was touched. Indeed, he didn't look the kind of man who could be broken that way. Look at the relaxed way he sat, without indignation, without demanding to know why he had been brought there. Winston started to tell him.

"You paid Suresh Banerjee $47,700. Why?"

Shrewd eyes behind rimless glasses summed up Winston. "You have Banerjee at Pokfulam?" Then, without waiting for an answer, "I could tell you I paid him for paper. Paper prices are always increasing. It is good business to buy stocks now." He paused, again looked shrewdly at Winston, somehow giving the impression he was already two moves ahead. "But I did not pay Banerjee for paper."

"For what, then?"

"For what he has told you already. I paid him for arms."

Winston was nonplussed. He had expected the usual evasions, denials, demands for legal representation. What was the man trying to do? Exchange co-operation for police help in mitigating his sentence? Let's put the boot in, Winston thought, and see how he likes that. "That makes it nice and simple," he said. "I'm going to take you downstairs and charge you."

"I have committed no offence," Chiao Te said with icy contempt.

"What the hell do you mean, no offence? Smuggling arms is a very serious offence."

"You only have jurisdiction in Hong Kong. The arms were never in Hong Kong. They were never intended to be in Hong Kong." He looked at his gold-banded watch. "At this precise moment the arms you are looking for are in four vegetable trucks trundling through the Portas do Cerco into Communist China. That is not an offence for which I can be charged in Hong Kong."

Indeed it wasn't. In fact, smuggling arms to China was something of which Pete Winston approved. But Watanabe had said differently. "What about the students?" Winston asked.

"I am Taiwanese," Chiao Te said. "I was an Officer in the Kuomintang. I have fought against Mao. Your Special Branch has a file which says I am suspected of being a Nationalist agent. What would I be doing starting an uprising in Hong Kong to kick the British out and bring the Communists in?"

What indeed? Winston felt his carefully structured world turning inside out. Chiao Te's facts were incontestable. For the first time he wondered if Watanabe had lied to him.

"Now," Chiao Te said, "your Special Branch will have a fact to put on my file." He shrugged. "That would end my usefulness to my government. Did Banerjee say much?"

"Enough," Winston snapped, still wondering about Watanabe.

"It will not be necessary for you to deport me," Chiao Te said. "I am making arrangements to leave Hong Kong. I have been in the service too long. I would like to go home, even if it is only to Taiwan."

Winston was still concerned with his own problem. There must be a plot, otherwise how could he justify the whole exercise in surveillance. He must have faith in Watanabe. He must press Chiao Te for more information. "Who is supplying arms to the students?"

Chiao Te stroked his chin with ink-stained fingers. "What would those students do with arms? You have been a soldier. Could you use a gun without being trained to?"

He leaned forward and stubbed his cigarette out in Winston's ashtray. "No one is supplying arms to the students," he said. "No one would be so foolish. If anyone was, we would have done something about it. In this matter, our interests are the same as yours."

More incontestable facts. More doubts about Watanabe. Kate had never believed in his theory of a students' uprising, either. She knew more students than he did. Could she be right? Chan too? No, there had to be an arms smuggler, somewhere.

"My information comes from an excellent source," Winston said.

"If the source is excellent, the results should be excellent." Chiao Te paused to study him again. "Does your source know how and when the arms are being delivered? Do you know how he knows?"

The man's logic was frightening. Winston wanted time to think. He changed the subject. "Why did you bribe the customs officer?"

"Bribe?" Chiao Te's eyebrows rose eloquently above his glasses. "What for? Did you find anything on that plane that shouldn't have been there?"

"But you still gave this customs officer money."

"I am godfather to his child," Chiao Te said. "What harm is there in that? Also, it stopped your surveillance operation."

"What were you frightened about?"

"Not about arms. I was concerned about what you might discover by accident." Chiao Te shrugged and smiled. "So a little falsehood. It is all part of the game."

A game in which he had been effortlessly outplayed, Winston thought resentfully. Conned like any dupey-dupe.

"These things happen," Chiao Te said, "when one tries to make facts fit theories."

To cover his embarrassment Winston pushed the telegram from Taiwan across the desk. "Explain that," he demanded.

16—TBI * *

Chiao Te took his time examining it. "Watanabe," he asked softly, "was he your source?"

Jesus Christ! The bloody gook was twenty moves ahead, not two. "Yes," Winston admitted reluctantly.

"Did you also ask yourself why Watanabe should tell you this?"

"Because he wanted to come to Hong Kong. He wanted to collect the remains of his former comrades."

"And so he spent a considerable time in the New Territories where the fighting took place?"

Winston hesitated. "No — no — I don't think so."

"You didn't verify his story." It was a statement of fact, a note of mild disapproval.

Winston nodded, flushing.

"And you didn't ask yourself why, if he wasn't dis-interring his comrades, he wanted so much to come to Hong Kong."

Winston shook his head. The man's thoroughness and logic made Thompson and the others he had worked with look like novices.

Chiao Te smiled. "The first lesson," he said.

Damn it, he seemed to be thinking Winston's thoughts before Winston himself realised he had them.

"Always enquire," Chiao Te went on, "never take anything on trust."

In a small voice, Winston asked, "Do you know what Watanabe was doing in Hong Kong?"

Chiao Te tapped the telegram. "Committing murder." He tapped the telegram again. "The sender of this telegram is my brother's son. He will go far in the Taiwan police. We are very proud of him. He has spoken to me about this case, because I have known Hiroshi Watanabe a long time."

"Are you saying that Watanabe went to all this trouble just so he could come here and kill someone?"

"No. The killings were forced upon him. Raghavan, the

Indian journalist knew too much. Saito Chu, the old man in Taiwan, talked too much."

"What about for God's sake!"

Slowly and patiently, Chiao Te told him. He told Winston about Bose, about the treasure, about Watanabe's involvement with the 82nd Bureau, of Watanabe's disappearance from Taiwan and his escape from Shatin Temple.

Every word stung like the barb on the end of a whip. That bloody flied lice gook, Chan, had been right. Right about the students, right about the murder, right about Watanabe. What on earth was Winston going to do? Plant arms somewhere? Suck up to the AC and make sure Chan would be even more discredited?

"And that is why I think Watanabe came to Hong Kong," Chiao Te finished. "To find something he had lost."

Winston had an eerie feeling of standing outside himself, watching himself react. Part of his mind was working uncontrollably. "You mean the treasure?"

Chiao Te got to his feet and walked to the door. "Perhaps." He paused a moment, looking at Winston. "My nephew thinks very highly of Inspector Chan. I am sorry I have not been able to meet him. He is too good a policeman to be lost to your force."

Winston asked hollowly, "What do you mean by that?"

"You know what I mean. Chan knows too much, too. Tell him to watch out for Wan Liu."

Chiao Te bowed courteously.

Winston stared wildly, feeling as if he was in a nightmare. "Is all this true?"

Chiao Te smiled. "You must decide that for yourself," he said. "That is the only way. And the only way you can make those decisions is by being true, inside."

Winston watched him go and reached for the telephone. She was sorry, the receptionist at the Peninsula said, but Mr. Watanable had left Hong Kong.

Winston stared uncomprehendingly at the whirring

instrument in his hand. Watanabe had gone leaving behind unsolved murders, and the problems of excuse and explanation, a sense of betrayal.

Slowly Winston replaced the receiver on its cradle, suppressing the anger and humiliation burning through him, the shameful realisation that he had been duped. In his own way, he thought bitterly, he had found the truth.

Excuses and explanations he could cope with. He was used to departmental intrigue, and Thompson and the AC liked him. They'd put it down to an excess of zeal, know that it was the only blemish on his record. But what about Chan? What, if anything, should Winston do about that?

He rested his head on his hands and thought about Chan, and about Watanabe. He thought a long time about Chiao Te and facts that fitted theories. Pete Winston thought a long time about the truth he was trying to find inside himself.

All right, he knew he was a bastard — Kate Farleigh had told him that often enough — but that didn't mean he was a coward, or that he could do nothing while someone else paid for his mistakes. His whole code was based on justice. That was why he had become a cop in the first place. All his life he had paid for what he had bought, he'd had nothing for nothing. The good he had earned and the bad he had deserved, and Chan was like that too. Besides, whatever else he felt about him, Chan was too damned good a cop to be chucked out of the force. There weren't many like him, as tough, as dedicated, or as good. Like him or not Winston had to admire him. Chan had proved the best of them all.

Slowly he raised his head, clear about what he had to do. He would speak up for Chan at the hearing. He owed Chan that at least — perhaps even something more. Yes, if he was to be true inside, he owed Chan an apology. He would go round and make it now. After all it was the decent thing to do.

*　　*　　*

244

Pete Winston stood in Chan's lounge, surrounded by Chan's furniture, listening to his children tossing restlessly and felt for the first time the enormity of what he had created. Li-li's dry eyed face in front of him mingled with a vision of Chan's burnt-out car.

"And then he — he — just went," Li-li said.

Just like that. No gun, no warrant card, nothing. Going after two murderers with his bare hands. Mad fool, Winston thought, mad crazy, brave fool. Mechanically he asked, "Why didn't he call the police?"

"Police!" Li-li said it as if it was a strange word in a strange language, polite enough to struggle to keep the bitterness out of her voice.

The suppressed bitterness stung. The fact that Mrs. Chan was too well bred to be overtly rude, stung even more. "I am sorry," Winston said, "it has been my fault," feeling better for saying it, but only slightly.

Chan had left over four hours ago, and if he wasn't back yet, only one thing could have happened to him. Winston's mind edged tremulously away from the horrifying possibility, as Li-li's must have done so often over the past hours. Grimly Winston forced himself to think about the fact that Richard Chan was dead.

If Chan was dead, it would be his fault. If Chan was dead, there would be no forgiveness, not from others, not from himself. Winston would be as guilty of that death as if he had driven the knife into Chan's gullet himself, and that he knew was the most heinous crime a policeman could commit — killing a brother officer.

Winston walked into the hallway, desperate for action. He picked up Chan's phone, feeling for the first time in his life, a total fear, that made his body tremble, his palms sweat. He forced himself to dial the station, forced himself to talk quietly. He gave instructions for Wan Liu to be brought to Wan Chai station immediately.

*　　*　　*

By the time Winston got back to the station, Wan Liu was there, surrounded by a whole squad of cops and his men sitting in the waiting area below.

"Get rid of the goons," Winston said to Sergeant Yim, "and take Wan Liu downstairs."

"But sir, we haven't charged him with anything."

"Later," Winston said.

Twenty minutes later it was all over. Wan Liu had not been able to take the dynamo attached to his balls. He'd admitted everything. His debt to Watanabe for eliminating his rivals many years ago, his help to Watanabe now in killing Raghavan, his sacrificial offering of Yong Po and Lin Yu, their capture of Chan.

Winston rushed from the cell, struggling into his jacket. "Charge him with being an accessory," he shouted to Sergeant Yim as he ran towards the street. "I'm off to Kwan Tong."

Cameron Wah's penguin-like figure rose to block his way. "I say, old boy — "

"Go, fuck yourself," Winston shouted and slammed him out of the way, knowing he could never live with himself if Richard Chan was dead.

29

A WHIRLING WORLD of stars and light and tall buildings, a rush of air, a brilliant white light that scorched his staring eyeballs. Chan's scream was still dying as his wheeling body smashed into the neon sign with a deafening bang and a maelstrom of incandescent sparks. Pain tore through his side, ripped along his arm. With a crackling sound, the sign sagged. Chan reached out, grasped the iron bar on which the sign was suspended, his muscles jarring with shock as they took his weight. Palms and fingers tore at the roughened surface. His body swung clear.

For a long moment he hung there, looking at the sign snapped nearly right through, a mess of wood and tin, trailing wires and shattered glass. Then he felt the blood trickling thickly into his armpit, the scorch of the burn across his body and his fingers began to slip. Desperately he clawed at the roughened iron, tearing away flesh and nails.

His strength was going fast. His arms felt like rods of fire, his palms as if they were gripping crushed glass. He remembered the school gymnasium, the exercise on the parallel bars. With a supreme effort he flexed his stomach muscles, knifed his legs up and locked them round the bar.

A moment or two of divine relief. His body began to tremble and his arms started to go all rubbery. He couldn't stop now. Not now. If he relaxed now, he would let go and fall. The sound of his harsh breathing filled his ears, his body was covered with cold sweat. Desperately he swung his legs in a scissor like movement levering his body round till he was astride the bar.

It was easier now, as long as he didn't look down, as long as the sweat kept out of his eyes and his body stopped shivering. He eased himself backwards and grasped the window ledge, waited for the shivering fit to pass. Then carefully, precariously he stood up on the narrow strip of iron and drew himself on to the ledge. Thank God the window was open.

*   *   *

Body filled with stiffness and pain, Chan sat upright in the back of the taxi as it moved along streets grown merry with people and the pimpling glow of lanterns. He held his arm out in front of him, the wound tied with strips torn from his shirt. It would need stitching, but later. The burn across his ribs had set up a constant smart and each movement of the taxi set up a new wave of pain.

The road to Shatin was a chain of purring metal and dipped headlamps, bordered by pavements thick with people and gigantic lanterns. Chan felt tired, lethargic despite the pain, in a way grateful for the delay, for the postponement of what he might have to do when he got there. They travelled in spasms, lunging between bumpers, engine fussing furiously. It took nearly an hour to get to Shatin.

Chan set off up the steps, doggedly, trying to will away the pain, ignoring the stiffness in his legs. He concentrated on each step as he climbed, willing his tired body to react. The way to the temple was filled with people, completely different to what it had been the previous afternoon. The music of the merry-go-round rose loudly above their high pitched conversations. What he was doing was crazy, Chan thought, preventing a crime, and he, not even a policeman.

248

But it wasn't only that. He was proving a point, satisfying an innate curiosity.

The climb was sheer agony. He had to stop often and rest, standing on the edge of the steps, avoiding the curious glances of the crowd. He knew he looked strange, especially on a festive day. The sight of his face in the mirror in the warehouse washroom had shocked even him. Swollen cheeks, puffed eye, face suffused with blood, his good eye red and protuberant. As he walked he kept his arm up, thinking that would prevent it bleeding any more.

At the top of the hill the temples were open and full of light. Crowds milled about in the courtyards, laughing and chattering. Chan picked his way to the topmost shrine, gingerly edged through the people standing on the steps and sauntering through the doors, staring and praying. The seller of joss-sticks was still behind his table, doing good business. Chan looked and saw that he was not too late.

He walked down to the lower temple, bought a Coke and ate skewered chicken and noodles like any low-class person. Low-class person or not it made him feel better. He sat at the table till past midnight, till the festival was nearly over. Crowds began to wend their way down the steep hillside, voices softer now, the atmosphere cloaked with expended excitement.

He went to the topmost temple where the joss-stick seller was putting away his stall. Opposite the temple was a balustrade and beyond it, grass and trees inclining steeply to the path below. Chan climbed over the balustrade and dropped down on the grass. Gratefully he rested his back against a tree and watched the lights stringing along the hill, one by one, go out. Trees and buildings turned to dark silver and the moon hung high and resplendent in the heavens, consummated.

Despite willing himself not to, Chan dozed.

He was awakened by the thwack of giant wings beating the air. He got up and crouching along the farther side of the balustrade hobbled along the hillside. Silhouetted against the moon was a skeletal shadow, topped by whirling blades, roaring loudly as it lowered itself to the ground. It was the structure he had seen the two white-overalled mechanics working on in the warehouse at Kwan Tong. Now it was lifesize and it was flying. There were three men seated abreast on the flying platform as it lowered itself on to the temple courtyard.

The craft landed in a flurry of dust and the engine died with a splutter. There was a moment of ear-aching silence and then the men stepped off the craft, the two men who had been in the warehouse and Hiroshi Watanabe. They started to walk towards the topmost temple, one of them carrying a tarpaulin, Watanabe and the other, carrying evilly glinting revolvers.

Chan kept pace with them as they walked, their feet crunching softly over the path, Chan's arm aching dully, his back stiffening from the unaccustomed curvature. He dropped to the grass with relief as they went up the steps and stood in the doorway, almost completely hidden by the darkened shadow of the verandah. There was a rasping of metal, a grinding of hinges, the sound of a bolt dragging across the floor. Then silence.

Chan edged his head over the balustrade and looked. Nothing. The temple was peaceful as a deserted lake. Chan thought he heard the scrape of leather below him, a long shuddering gasp of a man running, but there was nothing he could see there. He pulled himself painfully over the balustrade, crossed the path in three large strides and went up the steps on the sides of his feet.

He stood in the shadow of the verandah, well away from the door, his back pressed against the wall. He could hear Watanabe and the others moving inside the temple, the stifled gasps of their effort. After a few minutes they came out and went by, hardly six feet from him. They were carrying the statue slung in the tarpaulin between them, and it clanged against the cement as they went down the steps.

In the darkness, Chan moved after them. He stood on the top step and cried, "Stop! Police!"

The men whirled sideways on to Chan, one of the mechanics whipping his gun across his chest. Chan hurled himself forward off the steps. A brief airborne moment, the gun flaming in his face. Then the explosion echoing and re-echoing in his brain. He crashed, arms widespread into the men, pain wracking his body, his head scraping along the raw earth and his ribs smashed against too solid hips.

Someone writhed underneath him and something soft and heavy moved against his legs. Chan kicked and heard a yelp as he rolled clear, swivelling on to his back. One man was lying on his side, struggling for his feet and the gun. Chan rolled himself forward, in the same movement throwing himself at the man. His head crashed into a granite like fist and he fell on top of the man, stretching across his body for the gun. Watanabe's foot smashed down on Chan's outstretched hand. The man underneath him wriggled and tossed Chan on to the earth.

A shoe raked the back of Chan's neck, then the pistol had gone and he was staring at the blank faced statue, shining in the moonlight. There were gasps as the statue was lifted, Watanabe's voice saying, "Kill him." Chan threw himself across the tarpaulin, feeling the statue dig into his battered body and crumble as he landed.

He lay face down a jagged spur of pain stabbing through his ribs. He could hardly breathe and there was the warm kiss of blood running down his face. His gaping mouth sucked air. And something else. A smell of charnel houses and putrefaction more terrible than the insides of any mortuary. Chan knew he was smelling his own death as the tarpaulin was tugged away from underneath him and he was rolled helplessly on to the path. There he lay still, exhausted, shocked beyond any pain.

Watanabe and the two men were standing still too. They were staring petrified at the statue between them. Chan's leap had shattered the gold casting which lay like a broken shell, glistening in the moonlight, revealing the dried flesh and glistening bone of the decaying human body that had been underneath.

Chan retched and turned away, trying to blot out the vision of the grinning, long dead face. Bose's?

Watanabe's foot stopped him and Chan stared up at the dark barrel of the gun. He thought wildly of Li-li and the children trying to remember the words of the ritual act of contrition. The next moment there was a sharp crack. Watanabe's jaw dropped in surprise and his eyes widened. Blood petalled the front of his pale brown suit and his eyes rolled to the top of his head. Watanabe's body swayed and fell across the glistening, broken putrefying statue that he had risked so much to steal.

One of the men turned and broke away, running along the path towards the aircraft. The gun cracked again. The man screamed, cartwheeled to the ground.

Chan moved. At the end of the path was a lanky figure, arm now dropping the gun to its side, long hair fluttering in the breeze. Chan saw the second man raise his gun and flung himself at the gun hand. He missed and clouted the muzzle with his face. Red hot pain seared his cheeks, then a fist caught him in the middle and flung him sideways.

Chan clung on, feeling the gaping wound on his injured hand open. He worked his left hand free and landed two quick jabs to the man's body. Off balance, the blows had merely nuisance value. Chan let go of the man and stepped backwards. The gun came up again as Chan got a straight left through, snapping out smartly from his shoulder, flicking the man's head back. The gun exploded again with a sharp smell of cordite and a singeing spear of pain across the side of Chan's ribs. Chan closed in. Three swift jabs to the body, his wounded hand surging with pain, blood bursting through the primitive bandages. He stepped back, moved in with a hook just above the heart, an agonising right cross, then an upper cut that started somewhere near his knees and broke the man's jaw in two places, smashed his teeth together like a bag of crushed pebbles.

Chan watched the man drop, feeling the pain in his arm shoot all the way up his shoulder. Then he turned to the figure walking up the path towards him.

"Thank God you're all right, Charlie," Pete Winston cried.

*   *   *

They were seated on the steps of the temple, watching the uniformed figures moving busily around the courtyard. Chan rested his bandaged face against Winston's shoulder.

"You were right, Charlie," Winston said. "There weren't any arms. You were right about Watanabe, too. Right about everything."

"Sometimes you get lucky," Chan muttered. The pain killing injection was taking time to work.

"I got Wan Liu," Winston said. "He's the only one who'll live to face charges."

"And Banerjee?"

"He'll have to be deported, I'm afraid. He confessed too much."

"He meant well," Chan said and stood up. "I think I can walk now. I'd like to go home."

Winston walked beside him along the path to the courtyard. "Funny isn't it, about the statue of the old priest. You know they found that two years after he'd died, his body hadn't decayed. So they enshrined him in Watanabe's gold and kept him in the temple."

"Bose's gold," Chan said.

"The temple's gold," Winston said. "I don't think anyone will bother with it now."

They walked on, past the courtyard. Winston pointed towards the craft Watanabe had used. "So that's what they used the warehouse for," he said. "To assemble that

253

thing. It's a Kai-33 helicopter designed by the students of the Kharkov Aviation Institute. They used a few of them in Vietnam. They're light, cheap, portable and easily assembled. They fly with a motor car engine."

"They also used the warehouse to try to kill me."

Winston looked at Chan. "I know. I'm sorry. It was my fault."

They walked down the hill slowly, stopping from time to time to allow Chan to rest. Pete Winston said, "About the hearing, there won't be one. I will see the AC tomorrow and explain everything."

"You don't have to."

Winston laughed. "After all this?"

They walked in silence for a while. Then Winston said, "I would have spoken to the AC anyway."

It was Chan's turn to look at him. "Would you?"

Winston thought for a moment. "Perhaps I wouldn't, if I hadn't met Chiao Te. I must tell you about him one day."

Chiao Te, Chan thought. That was someone he should have seen. Then he remembered the case was over.

"You're a crazy bastard," Winston said, "going after all those people alone."

"You do what you have to do."

Winston thought that Chiao Te had said something like that. He smiled in the darkness.

Chan asked, "Why did you come alone?"

"A one per cent chance," Winston replied, "that you might be wrong. If you were wrong, I didn't want everyone knowing you had been after Watanabe again. I wanted to keep you out of trouble."

Chan felt embarrassed. "I'll always be in trouble," he said. "I'm the trouble-finding kind."

"Also, I owed you something."

"There's an old Chinese saying," Chan said. "The life you save belongs to you."

"Snap," Winston said.

Chan laughed. "Maybe," he said, "you are a bit of a crazy bastard too."

"You stubborn, flied lice, gook."

Chan laughed louder. "Bent, ex-pat plick," and suddenly he realised the pain was no longer as intense, and that there were some things you could only say to friends.